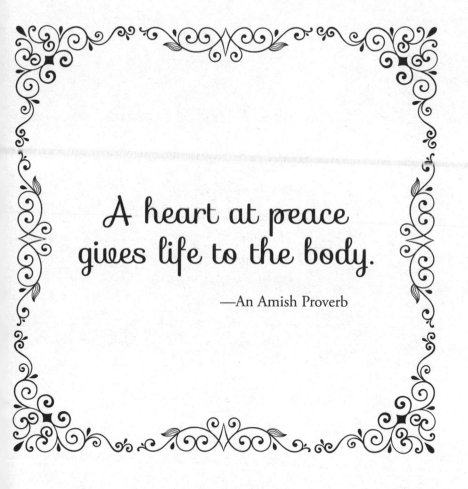

A heart at peace
gives life to the body.

—An Amish Proverb

Peace
LIKE A River

OLIVIA NEWPORT

Guideposts

New York

CHAPTER ONE

How her aunt Mitzi knew she was drooling over the cashmere-lined, hand-stitched, soft leather gloves in the Bloomingdale's catalog remained a mystery to Cheryl Cooper. But she should not have been surprised when she discovered the boxed gloves on a pantry shelf with one of her aunt's yellow envelopes taped to the gray paisley wrapping paper and Cheryl's name underscored with three curvy lines.

Still treating the gloves with admiration, Cheryl folded them carefully and assured herself they were secure in her jacket pockets. Since making a rapid decision a few months ago to move from Columbus and accept Mitzi's invitation to manage both her home and her quaint gifts and sundries shop in Sugarcreek, Ohio, Cheryl found at least one letter or gift every few weeks tucked away in an obscure spot. Last month it was the gloves, and Cheryl had taken to wearing them during her late-afternoon walks on the path running along the river on one end of the town. On some days it seemed silly to drive to a location just to get out to walk. Why not just walk there in the first place? But at this time of year, Cheryl fought the fading light if she wanted to get in a brisk constitutional after closing up the Swiss Miss and before settling in at home with a book, her supper, and her cat.

The note with the gloves had said simply, *When you warm up your fingers, know how much the thought of you warms my heart no matter how many miles separate us. Love, Aunt Mitzi.*

For a mid-February Monday, the day was uncharacteristically warm, even while the afternoon waned and genuine evening approached. As Cheryl loosened the sky-blue scarf swaddling her neck at the top of her burgundy jacket, she reached the highest point along the route she now took four or five times a week. From here she could look in one direction toward the orange orb sliding behind the rising evening shadows and in the other direction toward the festive lights of Sugarcreek. Some flickered off as businesses closed for the day, but others outlined store windows inviting visitors to enjoy the town's charm at any time of day.

How normal it all seemed now.

Only a few months ago, Aunt Mitzi's offer came out of the blue: *Come to Sugarcreek. Run my store. Live in my home. Free me to be a missionary in Papua New Guinea as I've always wanted.*

And what was there to keep Cheryl in Columbus? A job she'd lost interest in. A broken five-year engagement to a man for whom she'd waited far too long before realizing Lance was never going to be ready for marriage. Cheryl had friends and a church she enjoyed, but she preferred to believe thirty was not too old to build a new life somewhere different. That's what Mitzi was doing, and she was twice as old as Cheryl. Mitzi deserved to chase the dream of her youth. She and Ralph were married for forty happy years. Throughout her childhood and young adulthood, Cheryl saw this for herself. But Uncle Ralph had passed away several years ago.

Mitzi was on her own. Why should she not answer the call to missions that was as unambiguous now as it had been before she married? "Sixty is the new forty," Aunt Mitzi always said. She was in excellent health and a keen learner. Cheryl was delighted to launch her aunt's pursuit with the confidence that the Swiss Miss would be well minded in her absence, no matter how long Mitzi might be gone.

The agreement papers were signed, permissions authorized, Sugarcreek introductions made. Now instead of being chummy with the other assistant branch manager of the bank where she used to work, Cheryl's favorite companion was Naomi Miller. If anyone at the bank in Columbus had told her she would feel this attached to a farmer's wife ten years her senior, wearing the Plain dress and bonnet of the Amish, Cheryl would have laughed. Now Cheryl looked forward to the days each week when Naomi turned up at the Swiss Miss with breads and jams and sweet treats that sold faster than Cheryl could log them into inventory. Even more, though, Cheryl hoped Naomi would have time for a cup of tea and a quiet chat when she came in. Since arriving in Sugarcreek, Cheryl savored the small bits of her day that brought her pleasure— and they were bountiful.

For instance, for the first time in her adult life, Cheryl had time to walk along a riverbank, breathe deeply, and let peace lap against her spirit. She was hard-pressed to think what could make her want to give up this newfound habit. Even on frigid days, when most of the town looked forward to huddling beside their fireplaces, Cheryl anticipated her walks with enthusiasm.

Exhaling, Cheryl lowered the zipper on her jacket by four inches. This was the warmest day she remembered since before Thanksgiving, and the brisk mile and a half she had just power walked helped disperse heat beneath her layers. The river was a tributary of some sort of the Tuscarawas River, eventually tracing back to the Mississippi. Its movement had slowed after Christmas and through the weeks of January, but the temperatures had climbed steadily the last few days, and the sun was winter bright. Several times as she walked, Cheryl heard the crack of splitting ice on the water's surface and the escaping rush of the water gathering speed below.

Cheryl's gaze shifted from the setting sun to the slope of the stony riverbank about forty yards ahead.

Something looked unusual.

Trailing along the water's edge was a ragged path of oddball items. From this distance and in the shifting light, Cheryl wasn't sure what she saw—but she was certain it was more than the normal rocks, soggy soil, and patches of ice. She dipped her head forward to peer with more intention, but all she could make out was that the clutter looked as if someone had dumped a trash bin or the remains of a dilapidated garage. There didn't seem to be a pattern to the shapes and sizes of items, but her heart sank at the sight of the mess that would only get worse overnight.

She jumped when steps sounded behind her and immediately chastised herself. Anyone could walk along the river, of course, and she thought she had broken the habit of city fears. In Columbus, Lance constantly thought he should prepare for every bad thing that might happen, and Cheryl had absorbed his caution. After she moved to Sugarcreek, she embraced the notion that there was a difference between sensible circumspection, which she believed she practiced, and living under irrational fear, which she refused to continue doing. Life was too short to always be afraid.

But she admitted relief that the brisk footfalls she heard belonged to Rueben Vogel and not a stranger.

"Rueben!" Cheryl said. "What are you doing out here?"

"Same as you, I imagine," Rueben said. "Walking. Enjoying the river. Watching for the first star."

Watching for the first star. Cheryl liked that thought.

"I haven't seen you out here before," she said, "at least not this time of day."

"It is a new habit." Rueben's blue eyes twinkled. "I may be an old man, but I am not dead yet. Whenever I try to help around the farm, my daughter and her husband shoo me off. A body can only spend so much time rocking in a *dawdy haus*."

Cheryl laughed. "I always wondered what you did when you weren't playing checkers with your brother in my aunt's store."

"The farm is not far from here," Rueben said. "Perhaps a mile. No reason I shouldn't get out and about."

Cheryl pointed a thumb in the direction of the scattered trash. "Any idea what happened down there?"

Rueben twisted his head back in the direction he'd come from. "I'd better head back if I want to get home before my daughter calls me for supper and discovers I am gone."

"I've met your daughter," Cheryl said, teasing. "She's hardly a jailer."

He put a finger to his lips. "Shh. If the trees can clap their hands to praise *Gott*, they may also have ears."

Cheryl laughed again as Rueben pivoted his wiry frame and set a tenacious pace. Only after he was out of earshot did Cheryl realize he hadn't answered her question—did he know anything about the motley mess farther down the river? She was certain it had not been there yesterday, on Sunday afternoon, when she walked in full daylight. It could have been there as long as twenty-four hours or as briefly as one. She glanced in the direction she'd left her car, calculating that she could walk a few more yards before heading home for her own supper.

When she looked again at the strewn debris, she saw another man. He hadn't been there five minutes ago—at least he had not been within view from Cheryl's location.

But there he was. An Amish man in his telltale black trousers, jacket, and hat.

Cheryl couldn't make out who he was. Certainly she didn't know all the Amish men around Sugarcreek by name. She crept forward, watching. The wind kicked up, beginning to bite.

At first Cheryl thought the scattered items must belong to the man or he was responsible for them in some way. Why else would he be picking through the hodgepodge with as much deliberation as he exhibited? Perhaps a box tumbled out of a buggy on the road above the river. Maybe he was transporting a load as a favor for an *Englisch* neighbor. Or he might have a salvage business and had picked up a load. Any number of explanations might suit the circumstances. Cheryl felt sorry for the man. Restoring order to the wreckage was a most unpleasant close to the day. If she helped him, it would go faster. Clearing the shambles that marred the view would not have been entirely disagreeable if they at least had trash bags or boxes. Cheryl quickened her pace and then slowed in fresh realization.

The man was not trying to restore order. He picked up one item after another only to cast it aside without serious inspection. Cheryl couldn't tell what most of them were. Small shapes in the shadows from the distance were difficult to distinguish. He was interested in one particular piece of the detritus.

Cheryl watched, haunted by a sense that she ought to know this man. The temperature was falling along with the light. Cheryl rezipped her jacket against the wind.

The man untangled a rope or a small hose—Cheryl was not sure which—and extracted the item he had been fixated on all along. He held it in one hand and ran the fingers of his other hand along its length horizontally before turning it to stand on end. It was some sort of a thick stick with painted, worn stripes. Only when the man flipped it in the other direction and Cheryl saw the broad flat end now turned up in the air did she realize it was an old oar.

And the man's stature, now that she'd had time to study it, looked like Seth Miller.

Cheryl cupped her mouth and called out. "Seth!"

But the wind threw her effort back into her own face, and the man made no response. Instead, he kicked his work boots free of the nearest items, gripped the oar, and began walking in the opposite direction.

Chapter Two

Cheryl followed.

But the gap between her and the man was sufficient to require that she pick up her pace. She called Seth's name again, and for a slim fraction of a second she thought the man stopped. Or flinched. Or hesitated. Or the fleeting shift in his movement might have had nothing to do with Cheryl's summons. He did not turn toward her voice.

Cheryl slid down the bank closer to the water. The man's black clothing faded him further into the eclipsing surroundings, but Cheryl glued her gaze to the skulking, stocky form. In contrast, the oar caught moon slivers as he swung it in rhythm with his gait.

He moved with speed and purpose, following the topography with the ease of someone who knew well the land around the river. At a gentle bend in the water's flow, he took a sharp left turn as if he found the path he sought. Cheryl felt her disadvantage—a lack of knowledge of the ins and outs of access to the river formed by community habit rather than planning and signage. She always left her car parked in the same place and walked along a fairly level stretch of unpaved but well-tamped earth. Tonight she was venturing into less familiar territory.

The man escaped her field of sight. Cheryl was more convinced he was Seth Miller even as she was able to see less of him.

Seth's wife was Cheryl's best friend in Sugarcreek. Cheryl knew where the Millers lived with their blend of children from Seth's first marriage and the ones they had together.

And she knew they shared their evening meal on a predictable schedule. If the river wanderer was Seth, he was going to be late for supper.

Cheryl stilled and cocked her head to listen. Seth was a long way from home. He must have left a horse and buggy somewhere nearby. But Cheryl heard no whinny or neigh, no creaking buggy axle or stomping hoof, no brush of beast against vegetation.

Intending to pivot on one foot and hunt out the path Seth—if it was him—must have taken, Cheryl instead lost her footing. Her heel slid down the slope before settling in mud, her walking boot filling with cold muck before she reached out for a boulder she was certain would not move. Three more feet and she would have been in the frigid river. Grimacing at the thought, Cheryl heaved herself up the incline until she felt solid ground again.

Footprints, she thought. If someone had been there in addition to Seth, there would be evidence of multiple shoes or boots. Pulling her cell phone from her pocket, she snapped on the flashlight app.

One set of prints—but at least she could see where they led and find the trail.

It was narrow and perhaps did not deserve the *trail* moniker, but she found where the Amish man must have gone.

It was Seth. It was not Seth.

Cheryl couldn't make up her mind. Either way, he was gone, slipped from view more silently than Cheryl would have thought possible. And either way, she had a stronger sense of sinister activity than she would have imagined for any of the Amish she knew.

Despite the similarity of the man's build to Seth Miller, Cheryl resisted the notion Seth was miles from his own farm when he ought to have been tending his animals and washing up for supper. Suspecting him soured Cheryl's stomach, though in truth all he had done was claim an item that legitimately seemed abandoned.

Surely Seth would tell Naomi what this was all about. Naomi was outgoing and chattered freely. No doubt in the next day or so Cheryl would hear an explanation that made sense, or she would learn that everything was as it should be on the Miller farm. There was no point trying to follow farther tonight.

Her route back to her car would take Cheryl right past the damp litter again—right through it, in fact, if she chose.

If Lance were here, he would be standing well away from the water, close to the road, demanding that Cheryl leave the mess alone. What did it have to do with her? She wasn't being sensible. And he would have been right. It was dark, the promising warmth of the day now lost with the setting sun. She could hardly see where she was stepping, much less hope for any clues to explain the disarray. But Cheryl had seen enough mysterious activities in her months in Sugarcreek to feed her curiosity, and she could not cast out of her mind the image of Seth untangling that old oar.

Cheryl retraced her steps and paused at the edge of the upended pile of miscellaneous items. What had brought Seth here, and what had he seen? Once again using her phone for illumination, Cheryl surveyed what Seth's eyes must have observed only a few minutes ago.

A life jacket. Not entirely inappropriate along a river, but it was hardly swimming season.

A thin hose, the sort someone might bury in a flower bed to gently soak the ground rather than drench with a full-blast nozzle setting.

A man's brown loafer.

The most hideous green and orange garden gnome Cheryl had ever laid eyes on.

Three children's books featuring bunnies. Their condition saddened Cheryl as memories of her own favorite animal books wafted through her mind.

A woven laundry basket with a gash in one side. Cheryl realized now she had seen Seth lift the basket off the end of the oar midway through the process of removing the tangled hose.

One after the other, Cheryl handled the items between thumb and forefinger of one hand while inspecting them under the timid but steady stream of light from the phone she held in the other. It was all damp. Some of it was outright saturated, but not so soaked as to think it actually had been in the river under ice. None of it looked valuable, but it must have come from somewhere.

Cheryl blew out her breath. What happened to the peaceful walk she was enjoying just a few minutes ago? She couldn't leave now as if none of this had happened. Someone else would find these remains in the daylight. Someone else would ask questions. Someone else would grumble but clean it up.

But only she had seen Seth Miller extract the oar.

Cheryl dropped a gray cardigan sweater missing most of its buttons back into the mud and listened to the river. Flowing water was as secretive as it was peaceful, the current carrying away as much as it carried in.

An explosive crack jolted her nerves. Had she still been in Columbus, Lance would have concluded that the sound was a gunshot, proof that they lingered where they didn't belong. Cheryl lurched off balance, adrenaline bolting through her.

A car had backfired. That's all it was. Cheryl was certain. But it couldn't have been far from her, and the fact that she was oblivious to its presence even in the dark unsettled her. Her eyes flashed toward where she had left her Ford Focus. She snapped off the light on her phone and listened more intently than she had in weeks. Behind her, a motor gunned and headlights scattered beams through a path of trees.

Cheryl squatted, ducking below the rays.

That was no Amish buggy. Cheryl had not imagined a car could sound so angry—especially in a place like Sugarcreek with a whopping population of two thousand people.

Under one foot, Cheryl felt the slide of a stack of sodden files and shifted her weight to pull five manila folders from the mud. She turned on the light again. The top file now bore the cloudy print of her boot. One was empty, three were stocked with a handful of papers, and one overflowed. None had a label. Cheryl braced her stance, corralled the bulging folder against her abdomen, and started to peel back the layers. Even in daylight she would not have been able to make much of the faded pencil scratchings and blurred ink.

Cheryl Cooper, what are you doing? How many times had she walked through a park in Columbus and seen the litter of an overturned trash can? How many times on a windy day in her own front yard had she picked up ads and envelopes that had blown in from two blocks away? If she had come upon this scene two minutes later, she might have allocated it to the category of careless citizens satisfied simply to have the trash out of their own driveways.

Because it *was* trash. The life jacket lacked a buckle, the soaking hose was slashed, and the gnome's nose had broken off.

So why had Seth—Cheryl was convinced now the man was Seth—been so particular about rescuing the oar?

The folder held handwritten lists. One for the market with most of the entries crossed out. One for craft supplies, illegible with moisture. One stapled to the front of a mail-order catalog from three years ago. One an index of household chores. Cheryl pondered rhyme or reason. As she reached the more protected interior of the folder's contents, a greater number of complete words popped out. Calling the half sheets she encountered *dry* was an overstatement. She settled for *less wet*. They began to take on the form of business records, albeit thoroughly disorganized. Three ledger sheets had unlabeled numerical entries, but Cheryl could quickly see the math was off, as if someone knew she ought to keep better records but was not actually inclined to do so.

And then she saw the large scribbled *CC*. The letters could stand for anything, she supposed, but after thirty years of living with those initials, her own name jumped to the forefront of her mind. Reflexively, she tried to smooth the paper for a clearer look but only managed to smudge the writing. Cheryl was certain the word below the initials was *shop*, though it looked more like *hop* with a splotch in front. The numbers, more than the words, alarmed her.

The house number of Aunt Mitzi's house, which Cheryl now occupied, followed by sixteen digits that could only be a credit card number.

The sequence looked familiar. Cheryl was certain of the last four digits. Biting on one side of her bottom lip, she pictured the card number she had entered for an online order just a couple of hours ago.

This was *her* credit card number—or at least the one Aunt Mitzi had authorized her to use for store expenses.

Cheryl hovered the phone's light over the sheet more steadily, mouthing each number as she discerned it for the second time.

Knowing she was about to stir up irritation, Cheryl punched a number into her cell phone.

CHAPTER THREE

She listened to three rings and then the voice.

"Chief Twitchell."

"This is Cheryl Cooper," she said.

He missed the beat when he should have said, "How can I help you?" He was the police chief, after all. He was supposed to help.

"I'm sorry to bother you," Cheryl said, "but I have a situation."

"I was just about to lock up the office," Chief Sam Twitchell said.

Cheryl heard him close a file drawer and turn a key.

"Something happen at the Swiss Miss?" the chief asked.

"No, I closed an hour ago," Cheryl said.

"Then you can appreciate that I am trying to do the same."

Cheryl failed to see how it was the same at all. The stores along Sugarcreek's Main Street had posted hours. Crime could happen at any time. It seemed to her that Chief Twitchell had an obligation to at least hear her out.

"I was out walking along the river," she said, "and I came upon some items."

"I'm afraid you'll have to be more specific."

"I think you should come out here."

Another missed beat. "Now Cheryl," Chief Twitchell said, "we've been through this before. I know you get curious, but every odd happenstance does not necessarily mean a crime has been committed."

"I want to stop a crime," Cheryl said. She had his attention now and continued. "I think someone might be misusing the shop's credit card—and they have my address."

"And you made this determination while out walking along the river?" Skepticism rang in his voice.

"If you come out here, you'll see for yourself."

"My son has a band concert tonight. I promised I would be on time for a change."

"This won't take long."

"Can't it wait until morning?"

"Well," Cheryl said, "I suppose I could take custody of the evidence myself."

"Evidence?"

"Well, the stuff."

"So *not* evidence."

Cheryl set her jaw, relieved Chief Twitchell could not see the exasperation on her face. "I don't know what it is. That's why I called you. But if someone is monkeying with my credit card, I would like to nip this in the bud."

"Then I suggest you call the credit card company."

Cheryl was not going to admit this obvious action had not been her first impulse. In her mind, finding the number was entangled with larger questions. Resolving one piece would not explain everything.

"There's a bunch of stuff here," she said. She named the items she had identified so far. "Aren't you curious why someone would dump this by the river?"

"I don't get paid to be nosy."

"How can you keep the peace if you're not a little bit nosy about unusual events?"

The police chief was silent, and Cheryl knew from experience that his lips were working in and out.

"We have had a couple of minor burglaries lately," he finally said.

"It won't take you long to run out here," Cheryl said. "You can still get to the band concert."

"Yes, but without my dinner first," Chief Twitchell muttered.

"I'll wait for you." She described where she had left her car and the approximate distance to her current location.

"Fine," he said, "but I can't do anything about your credit card."

"Except perhaps find the person who is using my number."

"We have not established any fraudulent use, Miss Cooper. Let's not get ahead of ourselves."

Cheryl's stomach grumbled as she ended the call. Chief Twitchell was not the only one missing dinner. Most likely Seth Miller was not home yet either. Even Cheryl's cat, Beau, would be looking for his evening feeding soon. Her outing had lost its charm. If Cheryl had considered letting go of observing Seth's odd behavior, finding her own address and credit card number on a sheet of paper rekindled the fire to get to the bottom of this unusual turn the evening had taken.

Cheryl found the flat edge of a boulder and perched on it.

Seven minutes later, Chief Twitchell arrived, the hesitation in his step obvious. He came armed with a battery-powered wide beam of illumination. Cheryl realized the presence of smaller, darker items she had not noticed earlier settled into the mushy ground. Garden hand tools. An empty cylindrical bird feeder. A child's sand bucket.

"None of these things has anything to do with the others," Cheryl said.

"Except they're all here," Chief Twitchell said. "They did not arrive randomly and independently."

"So you do think there's something going on?" Cheryl's heart rate kicked up.

"Nothing as criminal as what you're imagining." Chief Twitchell handed the light to Cheryl and removed a phone from his shirt pocket. "I'll get some pictures for the record."

"So you're going to investigate?"

"I don't expect it will take more than ten minutes tomorrow morning. I'll look at the lists of items from recent unsolved burglaries, and we'll know where these things came from."

Cheryl bit down on her lower lip again, refraining from pointing out the more important questions—who was the thief, and why?

"I suppose you've touched everything?" Chief Twitchell snapped a couple of photos.

Cheryl shrugged. "Some of it. The papers, obviously."

"If you really thought this was evidence of some sort, you should have left it alone."

Cheryl turned her head from his view to allow herself to roll her eyes.

"If this doesn't match any reports I have on file," Chief Twitchell said, "then my guess is someone made illegal use of a public trash bin to dispose of household garbage. If I get lucky, I might write out a ticket. But that's unlikely. Did you see anyone while you were walking?"

"I spoke to Rueben Vogel. He was out having a walk too."

"What did you talk about?"

"Nothing in particular. He doesn't like feeling housebound on his daughter's farm. Honestly, he hardly stopped long enough to say more than a polite hello."

"These could be his things, I suppose."

"Rueben? You can't be serious. Besides, what would he be doing with my credit card number?"

"You'd better show me the papers." Lackluster, Chief Twitchell put out a hand.

Cheryl placed the thickest folder in his grasp.

"Did you see anyone else?" He flipped through a few sheets of paper, making no effort to persuade her of genuine interest.

Cheryl drew in a breath. "I saw another Amish man. I was up there." She pointed. "He was down here poking through things."

"A name would help," Chief Twitchell said.

"I'm not sure. It might have been Seth Miller."

Chief Twitchell didn't ask what Seth was doing. Cheryl said nothing about the oar.

"What happens next?" she asked.

"I'll track them both down and talk to them. See if they saw anything," Chief Twitchell said. "Some of the young ones have phones, if they can get away with it, but the old geezers don't. Either way, I don't think you have to bother any more about it."

Cheryl opened her mouth to protest, but she could already hear his repeated response. *Call your credit card company.*

"I guess I'll put as much of this as I can in the trunk and the rest in the backseat of my squad car," the chief said. "Then I'll give you a lift back to your vehicle, and we'll both be on our way."

Cheryl nodded and began to help pick up the dank items and arrange them in the trunk. Ten minutes later she was in her own car. As the police chief drove away, Cheryl thought how quiet the police car was. She'd forgotten to tell the chief about the backfiring that startled her and the car she had not even noticed before it raced away.

Tomorrow, she thought. If she called Chief Twitchell again now, he was likely to hang up on her. She put the key in the ignition and turned it. Perhaps she would come back in the daylight and look around again. Just in case.

At home, Cheryl left the car in the driveway and let herself in the back door of her aunt's cottage. Mitzi had been emphatic that Cheryl feel free to make whatever changes she liked to the home, but for the most part Cheryl left things as they were. Memories of childhood visits tumbled out of every cupboard or closet she opened, and Cheryl relished them. When the weather was warmer and she could have the windows open, she might put a fresh coat of paint on the walls, but she doubted she would change the color.

She fumbled for the light switch inside the kitchen door. Too late she realized she had stepped on the cat's tail. Beau snarled and darted. Cheryl focused on halting a fresh flow of adrenaline.

"Beau, come here," she said.

The cat circled the kitchen table before going underneath and jumping onto one of the chair cushions. Cheryl gently slid the chair out and scooped up the cat.

"It's all right," she said. "Nobody's trying to hurt you." She was talking to herself as much as to Beau. Watching Seth do something that made no sense, sliding around in the mud, jumping at a car she hadn't realized was there, finding personal information in an unexpected place, picking through waterlogged rummage—none of this had been on Cheryl's to-do list when she drove out to the river's edge. *Watch the sunset. Feel the marvel of her body in motion. Breathe deeply of fresh air. Listen to the water swirl around rocks. Pray.* Those were the things she had gone to the river to do.

Before she even removed her jacket, Cheryl set milk, unsweetened cocoa, vanilla, and sugar on the counter. Suddenly hot chocolate warming her gullet and holding her cat in her lap were all she wanted for the evening. Holding Beau in one hand, Cheryl shirked out of her jacket and hung it over the back of a chair. Aunt Mitzi had been the one to teach Cheryl that hot chocolate worth drinking did not come from a dry mix in a cardboard box. Hot chocolate was one of the few things Cheryl could manage to cook. She pulled a saucepan from the back of the stove and began the patient process. Beau inched his way up her shoulder and draped himself there.

Cheryl's mind drifted to Naomi's kitchen. Naomi's stove and refrigerator were powered without plugging them into outlets, but otherwise the process of storing and preparing food was the same. Of course, Naomi cooked every night for a houseful. Levi, Seth's oldest son from his first marriage to Ruth, lived and worked on the farm, and so did Caleb. The three children Seth and Naomi had together—Eli, Esther, and Elizabeth—were there as well. Cheryl didn't imagine the spacious Miller kitchen ever was as quiet as the cozy room in which she stood and stirred cocoa and sugar into milk.

Naomi was the reason Cheryl couldn't let go of the night's events. She could not stand the thought that somehow Naomi might be hurt by them.

Cheryl sat on the couch in the living room to drink her hot chocolate and scratch Beau's neck. There she dozed, eventually rousing enough to move properly to bed and sleep soundly.

When she woke in the morning, she knew the most important thing she would do all day was talk to Naomi. Naomi supplied jams, breads, and other treats to the Swiss Miss, but Cheryl could never be sure when Naomi would bring something in. They didn't need a schedule because the homemade goods sold within hours—minutes sometimes—of when Naomi or one of her children dropped them off.

Normally when Naomi came into the shop, Cheryl's heart lifted at the sight of the married Amish woman who had befriended the new kid in town. Cheryl would drop whatever she was doing to chat for as long as Naomi could stay. Sometimes she plugged in the teakettle in the small office at the back of the shop, and the two of them would have a catch-up visit even if only two days had passed since their last conversation. Today Cheryl didn't want to gamble. She must talk to Naomi.

What was Naomi's husband doing wandering along the river when he should have been home on the farm for supper?

Something was wrong.

The walk to the Swiss Miss was only four blocks. It rarely made sense to take the car, even in frigid Ohio winter weather. Parking was too much trouble to bother with, and Cheryl enjoyed a brace of fresh air.

Sugarcreek was a charming village. Cheryl had thought so even as a girl visiting Aunt Mitzi and Uncle Ralph. Restaurants, crafts, antiques, handcrafted furniture, collectibles—Sugarcreek held enough interesting shops with a twist of history to make visitors feel as though they were stepping into a Swiss village, complete with the world's largest cuckoo clock and murals painted on the sides of buildings. The Swiss Miss was built in the same cottage style as Aunt Mitzi's home. Painted a crisp cream color, the outside featured cornflower blue accents and adorable red shutters. The turret-shaped room on one side of the building piqued

Cheryl's imagination after living in boxy apartments in Columbus for so long.

Cheryl unlocked the front door and set to work unpacking the latest shipment of Valentine's Day items and arranging them on shelves. The four days until Valentine's Day would bring in steady traffic as both townspeople and tourists looked for unexpected sentimental gift items.

Lydia Troyer, with her long striking black hair, came in through the front door just after Cheryl turned the sign from Closed to Open.

"Am I late?" she said.

Cheryl glanced at one of six cuckoo clocks that ticked a ragged rhythm next to each other on a shelf. This was a gesture of habit. She didn't need to look. The clocks had all crowed a few minutes ago, so there could be no doubt that the time was shortly after ten.

"Right on time," Cheryl said.

Lydia's hours in the store were not as predictable as Esther Miller's, but Cheryl knew she was lucky to have her—though the Amish would not say it was luck. God's will. Either way, Lydia might be just the answer to the challenges of the next few days.

An Amish teenager enjoying *rumspringa*, Lydia dressed in nice tops over her latest-style jeans with her trim cell phone creating a slight bulge in a back pocket. Her hair was clipped back out of the way but not hidden under an Amish prayer *kapp*. Lydia sometimes had to acquiesce to her family's household schedule when arranging rides into town to work a few hours each week for Cheryl. Rarely did Cheryl have a fixed appointment, so extending flexibility to

Lydia was an easy grace. Today, though, Cheryl was eager for Lydia's arrival so she could be free to leave the Swiss Miss and drive out to the Miller farm. First she had to wait for the morning tour bus from Annie's Amish Tours. While the winter tourist traffic was nowhere near what it was in the summer, the tour bus company was mindful of particular interest around holidays. Cheryl had already been warned that the days before Valentine's Day would bring both morning and afternoon buses. Visitors would disembark across the street from the Swiss Miss and then browse the immediate shops before moving down the street. Even if they didn't make a purchase, Cheryl felt better if two shop representatives were present. It wouldn't be fair to leave Lydia alone with the glut of questions and shoppers.

The clocks announced eleven before Cheryl could consider leaving the shop. Esther Miller would be in at noon for her three-hour shift. Lydia wouldn't be alone for long, and Cheryl would be back well in advance of the afternoon bus. She gave Lydia some simple instructions about moving items around to feature Valentine's gifts more prominently.

Striding the four blocks home for her car, Cheryl resolved not to alarm her friend, nor offend her. Somehow she would figure out how to tell Naomi what she'd seen and await the simple explanation that Seth surely had provided to his wife. Two miles out of town, Cheryl drove past the maze the Millers operated in the summer and fall, lying idle in the winter months. A creek ran along the property line. Someday Cheryl intended to follow the creek and discover where it met up with the river. For now, she drove through the old covered bridge that spanned the water like a tunnel of history. On the other end, the Millers' white house came into view. Cheryl parked along the fence enclosing a pasture where three Morgan workhorses grazed, awaiting their summons to the day's labor.

Knowing Naomi was likely to be in the home's enormous kitchen, Cheryl walked around the side of the house and knocked on the rear doorframe. Naomi opened the door within seconds and brightened at the sight of Cheryl. The meaty fragrance of stew simmering on the stove made Cheryl instantly ravenous. On the long, sheet-covered table in the middle of the room was evidence that Naomi was sorting household laundry. Swiftly she put on water to boil and set out two cups before pushing the laundry to one end of the table and giving the wood a quick wipe with a damp rag.

Cheryl told the story of finding the rummage and discovering her credit card number.

"It sounds like it was thrown away," Naomi said as she poured steaming water into the cups. "Perhaps weeks or months ago."

"But someone could still have it." Cheryl dipped her tea bag up and down several times. "Or it could have been copied."

Her wallet was stolen once. Lance had warned her not to leave it in the car while they hiked. Cheryl was tired of his haranguing and left it just to make a point—one that backfired. They returned to find the passenger window smashed and her wallet removed from under the seat. Canceling her credit cards and replacing all of her identification had been a nightmare she hoped never to repeat. But she might have to, at least for the card she used in the shop's transactions. Lance would say that a hacker who had one card number could find everything else. Cheryl shut his voice out of her head. Lance was nothing more than a bad habit she needed to break.

"I have a feeling there is something else on your mind." Naomi sweetened her tea.

Cheryl moistened her top lip. "Before I found the papers, I saw somebody looking through everything."

Naomi raised an eyebrow.

"I'm pretty sure it was Seth," Cheryl said softly. "He was acting…peculiar."

"He was late getting home last night." Naomi abandoned her tea and moved to a laundry pile of Seth's dark trousers. "I try to give him space. He turns quite moody every year around this time."

"Why?" Cheryl asked.

"It is a long story," Naomi said, "and not all of it is mine to tell. I am pretty sure I do not even know everything."

"Something to do with Seth?"

"I sometimes wonder how things would have been if I had been his first wife," Naomi said, checking pockets. "But I cannot change that. I just have to trust Gott."

"I don't understand. Is there something in Seth's past you don't know about?"

"I am not sure. There could be a lot I do not know. I am not originally from this community. My family's farm was in Dalton, about thirty miles from here, but my parents had many relatives in Sugarcreek. We visited often while I was growing up, and I had many cousins and friends here. Through those connections, I eventually met and married Seth." Naomi picked up another pair of her husband's pants and pushed her fingers into a pocket. They came out wrapped around a tightly folded piece of blue paper. "*Mmm.* I always check the pockets, but I hardly ever find anything. Seth is not a careless man."

Cheryl held her tongue while Naomi unfolded the bit of paper.

Naomi gasped and pushed the note toward Cheryl.

I am back, it said in ragged block letters. *How could you steal someone's life and walk away? I will be there on the anniversary. Make sure you are. Or else.*

Cheryl looked up at her friend's blanched face.

"Our wedding anniversary is on Friday," Naomi said.

"The day before Valentine's Day," Cheryl murmured. "Then we have three days to figure this out."

Chapter Four

"You cannot tell anyone," Naomi said.

"But this is some sort of threat," Cheryl countered. "Chief Twitchell should know."

Naomi shook her head. "If Seth thought it was something I needed to know about, he would have told me."

"So you're just going to ignore it?"

Naomi reclaimed possession of the note and creased it along the fold lines. "The Bible tells me not to worry but to be thankful and take everything to Gott in prayer."

Cheryl knew the verse from Philippians. *"Do not be anxious about anything, but in every situation, by prayer and petition, with thanksgiving, present your requests to God."* The words did little to settle her mind.

"It's not that simple," Cheryl said.

"Of course it is."

"What happens when Seth realizes the note is missing?"

"He will ask me if I have seen it." Naomi pressed the note between her palms. "That's what he always does when he misplaces something—which is rare."

Cheryl met Naomi's eyes. "And if he doesn't ask you?"

Naomi shrugged one shoulder. "Then it is not important. If he is not worried, why should I concern myself?"

"So you'll just wait to see what happens on Friday—your anniversary?"

"We never make a big event of the day," Naomi said. "The cows will still need milking, and the children will still be looking for their supper."

Cheryl slowly ran her tongue along the arc of her upper lip. "If you're sure that's what you want."

"I am." Naomi picked up an armful of her husband's trousers. "I had better get started on the laundry. Promise you will not tell anyone."

Cheryl leaned back in her chair. At that moment, she only wanted to do what would put Naomi at ease.

"Promise," she said.

Its words permanently impressed in her mind, Cheryl left the note with Naomi. She stood up.

"I should get back to the shop. I could give Esther a ride, if she'd like."

"She is not here," Naomi said. "She had errands, and she does not mind walking to town even in the winter. She says she uses the time to pray, and I think she also likes the independence."

Cheryl glanced at the kitchen clock. At this rate, Esther might get to the Swiss Miss before she did. Back in her car, Cheryl took a moment to circle past the Millers' petting zoo and wave at eighteen-year-old Elizabeth feeding the pygmy goats. Cheryl arrived back at the Swiss Miss feeling more jumbled than when she left.

"I am not sure you have enough Valentine's Day goods," Lydia said as she straightened the remains of a shelf that had been full when Cheryl left two hours ago. "People have been asking about the buttercream fudge from Heini's. Do you want me to call and order more? I think we could sell twenty pounds if we had it."

Certain that sales of chocolate in any form would increase as the calendar approached Valentine's Day, Cheryl nodded. She had stocked the shop for the holiday based on instinct and Christmas traffic. Now she realized she should have looked for her aunt's records from last February.

"They have the credit card on file, right?" Lydia moved toward the office.

"Yes," Cheryl said.

"That makes things easier."

"But don't use it."

"Do not use the credit card?" Lydia scrunched her face. "Are you turning more Amish than I am?"

"I'll give you another card." Cheryl reached into the purse that hung from her shoulder. She had two credit cards of her own, one she used for convenience and paid off each month and the other she reserved for emergencies. She extracted the backup card.

"What is wrong with the shop's card?" Lydia asked. "Are we over the limit?"

Aunt Mitzi had a generous business line of credit. They couldn't possibly be over the limit with normal purchases.

"I think someone has the card number," Cheryl said, handing Lydia the replacement card.

Lydia laughed. "*Ja.* Everybody your *aenti* has ever done business with."

The girl spoke truth. Cheryl scanned the shop and realized the number of vendors the shop did business with added up quickly. If she called the credit card company and suspended the card, a lot of automatic payments would go off the grid. Her years in a bank told her the standard line was it would take a week to ten days to get a new card in the mail. In the meantime, she could spend valuable hours tracking down Web sites and changing to a personal card only to change again when the new business card arrived—and all because of a frivolous panic.

"Maybe it's nothing," Cheryl said. "But what's Valentine's Day without chocolate? So for this one order, let's use a new card. I'll straighten things out."

She would assess the risk by looking at the account online to isolate any unauthorized activity—if there was any.

Lydia retreated to the office, and Cheryl heard her calm voice on the telephone. She did very well for a teenager who had not grown up with electronics. Esther was also part of the backbone of the Swiss Miss. She came in every day for three hours, and bit by bit Cheryl was training her to help with the shop's books and invoices. Esther would be helpful in detecting whether anything was off on the credit card account.

The shop door jangled, and Marion Berryhill from the bookstore down the street caught Cheryl's eye.

"I don't know what his problem is," Marion said, "but he needs to get over it."

"Who?" Cheryl removed a heart-shaped red candy dish from its box and set it atop four identical boxes to display their contents.

"Seth Miller. I know he's not the most outgoing person in town, but he just about knocked me over without so much as a hello."

"Seth?" Cheryl's ears perked up. "Just now?"

"He was marching off somewhere," Marion said.

Cheryl moved toward the door. "Which direction?"

"That way." Marion pointed. "Do you still have those cards of decorative buttons?"

"We moved them into the turret room." The cozy curved space on one side of the old house, opening up to the main room, had quickly become Cheryl's favorite feature. When she'd approached Jacob Hoffman about building custom-made shelving to nestle in the curves, he instead pointed her to a man in Berlin who came and measured and sketched and photographed the space where Cheryl envisioned creating a cozy area to display unique merchandise that would honor and inspire traditional crafts.

She hesitated about helping Marion find the buttons and instead wrapped her fingers around the door handle. "Lydia will be right out to help you."

The oar and the note. What did they have to do with each other, and what did they have to do with Seth? The straightest line to the truth would be a direct question of the one person Cheryl was sure was involved with both items.

Outside, she looked in both directions down the sidewalk and saw no sign of Seth.

"*Or else,*" the note said. Or else what? Cheryl didn't have a wedding anniversary, but if she did she wouldn't want a vague ominous threat hanging over the day. The pallor of Naomi's face when she unfolded and read the mysterious note was an image Cheryl would not forget.

Cheryl reversed her steps without turning around—and ran into a solid obstruction.

"Seth," she said.

"No, it is just me."

Cheryl would know that voice anywhere. She spun around. "Levi!"

"Are you disappointed?"

Cheryl supposed Levi looked like his mother, Seth's late wife. His blond hair and blue eyes were such different coloring than Naomi's children, his half siblings.

"Don't be silly," she said.

"Are you looking for my *daed*?"

"Someone said he was out here."

"Yes, we came into town together. What did you need?"

Cheryl was tempted. Sorely tempted. If she confided in Levi, he might have an explanation. He knew his own father's moods. Levi was a grown man, a decade older than Seth had been when he married Ruth. He was thoughtful and insightful, and he probably understood more of the family dynamics than anyone gave him credit for. If she asked him now, the whole matter could be put to rest.

She doubted it, though. And she had promised Naomi. *"You cannot tell anyone."* If Cheryl had caught up with Seth, speaking candidly to him would not have broken a confidence. But speaking to his son was a different matter.

"It's nothing," she said. "I'd better finish my errands so I can get back to the store." Esther would arrive momentarily, but the next three hours would be the busiest of the day.

"I will walk with you, if you like," Levi said.

Under any other circumstances, Cheryl would have taken Levi up on his offer. The hardware store, the bookstore, the Honey Bee Café, Yoder's Corner—any of those destinations would have provided the welcome diversion of Levi's company.

But Cheryl had decided to go see Chief Twitchell, whose office was just down the street. She couldn't tell him about the note, but she could ask if the items from the riverbank matched any of his burglaries.

"I don't want to hold you up," Cheryl said to Levi.

"I do not mind."

"No, really. I'm just going to be running around in a hurry."

Levi nodded. "Next time."

Levi crossed the street. She had not meant to hurt him, but maybe she had. Cheryl released her breath and lit out for the police station.

"Hello, Delores," she said when Chief Twitchell's receptionist looked up. "Is he in?"

Delores raked fingers through her dark frizzy hair and waved Cheryl in. "Good timing. He just told me he was going to have to find you."

Cheryl passed through the frosted door to the inner office, where Chief Twitchell's eyes arced upward under his salt-and-pepper hair.

"Now, it can't be more than three minutes since I asked Delores to track you down," he said. "If she keeps up this efficiency, I might have to give her a raise."

"Did you find the report?" Cheryl eyed the green vinyl chairs and opted to remain standing.

Chief Twitchell tapped a folder that apparently had earned its place at the top of the pile on his desk. "This report just came in a week ago. A shed in someone's backyard was broken into. Do you know the Thatchers?"

"I know Mrs. Thatcher," Cheryl said.

"Rob and Dianne are good people, even if they do anchor the oddball list," Chief Twitchell said. "How do you know Dianne?"

"She does beautiful cross-stitching. My aunt warned me that she wasn't organized enough to be regular, but that if she ever brought in any table linens, I should take them because they are a hot item."

"Table linens, eh?"

"Napkins, place mats, runners. That sort of thing."

"And has she supplied any of these items to you?"

Cheryl nodded. "A couple of times."

"And did you pay her for them?"

"Of course." The light clicked on in Cheryl's head. "I remember I was surprised to find out she takes credit cards. I gave her my number over the phone."

"There you have it." Below his long nose, Chief Twitchell set his mouth smugly. "Case solved."

Not quite. "We still don't know who had access to the credit card number after it was stolen."

"Teenagers," Chief Twitchell said. "We've had several cases of minor vandalism or burglary in the last couple of months, and they've all traced back to the same bunch of kids."

"How can you be sure the same kids were behind this break-in?"

Chief Twitchell pushed back in his chair. "I graduated the same police academy as your fancy Columbus officers. I assure you I am capable of followin' through and settlin' this matter."

Cheryl opened her mouth, closed it, and opened it again, then said, "I did not mean to imply otherwise."

Chief Twitchell took a sheet of paper from the folder at the top of his pile and pushed it toward Cheryl. "This is what the Thatchers reported missing."

Cheryl scanned the list. Life jacket. Garden tools. Clothing. Business records. The items strewn along the river were accounted for.

Except for one. No oar.

"Is this a complete list of what was stolen?" Cheryl asked. "Or is there a second page?"

"No second page," the chief said. "As to whether it's complete, we only listed what the Thatchers could recall. Can you name every item in your garage or basement?"

She pushed out a sigh. "No. I'm sure I can't."

Chief Twitchell punched numbers into the phone on his desk and then hit the Speaker button.

Four rings. Cheryl was expecting an answering machine to kick in when a voice came on.

"Hello?"

"Rob, this is Chief Twitchell."

Cheryl leaned in to listen.

"I think we found the items that went missin' from your shed," Chief Twitchell said. "I've logged everythin' in and taken all the photos I need, so we should be able to return your belongings soon."

"Are you talking about that junk my wife doesn't want me to see?"

Chief Twitchell chuckled. "Well, now, I'm not goin' to get in between you and Dianne, but we recovered some items that match what the two of you put in the report."

"Was it those kids again?"

"Innocent until proven guilty," the chief said, "but I'll go out and talk to their parents this afternoon."

"All I have to say is good riddance to most of that stuff," Rob said.

"There were some business records," Chief Twitchell said.

"Every now and then Dianne gets scared the IRS will come after her, but I don't know anything about her files. If they audit her, we're sunk."

"We'll be in touch about returnin' everything." The chief ended the call and turned to Cheryl. "Looks like we've wrapped this up."

"But we don't know where these things have been," Cheryl said. "Anybody could have seen the papers."

"You let me know if there's any funny business on your account, and we'll have somethin' to work with." Chief Twitchell stood up as if to usher Cheryl out. "But without evidence of a crime, I have nothin' to investigate."

"What about Seth? And Rueben?" Cheryl asked, refusing to budge. "They might have seen somebody. Don't you need witnesses to build a case?"

Chief Twitchell sighed. "I'll talk to them. And I will talk to the boys. But let's not make this a bigger situation than it really is."

CHAPTER FIVE

Cheryl wasn't outside the police station for more than seventy-three seconds before she pivoted and hustled back inside.

"Delores!" she said. "Tell Chief Twitchell to come quickly."

"He's not going to want to," Delores said.

"Do you want to spend all day looking for an Amish man who doesn't carry a phone?"

"You sold me." Delores pushed back from her desk.

Cheryl stood in the doorframe, one foot inside the police station and the other outside while she tracked her prey.

The chief appeared. "I was under the impression we concluded our business."

"Seth Miller is right down the street. Now's your chance." Cheryl took the chief's jacket off the hook beside the door and tossed it at him.

He caught it with a sigh, but he put his arms through the sleeves. Cheryl set a pace that would allow them to intersect with Seth's path before he disappeared from sight again.

"Mr. Miller," the chief said. "I wonder if I might have a word with you."

The expression Seth offered was both expectant and reluctant.

Chief Twitchell glanced at Cheryl. "We recovered some stolen items from the riverbank last night. I have a witness who places you there."

Subtle. But Cheryl didn't care if Seth knew she was the witness. She had questions, and she wanted answers.

Seth looked from the police chief to Cheryl and back again but volunteered no information.

"How about if I buy you a cup of coffee?" Chief Twitchell said. "You might have seen somethin' you didn't realize was significant."

Seth nodded slowly.

"Yoder's Corner all right?" the chief said.

Another nod.

Inside her boot, Cheryl's toe tapped with impatience.

"This won't take long," Chief Twitchell said.

The two men turned shoulder to shoulder toward Yoder's Corner, where August cooked and Greta kept the food and coffee coming. Cheryl stayed a few steps behind them, walking not back toward the Swiss Miss but away from it. Esther was reliable. She would be there soon, and the girls were more than capable of handling the shop. So far Seth had not said so much as good morning, but it was a good move on Chief Twitchell's part to invite him to the place with the best cinnamon rolls in eastern Ohio. That should soften him up. Cheryl did not want to miss this conversation.

"Table for two, please," Chief Twitchell said to Greta.

Cheryl flinched. If the chief saw her response, he ignored it.

Greta raised her eyebrows, and Cheryl muttered, "Table for one, I guess."

Fine. Cheryl didn't have to sit at the table with Chief Twitchell and Seth Miller. Her hearing was plenty sharp. But she wasn't leaving this to chance. When Greta led the police chief and Seth toward a table against the rear wall, Cheryl eyed one nearby and followed a respectful but determined five steps behind. A wide post gave the illusion of privacy in the back corner, though Cheryl doubted it blocked much sound. Unless the men whispered, she would be able to hear, and Chief Twitchell couldn't do anything about it.

"I see Rueben Vogel is here." Chief Twitchell gestured across the room toward the gray head bent over a cup. "Greta, would you ask Rueben to stop by?"

Avoiding Seth's eyes, Cheryl rearranged the napkin and silverware at the table next to Chief Twitchell's. She hadn't noticed Rueben sitting quietly at the table nearest the kitchen. Now she watched as Greta ambled across the room, spoke to Rueben, and pointed toward the police chief. It looked like Rueben had finished off a cinnamon roll. Greta picked up his plate and coffee mug. Rueben scooted his chair back, found his balance, and crossed the room.

"Greta says you wanted to see me," Rueben said.

"I understand you were walkin' along the river last night," Chief Twitchell said.

"That's right."

"Did you notice who else was out there?"

Rueben looked confused and glanced at Cheryl. "Well, Cheryl Cooper was there, but I am guessing she's the one who told you I was there."

"That's right."

Cheryl smothered a smirk.

"I mean, did you see anyone else?"

"I do not expect it is a crime for folks to take a stroll." Rueben stroked his beard.

"So you didn't see anythin' unusual?" Chief Twitchell turned his coffee mug over so Greta could fill it.

"Saw some birds I thought would have been in Florida at this time of year if they had any sense."

The laugh escaped Cheryl's throat.

"Any unusual non-livin' items?" Chief Twitchell persisted, but Cheryl still hadn't heard Seth utter a single syllable. "Somethin' that looked like it didn't belong on the riverbank?"

"I do not know what you're talking about, Chief Twitchell," Rueben said. "I do know it is time for me to head on home. My daughter will be looking for me to make sure I get my nap."

Rueben winked at Cheryl, and she couldn't help but smile. If she had to pick favorites among people in Sugarcreek, Rueben would be at the top of the list.

Chief Twitchell waved off his irritation and turned to Seth. "Now, I'd like to hear what you saw last night at about half past five."

Seth cleared his throat. Cheryl watched Rueben mosey across the restaurant and out the door.

"Seth, were you on the river last night?" Chief Twitchell asked.

"Near the river. Not on it." Seth raised his coffee mug to his lips.

"And what did you see?"

"Water. Rocks. Plenty of mud, I'll tell you that. The usual."

"Perhaps you can think along less usual lines." The chief loaded his coffee with creamer. "It might help if you tell me why you were out there."

"I grew up not six miles from here," Seth said. "I am hardly a stranger along the river."

Greta paused at Cheryl's table, a fist wrapped around the coffeepot's handle. "Would you rather have tea? I know you sometimes drink tea."

Cheryl turned over her mug. "Coffee's fine." She would do whatever necessary to urge Greta on.

"We'll have some fresh cinnamon rolls in about ten minutes," Greta said, her eyes taunting.

"Just coffee today," Cheryl said. She'd missed Chief Twitchell's last question and Seth's response.

"I could bring you a copy of the *Budget*," Greta said as she poured coffee. "It is last week's edition, but it is still interesting. I know you sometimes like that too."

"Not today, thank you." Cheryl had missed another exchange between the men.

"All right then," Greta said. "I'll leave you be."

Yes. Please. Do that.

At last Greta moved on, freeing up Cheryl's view of the chief's table.

"So that's all you saw?" Chief Twitchell said.

Cheryl sighed into her coffee. If Seth had explained his reasons for being at the river instead of home for supper, she'd missed it.

"I did not see Rueben, if that is what you are asking," Seth said.

"I have no reason to doubt Rueben," Chief Twitchell said.

Cheryl did not doubt Rueben either. It was Seth who stirred up questions. Seth whose eyes gave him away when he teased his children. Seth who was a hardworking family man. Seth whose wife trusted him. Seth who welcomed Cheryl into his home frequently but who last night had ignored his name coming from her lips.

Seth who picked an old oar out of a pile of junk.

And did what with it?

That's what Cheryl wanted to know. Of course, Chief Twitchell knew nothing about the oar—not that it had been stolen and not that Seth had carried it off. Cheryl had no way to be certain the oar had been among the stolen items. It wasn't on the Thatchers' list.

Even more important, Chief Twitchell did not know about the note Naomi pulled from her husband's pants.

"How about a car you didn't recognize?" Chief Twitchell asked Seth.

"I drive a buggy, Chief Twitchell," Seth said. "Why would I pay any attention to the *Englischers'* cars?"

"I'm just trying to narrow down who else might have been near the river yesterday afternoon," the chief said. "But it doesn't matter. I know where the stolen items came from, and I'm pretty sure I know who took them. It's just a matter of making sure the confession includes both the burglary and the disposal."

Seth swigged the last of his coffee. "Am I free to go?"

"I'd be happy to buy you a cinnamon roll," the chief said.

"No time for that. Thank you for the *kaffee*."

"Thanks for your help."

Seth gave a slight nod at Cheryl on his way out. Chief Twitchell leaned back in his chair and crossed his arms over his chest.

"So did you get all that?" he said.

Cheryl was determined to contain her exasperation.

"Just as I thought," the chief said. "Neither one of them was much help. They didn't see anybody. They don't know anything about the items."

Cheryl opened her mouth and clamped it shut again. Chief Twitchell was settling for unconvincing responses. But she had little argument to counter with. Seth had not lied—at least not as far as Cheryl heard—but couldn't the chief of police detect that he was withholding something?

"It's the teenagers I need," Chief Twitchell said. "They'll be out of school in a few hours."

The restaurant's front door opened, and a band of tourists came in. With their cameras, sturdy walking shoes, and shopping bags, they weren't hard to spot.

Cheryl bolted to her feet. She yanked her cell phone out of her pocket to check the time. Even if Esther had arrived, Lydia would be getting antsy to be on her way.

"Now I think I'll have one of those fresh rolls," Chief Twitchell said.

Cheryl tossed a couple of dollar bills on the table and steered toward the door.

Back at the Swiss Miss, she caught Lydia's eye. "Sorry. I didn't mean to be gone so much today."

"You can pay me in chocolate." Lydia began to gather her personal belongings. "Heini's says they have someone coming this way tomorrow, so they will deliver."

"Perfect. Thank you for staying all this time."

"We sold a few things," Lydia said. "And I found this on the counter."

Cheryl took the envelope Lydia held out. Levi's name was scripted neatly on the front. "That's odd."

"I did not see who left it," Lydia said. "Things were busy while you were out."

"It's too bad it didn't turn up earlier." Cheryl turned the envelope over to inspect the seal. "I ran into Levi today. I could have given it to him."

Lydia put on her coat and buttoned it up. "Do you want me to try to find him?"

Cheryl glanced out the door. She certainly was not inclined to go looking for Seth at the moment. Levi could be anywhere in town.

"I'll keep it for now," Cheryl said. Esther could always take it home to her brother.

She hit a button to open the cash register and tucked the envelope under the drawer.

Chapter Six

D
o you need me tomorrow?" Lydia's dark eyes questioned.

"Yes, please," Cheryl said. "Every day this week, if you're able. Whatever hours you can manage."

"I will see what I can do. See you." Lydia tucked her cell phone into her jeans pocket and headed for the door.

Four days until the evening of Valentine's Day, when it would be too late for gift-buying.

Three days until Seth's and Naomi's anniversary, when "*or else*" would happen.

The week promised to be busy. Cheryl would need all the help in the shop she could arrange.

At the table near the front window of the shop, Rueben Vogel sat playing checkers with his brother, Ben, who had left the Amish church decades ago but never abandoned his brother. An older Amish woman browsed an aisle of knickknacks. Cheryl fished for her name. Mrs. Lehman. She came in to look on a regular basis but rarely bought anything more than a piece of fudge. On the far side, two younger Englisch women with small children in strollers gabbed about how to plant the suggestion in their husbands' minds to come in and buy the teapots they eyed as Valentine's gifts.

On her way out, Lydia paused at the checkerboard. "You have at least three possible jumps, Dr. Vogel."

Ben Vogel gave Lydia a playful scowl and shooed her off. As the door closed behind the girl, Cheryl ambled over to the brothers. Lydia was right. Ben had at least three jumps, but they were all traps. The brothers played checkers in the shop three or four times a week. In the last few months, Cheryl had seen enough of their strategies to know Rueben was ready to pounce. Ben had a few tricks of his own, but when he was ready to go home, he would march his pieces right into his brother's snares.

"Did you really not see anything on the river the other night?" Cheryl asked.

"I saw you," he said. "I saw the sunset. I saw a hungry squirrel and wished I had something to give him, but I am pretty sure my daughter counts the walnuts in her pantry."

Cheryl's mind churned with reasons Rueben would avoid saying he saw the stolen litter. None of them were any good, and she was left with the reality that he simply had not lifted his eyes the way she had at that high point of the walk. He talked to her without looking over her shoulder, and he must not have heard her question when she asked what he supposed happened. Rueben Vogel had gone reluctantly into his aging years, but he was hardly the sneaky type.

Ben slid a checker forward and somehow managed to avoid a trap. "How's the boy?"

Puzzled, Cheryl saw Ben glance at Rueben. Did he mean one of Rueben's grandsons on his daughter's farm?

"Keeps to himself." Rueben moved a checker.

"Surprised to see him," Ben said.

"Me too."

"Hardly recognized him."

"A daed knows his *kinder*," Rueben said.

"Of course. Been years."

"Thirty."

"Is he coming into town?"

"Doubt it."

"Why'd he come?"

"Hasn't said."

Cheryl turned up one side of her mouth in a hesitant smile. For years the brothers played checkers in silence. This was Rueben's way of shunning Ben for leaving the church to become a doctor. Although Rueben wasn't shunning now, their exchanges still barely qualified as conversation.

Mrs. Lehman had wandered over to watch the competition. "Are you talking about the racing boy?"

Cheryl was tempted to pull a small notebook off the shelf and start keeping notes so she could later figure out what everyone was talking about. She almost missed Rueben's nod in answer to Mrs. Lehman's question.

"Those were beautiful days on the river," Mrs. Lehman said, inhaling as if breathing in a treasured memory. "We should start the races up again. The young people would like it. Would they not, Cheryl?"

Cheryl lifted her shoulders in a half shrug. "I'm a little lost."

"Long time ago." Ben's finger slithered toward a checker to nudge it forward.

Rueben executed a victorious triple jump. Ben crowned the piece that now sat in the center of the first row of squares.

"I think we all see where this game is going," Ben said.

"Maybe," Rueben said. "Maybe not."

Cheryl creased her brow. Were they still talking about checkers?

In reflex to a shadow settling outside the shop window, Cheryl turned her head. Seth Miller leaned one shoulder against the building, his gaze vaguely aimed at something down the street. Cheryl glanced at Mrs. Lehman and the two women with strollers, who had progressed to the display of cuckoo clocks equally as quaint as the teapots. She could keep an eye on the shop and speak to Seth at the same time. Cheryl stepped outside.

Seth's head turned at the sound of the bell on her door. "Oh. Thought it might be Naomi coming out."

"I haven't seen her today," Cheryl said. "I thought you came into town with Levi."

"That's right." Seth turned his head away again.

"Seth," Cheryl said, "what's going on?"

"I came into town to look at some equipment catalogs at the Amish general store, got waylaid by the chief of police—thanks to you—and now I am waiting for Mrs. Swartzentruber to drop off my wife following their lunchtime visit. We will collect Levi, probably at the hardware store, and we will all go home. We would wait for Esther, but she prefers to walk. I believe Naomi will have some items for you, which is why I am standing outside the Swiss Miss."

On any other day, Cheryl might have thought Seth was teasing her with this sudden outpouring of detail. Today it felt evasive.

"I saw the oar," she said softly.

He said nothing.

"I saw you take it out of that pile of stuff that was stolen."

More silence.

"Everything in that pile was broken in some way," she said.

"Maybe not," Seth muttered.

"You were quite deliberate."

"I usually am."

That was true. As Naomi had said just a few hours ago, Seth was not a careless man.

"Why did you take it?" Cheryl asked.

"Why does it matter to you?" Seth countered.

"I care about Naomi. It is not like you."

"This has nothing to do with my wife."

"I can't help wondering why you wanted it."

"It is not anything you need to worry about."

"I'm not *worried*, exactly."

"Then it is not anything you need to be nosy about."

His words stung. Questions spun through her mind, but she clamped her mouth closed.

"The oar will be where it belongs soon enough."

Where? Cheryl wanted to know. *Why?*

"I will go look for Levi." Seth stepped away from the shop's wall. "If Naomi comes, please tell her I am at the hardware store."

"Of course." The men in town seemed able to spend hours poking around that little store jam-packed with bits of metal in every formation Cheryl could imagine and gadgets for every task. Cheryl rarely went in without a specific item in mind.

Seth paced away, not in a hurry, not lingering. Nothing in his physical demeanor suggested this was not an ordinary outing into town—although Cheryl could not help wondering why Seth had been moving up and down Main Street for so long. No one else watching him would think twice about what they saw.

Cheryl turned to the shop door and nearly collided with Ben.

"Game over?" she said.

Ben smiled. "With Rueben, it is always game on."

Inside, Rueben was restoring the checkers to their wooden storage box.

"Triumph?" Cheryl said.

"I do not like it when he lets me win." Rueben set the box precisely in the center of the checkerboard. "Next time I will not make it so easy for him to do that."

"It's all in fun," Cheryl said. "What was all that talk about the river races? And do you have a son visiting from out of town?"

Rueben nodded toward the counter at the front of the store, where the two Englischer women stood with a couple of items to please their children. Smooth-sanded wooden toys, carved in one piece without moveable parts that might be choking hazards, always seemed to attract parents of children still in strollers. Abandoning her questions—for now—Cheryl took her place behind the counter and rang up the two sales on the ancient cash register. The cash and credit card receipts she saw in the drawer told her Lydia had done brisk business.

As she watched the customers leave, Cheryl realized Rueben and Mrs. Lehman had slipped out as well. At the counter, an older customer labored over a check. Occasionally people still wrote checks with entire account numbers spread across the bottom. Cheryl liked to think the debit and credit card numbers were more secure. The old cash register made for a good show, but Aunt Mitzi had made sure people felt safe using their plastic.

But the store's credit card number was scrawled on that sheet of paper still in Chief Twitchell's office. And Cheryl wanted to know where it had been.

The bell jangled, and Naomi entered.

Cheryl looked up. "It's not often I see you twice in one day."

Naomi's sunny smile contrasted with her husband's grumpy face outside the shop only a few minutes ago.

"Oh, I saw Seth," Cheryl said. "He said to tell you he would be in the hardware store when you're ready."

Naomi's smile faded. "How was he?"

Cheryl took Naomi's elbow and steered her into the turret room. In its current state of sparse displays, few customers lingered there. "Actually, I've seen him more than once today."

Naomi raised her eyebrows and set the basket she carried over one arm on an empty shelf.

"I was there—sort of—when Chief Twitchell asked Seth what he'd seen last night." Cheryl recounted the details of the encounter at Yoder's Corner. "When I talked to you earlier, I left something out."

Naomi fidgeted with the basket.

"Seth took something last night," Cheryl said. "An oar. But he didn't mention it to Chief Twitchell, and the Thatchers didn't have it on the list of items taken from their shed."

"But we do not even have a boat," Naomi said. "Seth has always refused to let the children enjoy recreation on the river."

Cheryl watched the shifting countenance of her friend. "Does an oar have something to do with the part of the story you said is not yours to tell?"

"I have no idea," Naomi said.

"Or the note?" Cheryl said.

Naomi waved a hand. "I have been praying all day, and I am not going to worry about the note."

Cheryl paused. "It sounded threatening to me, Naomi."

"We do not even know if it was meant for Seth."

"It was in his pocket."

"Maybe he is helping a friend."

"But it referred to your anniversary."

"I have peace in the decision to trust my husband," Naomi said. "Whatever the note means, Seth will take care of it. 'A heart at peace gives life to the body.'"

"And the oar?"

"If he wanted it, he had a good reason. I trust him."

Cheryl had no words. She had never been married. Even while she was engaged to Lance, she would not have been satisfied with trusting odd behavior. Perhaps she had never loved him at all—not the way Naomi loved Seth.

Or maybe love was blind.

"I brought you some scrumptious things." Changing the subject, Naomi unfolded the towel that lined the basket. Inside were several sealed containers. With a sly grin, she popped the corner on one of them and removed the lid.

"Valentine's goodies!" Cheryl's eyes feasted on the assortment of heart-shaped cookies thickly frosted in red and pink.

"Rachel Swartzentruber is quite the baker, you know. She was taking these out of the oven when I arrived, so we frosted them together. There are four dozen here, and I am sure she would do more for you if you wanted them."

"The tourists tomorrow afternoon will snatch these up."

"I can hear the cash register dinging already."

"Oh, that reminds me!" Cheryl walked to the counter, opened the register, lifted the drawer, and removed the envelope with Levi's name on it.

"What have we here?" Naomi took the envelope.

"I admit I'm curious."

"It is handwritten with no return address."

"Quite the mystery."

"I had better get down to the hardware store." Naomi tucked the envelope into the outer pocket of her purse. She caught Cheryl's gaze. "It will all work out. Whatever it is, it will be just as Gott intends."

Cheryl swallowed hard.

"Let it go," Naomi said. "Just let it go. Seth will work it out."

Naomi was one of the wisest people Cheryl had ever known. But the smile on her face was artificial. Cheryl knew the difference. "Let it go" didn't seem like the right advice in this situation. Not with "*or else*" folded up in Seth's trousers.

CHAPTER SEVEN

Early the next morning on her way into the Swiss Miss, Cheryl popped into Hoffman's Furniture store. Like many of the shops along Main Street, the front door was unlocked before official business hours began. Jacob was Mennonite, not Old Order Amish, but he sold copies of the *Budget*, which came out on Wednesdays. Sometime during the night, Cheryl had decided this week's edition might be important to peruse. Sitting on the stool behind the counter at the Swiss Miss, she opened the weekly Amish newspaper. She read it nearly every week now, tucking away what she learned about the Amish from reading it and understanding the people she saw on the street better every day.

This week, though, she flipped past the stories and news and went straight to the personal ads. Maybe whoever left that note for Seth would communicate another way as well—or with someone else. Reading personal ads was like reading teasers for much bigger stories. The small bits they revealed stirred her imagination to what they might mean. People selling farm equipment might be moving. A cryptic ad looking for Leah or Aaron or Isaiah might be a parent seeking news on an adult child who had left the district. An elusive description of a found item might be a way of hoping the true owner did not recognize it.

But today there was nothing. This week featured fewer ads than usual, and none of them sounded remotely like the note in Seth's pocket.

Cheryl folded the paper and left it on the counter. Curious tourists sometimes liked to turn the pages. It was time for Cheryl to get down to business. She would sweep the floor, dust the shelves, and make a list of small organizational tasks Esther could complete if traffic through the store lulled. Esther could also take a deposit to the bank. With a little bit of training, Naomi's daughter had proven surprisingly adept at tracking financial records using computer software. Cheryl had gotten over her surprise months ago at how many of the local Amish businesses relied on telephones and computers to make a living. Seth's and Naomi's enterprises were no different. Although they did not keep a phone in their home, the maze and petting zoo on the Miller farm relied on modern communication to handle group reservations, electronic payments, feed for the animals, and veterinary bills. A phone shack, far enough away from the house so as not to disturb activities within but convenient to the two businesses, served the family's needs.

So far Cheryl had not detected anything odd in the online record of the shop's credit card—she had looked four times—but even after several months in Sugarcreek she was still getting used to the way vendor names appeared on invoices and payments for the shop's business. Esther could have a look too. A second set of eyes would make Cheryl feel better.

More fudge, she wrote on a half sheet of paper. Lydia's estimate of twenty pounds seemed low.

Cheese. Heini's used Amish milk in their cheese, a tidbit of information that seemed to appeal to tourists.

Pay for cookies. Cheryl was certain the Valentine's cookies would sell well, but if she lost track of the detail of paying the bakers, Rachel Swartzentruber and Naomi Miller were unlikely to mention it.

List of vendors. As long as Cheryl would enlist Esther to watch for erroneous credit card transactions, they might as well gather a list of suppliers whose invoices were automatically paid with the card. It would be a good starting point for updating all the accounts.

Ugh. Cheryl hated the thought.

When the shop's front door opened, Cheryl expected one of the townspeople. Cheryl's habit of arriving early and not bothering to lock the door behind her was common. Most of the town did not come to life until shopping hours began at midmorning, but the Sugarcreek regulars knew they could find shop owners and managers already at work.

What was it about Levi Miller that made her heart threaten to skip a beat? He wore a warm black jacket, but she saw the top of his white shirt just above the zipper. His blue eyes caught morning light and seemed a deeper shade.

"I just wanted to say thank you," Levi said.

"For what?" Cheryl put her pen down.

"For being sure I received that envelope."

"Oh. Right." Cheryl still did not know how the envelope had made its way into the shop the previous day.

"Someone gave me tickets to the Sugarcreek Valentine's Day banquet on Saturday."

Cheryl perked up. "They're raising money for playground equipment, right?"

Levi nodded. "Along the river—but not too close to the water."

"A worthy cause." Cheryl sought his gaze. Why had Levi thought it was important for her to know the contents of the envelope?

Cheryl had made a contribution to the project in the name of the Swiss Miss and another in her own name, but she had declined purchasing tickets to the banquet. The idea of buying one ticket and going alone held no appeal, and if she bought a pair she would have to find someone to go with her. Buying tickets and not showing up hardly seemed fair to the people planning the event.

So she had not bought tickets.

But here was Levi Miller, in possession of tickets, talking to her.

What would she wear to go to a town dinner with an Amish man? Valentine's Day called for red, but the only red dress she owned was sassy, slightly too smooth fitting. It would send the wrong message.

Navy-blue was a better message. Navy-blue with a small white print. Stately rather than sassy. That was it. She had the perfect belt, and she could wear the pearls Aunt Mitzi had figured she would never need in Papua New Guinea.

Or yellow. The yellow dress was longer and had a higher neckline. And it was livelier than navy without being immodest.

Cheryl prepared for the invitation. Of course she would say she would be delighted to go. Attending alone or scrounging up a companion was one thing. Accepting an invitation from Levi Miller was a different matter entirely.

Should she offer to drive? Should she say his buggy would be fine? Would this be an official date, or just two friends supporting a community effort? Would Seth and Naomi be glad to see them together, or confused about what a budding relationship between Levi and an Englischer would mean?

"So anyway," he said, "I just wanted you to know I appreciated that you made sure I got the tickets."

"Of course."

"I also wanted to ask about something else."

Something else. Not the banquet.

Stones sank in Cheryl's stomach. The moment had passed. He was not going to ask her. She had fretted through her wardrobe and her romantic status for nothing.

"Did my *maam* seem all right when you saw her yesterday?"

Now her stomach clenched.

"I found her sitting by herself after Daed and everyone else went to bed. Her Bible was in her lap, open to Philippians, but I do not think that is what she was thinking about."

Cheryl's brain flashed a Proceed with Caution sign. "I don't think yesterday was the greatest day she ever had."

"It was as if just getting through the day was all she could manage," Levi said.

A heart at peace gives life to the body. Maybe trusting Seth was not as easy for Naomi to do as it was to speak the words.

"She and Daed circled around each other all through supper and clearing up. He took twice as long as he needed for the evening barn chores. He did not want Caleb or Eli or me to help him. It was as if he wanted to be somewhere else—no, it was like he *was* somewhere else. My sisters could not wait to go up to their bedroom and get away from whatever is going on."

"Has anything unusual happened at home?" Cheryl asked, unsure what clues Levi might hold.

"It happens every year," Levi said. "Their anniversary gets close, and Daed goes into a shell. I think the older we get, the more we realize something is going on. We all just wait for it to be over."

"It always gets better?" Cheryl said.

Levi nodded. "It takes a few days, maybe a week. Then he comes back to us like it never happened."

"Then things will get better."

Levi shook his head. "It is different this year. Something happened yesterday that made it worse. I do not know what it was, and they are not talking to each other."

Cheryl took a deep breath and exhaled slowly as she considered her options.

"I saw your dad out by the river on Monday," she said.

"He was late for supper."

Cheryl nodded. "I figured he would be."

"And he had mud on his boots. Maam asked him not to walk through the house that way."

"Did he bring anything home with him?" Cheryl asked.

Levi shrugged. "Such as?"

"An oar."

"What would he do with an oar? We do not even have a boat."

"That's what your maam said."

"Because it is true. Daed hates the water."

"He was pretty determined to get that oar." Cheryl described the process she had observed. "When I tried to talk to him about it yesterday, he basically said it was none of my business."

"He likes you. You know that, right?"

"Yeah. Well. It didn't seem that way yesterday." Cheryl settled on the stool behind the counter and wished she had a chair to offer to Levi. "So I wondered if he took the oar home."

"If he did, he hid it. I have not seen it."

"But why would he hide it?"

"Are you sure it was an oar? You said it was dark."

"It was *getting* dark at that point. One moment you can see fine, and the next, things start going gray. But I saw enough to know there was some kind of pattern of paint on the handles. Stripes. I think there was something on the paddle ends too, but it looked more worn."

"I suppose the end that was in the water would be more faded," Levi mused, "but I do not see where this takes us."

"I've seen that pattern somewhere before," Cheryl said. "I just can't think where. If I could figure out why it looked so familiar, it might mean something."

Levi wiped an open hand across his eyes. "Their anniversary is the day after tomorrow. I hope this oar business has nothing to do with anything."

The oar was odd. The note Naomi found in Seth's pocket worried Cheryl more.

"Is there something else?" Levi asked.

Cheryl hesitated. "No." She had promised Naomi.

"Are you sure?"

She met Levi's blue eyes. "Yes."

"Then I will let you get back to work." Levi adjusted the tilt of his hat. "Let me know if..."

Cheryl nodded. As soon as she could tell Levi more, she would. When he was gone, she looked at the one clock in the shop she trusted to give her accurate time amid the clatter of cuckoos. She still had an hour before she had to be ready to open the shop. That was enough time to pick up some quilted Valentine's place mats she'd commissioned from the Sugarcreek Sisters Quilt Shoppe next door and check in at the Artistic License studio across the street, next to the Honey Bee Café, to see if they had any small hand-painted vases they might like to sell on commission. Artsy vases in the Swiss Miss shop window caused people to slow their steps long enough to wonder what else might be inside.

Seth Miller was not the only one to go into a funk around Valentine's Day each year. Cheryl had no one this year, not even a friend to invite to the banquet. She'd spent five years engaged to Lance and dated him for a solid year before he put a ring on her finger. But half the time he forgot about Valentine's Day or made such an insulting effort that it would have been better if he had overlooked the date completely.

Lance was the past. *Stop thinking about him so much.* Maybe she needed to get past these next few days as well. The lurking question was whether anyone was in her future. As much as she was drawn to Levi, a relationship seemed impossible.

Relationship. She hated that word. Lance had been a relationship. She didn't want a relationship. She wanted love she could trust.

Cheryl closed the front door and made sure it was locked behind her. She had to find out what the note meant, and she only had two days.

"Or else."

The sound of her own cell phone jolted her out of her preoccupation.

"This is Chief Twitchell," the voice said. "I talked to the boys last night."

Cheryl stopped walking. "And?"

"And one of them admitted he had copied that credit card number. He showed it to a kid at school who is supposed to be some kind of IT genius. Says the kid took a picture with his phone, but our boy didn't see it for himself."

"A hacker," Cheryl said.

"Maybe. You know how teenagers are. Braggin' and exaggeratin'."

Cheryl exhaled. "There must be some kind of a crime involved here."

"We're not sure anyone has actually done anything fraudulent."

"Yet."

"The only way to see if anybody will is to let it happen first," Chief Twitchell said. "Then we could trace the activity."

"Why should I take that chance?"

"I'm not sayin' you should. I just want to be clear that the Sugarcreek Police Department does not have the resources to go after a *possible* illegal action by a *possible* individual who might *possibly* know what he's doing."

Chapter Eight

All morning between customers, Cheryl considered her options for how to spend her time during the next two days.

Goal: Get Seth to open up about what was going to happen on Friday. Strategy: Shock him by telling him I know about the note. Offer to help.

Goal: Find out what Seth intends to do about the note. Strategy: Arrange for Lydia and Esther to watch the shop and then lurk wherever Seth goes. Confront as necessary.

Goal: Persuade Naomi that the situation is potentially serious. Strategy: Ask to see the note again. Point out tone and word choice.

Goal: Determine the meaning of "or else." Strategy: Tell Levi about the note and enlist his help with his parents.

Even Cheryl was not convinced any of these approaches would bring desirable results. How could she entice anyone to cooperate? Yet the idea of doing nothing and waiting for Friday's disaster was unacceptable.

Lydia arrived just before noon, which allowed Cheryl to take Esther into the office and calmly explain the credit card conundrum. As she listened to herself talk, Cheryl could hardly believe she was explaining the financial challenge to a teenager.

"We'll have to figure out how much cash flow we'll need for the next couple of weeks," Cheryl said. She hadn't canceled the card yet, but she might have to.

Esther chewed her bottom lip. "It is the middle of the month. Most of the accounts come due at the end of the month, right? Payroll and utilities are the main things."

Cheryl would do without her own salary for the time being, but it wouldn't be fair not to pay Lydia and Esther.

"Let me see the bank account balance." Cheryl hunched in toward the computer, clicked a few keys, and entered a password. The bank account displayed.

"At least we are not broke," Esther said. "And we will have the daily deposits."

"The bigger question is, how many of the vendors get their payments automatically charged to the shop's credit card?"

Together they scrolled through the transaction history.

"Looks like most of them," Esther concluded.

Cheryl wasn't surprised, even with dozens of vendors. Aunt Mitzi always thought it was easier to pay one bill. And a lot of the suppliers were small businesses. They did business with the Swiss Miss because they knew they'd be paid promptly.

"Would you feel comfortable working on changing the payment method online temporarily?"

"I could try."

"You can do it," Cheryl said. "I see the way you've learned to use the computer. Usually you just have to log in to the site and find the place where you can update our account profile."

Esther's nod was slightly more convincing.

Cheryl wrote a Web site, user name, and master password on a scrap of paper. "Start with this site. From there you can automatically log in to any of the vendor sites you see listed."

"What if something doesn't work?"

"Write me a note." Cheryl pulled her emergency credit card from her wallet and put it on the desk. "Here's the new card number. If you can't change a profile online, try calling to give them the new card."

Esther eyed the card. "Won't they want to talk to you before they make changes?"

"Make me a list of who I need to call. But put on your best authoritative voice and see what you can do. Today you are the assistant manager of the Swiss Miss."

If Cheryl did not enlist Esther's help, she could spend the next two days running back and forth between the phone, the computer, and the front counter with no time for her other priorities. She tilted her head and looked at the bags under the trustworthy and temporarily deputized assistant manager's eyes.

"You look a little sleepy," Cheryl said. "Do you feel all right?"

Esther blew out her breath. "I am fine. It is just…busy at home too."

Busy. It was not the word Levi would use, but Cheryl could see that the tension in the Miller home was taking its toll.

"If you need to talk about anything," Cheryl said, "you know I'm here for you."

Cheryl meant what she said. She would willingly listen to any troubles Esther experienced. And she guiltily hoped for more information about what was happening in the Miller house.

Both their heads turned toward the rap on the open office door. Lydia stood there.

"I thought you were going home today to try to Skype with your aenti without distraction," Lydia said. "It is on the calendar."

Cheryl jumped up.

"Isn't it the middle of the night in Port Moresby?" Esther said.

"Some would call it very early in the morning." Cheryl jammed her wallet back into her purse and slung it over her shoulder. "But her e-mail said this was the best time."

Cheryl hustled the four blocks home to the cottage so similar to the house Aunt Mitzi had transformed into the Swiss Miss twenty years ago. She snatched up her laptop and pushed the button to power it up, drumming her fingers on the computer while she waited. Already she was seven minutes behind schedule.

The screen came to life, Cheryl logged into Skype to initiate the call, and a few seconds later her aunt's grin beamed across the fourteen-hour time difference. Cheryl settled into the cushions with the cat stretched across the back of the couch.

"Tell me all your news," Aunt Mitzi said. "How are the Millers and the Swartzentrubers and the Troyers and the Berryhills—and everyone?"

"They all miss you," Cheryl said. "It helps me a lot that they all know how you ran your business. If I run into a problem, I just have to ask what Mitzi would do, and someone knows the answer."

"I hope you're not running into any serious problems."

"I started walking along the river," Cheryl said, deciding not to waste valuable minutes on the credit card question. Her aunt couldn't do anything about it from the other side of the world, so why worry her?

"It's beautiful on the river any time of the year," Mitzi said.

"It's warmed up a little bit. We had some ice on the water, but it's been thawing. It's pretty in a wintry way."

"Send pictures!"

"I will," Cheryl promised. "I heard there used to be summer races on the river."

"Not for decades now," Mitzi said. "At least thirty years. I saw one or two myself, but then they stopped and I never knew why."

"I wonder if Seth was involved. Something odd happened the other day." Cheryl started in on her story of Monday evening, but a few sentences in, she realized the image of her aunt had frozen on the screen.

This was a terrible time for a failed Internet connection.

"Aunt Mitzi? Can you hear me?"

No response. The cat dropped into Cheryl's lap, and she gently but firmly nudged him to the floor. She sucked in her lips. Modern technology that let her talk to her aunt halfway around the world was wonderful, but it depended on a strong steady Internet connection. The missionary guesthouse where Mitzi sometimes stayed when she was on the outskirts of Port Moresby featured unreliable service.

"Aunt Mitzi?"

Mitzi's picture began to jerk in slow motion. Bits of her voice came through. "Hesitate... try again... look deep... it's there somewhere."

And then the connection cut out completely. Aunt Mitzi's frozen face disappeared.

Quickly, Cheryl tried calling again, but she got no answer. She switched to e-mail, unsure how much of the car account Mitzi heard—or whether the choppy phrases Cheryl heard were in response to the story or unrelated.

You still there? I didn't hear everything you said. Can we keep going on e-mail? Cheryl hit the Send button.

Persistent, Beau climbed back into her lap. As a compromise, Cheryl pulled him off the keyboard and arranged him in the part of her lap not occupied by the laptop.

Three minutes. Five. Nine. Eleven.

Finally Cheryl gave up. The connection was gone, and no doubt Aunt Mitzi had a full day ahead of her. Why else would she be up and dressed at four in the morning?

"Two days," she said to Beau as she set him on the floor again. "How am I going to figure out what Seth is up to in two days? Especially without Naomi's help?"

Cheryl was tempted to put the cat in the car and drive somewhere to investigate. She had to know where Seth was going, who he was talking to, what he was buying, whether he mailed anything. Now she wondered if the note in his trousers had arrived in the family mail, been tucked in among the business mail for the Miller Maze and Petting Zoo, or been left somewhere only Seth would find it.

But there was the matter of keeping the store accounts safe. Seeing her aunt's faraway face, even for a few minutes, reinforced Cheryl's determination to keep the business in thriving health.

Halfway back to the store, Cheryl realized the credit card number was tied to the bank account because Mitzi had always paid the credit card bill online. Changing the card was not enough. The bank account itself was at risk.

She groaned.

In the store, Cheryl looked at the row of clocks to confirm she had a few minutes before the afternoon tourist onslaught arrived. She approached the counter to get out the cookies Naomi had brought in yesterday.

"So what did he do with them?" Lydia was asking Esther.

"Who did what?" Cheryl asked. She snapped the lids off the cookie containers and looked around for a display tray.

"Levi." Lydia giggled. "Esther said the envelope had tickets to the banquet on Saturday."

Cheryl almost said she already knew this juicy tidbit, but the girls' giggling made her reconsider.

"He just put them back in the envelope," Esther said.

"Do you think he will take someone?" Lydia said.

Not me. Cheryl began arranging cookies. They were thick butter cookies with generous frosting. A dollar apiece would seem like a bargain.

"I cannot think who he would ask," Esther said.

"Mrs. Lehman's daughter," Lydia suggested.

Heidi. From the few times Cheryl had seen Heidi Lehman, she judged her to be a lovely young woman. So why didn't she like the thought of Heidi with Levi?

Esther shook her head. "I do not think my *bruder* is interested in anyone right now. I am not sure he will ever get married. Besides, at our house Valentine's Day never is a big event."

"Let's get back to work." Cheryl heard the bite in her own tone. She wasn't usually that kind of boss. "Sorry. We just have a lot to do today."

The bus pulled up across the street a few minutes early. Cheryl wished she had grabbed a sandwich while she was at home, lest she decide to eat three enormous frosted heart-shaped cookies for a late lunch. The pace in the shop didn't let up all afternoon. Esther stayed longer than usual to get through most of the vendors. Cheryl managed what she could with the bank over the phone and made an appointment for early the next morning to sign forms.

Was it all for nothing? She hoped so.

When she locked the shop at five o'clock without cleaning up, Cheryl paced home, changed into walking boots, and grabbed her car keys. As she pulled up to her usual parking spot, the sky unloosed an exquisite palette of orange and red. Breathing in deeply and out slowly, Cheryl eased out the day's aggravations and began a low hum. The path was familiar, though she felt more alert since finding the mess two days before and hearing the car gunning out of the adjoining woods. Today she heard the crunch of steps behind her, just as she had on Monday.

Rueben. With a smile, she turned around.

And saw no one, not even a squirrel darting across the path.

Yet she was sure she had heard something. Someone.

The slight drag in the steps she'd heard suggested booted feet with a faint, ambiguous squeak in the gait.

She watched the growing shadows, scanning the landscape to find the one-to-one correspondence of solid form to contorting gray shapes. The sinking sun unrolled a dusty carpet over the riverbank. On most days when Cheryl walked, she gave herself to the sensation of settling into the peace of the river in these moments when every few seconds the scene shifted with the waning light. Below the path, water flowed freely, tumbling over rocks and gurgling around stray low-hanging tree branches. She knew how far she would walk before the river sounded louder, where it would diminish around a bend, where the color deepened.

This was her place of peace, for both body and spirit. Most evenings the sunset satiated her spirit and the river's moist air her lungs. But that's not what she felt right then. Not at all.

Her hands in her jacket pockets, Cheryl walked with spry steps, determined to reach her usual goal before turning around. Perhaps she might still run into Rueben.

There. Again. A crunch, a snap. A slight modulation filtered through what Cheryl was accustomed to hearing. She stopped again. The sound stopped. Cheryl looked at her own feet, reassuring herself she was not causing her own suspicion. When she moved again, she stepped slowly enough to listen clearly.

Somebody was there. Watching her. For a split second she thought she saw the flash of a wide, worn brown boot. But if Chief Twitchell had asked for details, she would not have been able to provide them, and the impression was gone.

She could go home now. The walk was spoiled anyway. But if she turned around, she would walk right toward whoever was hidden behind her. Instead, she increased her pace until she came to a path that rose toward the road and returned to her car by walking on the gravel shoulder.

CHAPTER NINE

Cheryl let herself in the back door of the cottage. Whatever—or whoever—had unnerved her on the path now prompted her to be sure the latch turned.

Beau circled her ankles in a greeting that said, *You took too long, but I'm glad you're here now.*

Cheryl picked up the cat. "Have you been waiting for me?"

Beau meowed in a less than friendly way, and Cheryl took his face in one hand to look into his eyes.

"We're both hungry," she said. "Let's do something about that."

Cheryl opened a can of food, dumped it in Beau's dish, and set it on the floor. Beau inspected but did not eat.

"You're in a mood," Cheryl said as she opened the refrigerator in search of leftover shepherd's pie. She hadn't made it herself. If she had to cook for a family the way Naomi did, or so many other wives and mothers, everyone would starve.

After she finished eating and settled on the couch in the living room with a book, she expected the cat would stretch himself out behind her shoulders or curl next to her. She had read forty pages before she realized Beau wasn't there. Instead he still drowsed on the kitchen floor, his food untouched, and Cheryl heard little from him during the evening. At bedtime, ready for a small snack, Cheryl found few options. Opening one cupboard after another, she met with disappointment. In addition to being an unimpressive cook, she was an unreliable grocery shopper. As a last resort, she stepped on a stool and opened the usually out-of-reach cabinet above the refrigerator. Perhaps an unopened box of crackers had found its way up there before Aunt Mitzi left.

Instead, Cheryl found a note taped to the inside of the cupboard door. It said simply, "For Cheryl. 1 John 3:1–2. Love."

Forgetting her hunger, Cheryl pulled the note off the door and went out to the living room for her Bible to look up the passage.

"See what great love the Father has lavished on us, that we should be called children of God! And that is what we are! The reason the world does not know us is that it did not know him. Dear friends, now we are children of God, and what we will be has not yet been made known. But we know that when Christ appears, we shall be like him, for we shall see him as he is."

Cheryl's throat thickened. That note had been there for months, and she found it during the week when she wondered whether she would ever know love. Maybe the Amish were right and there was no such thing as coincidence. She left her Bible open on the coffee table as she began to turn off lights and check the locks. Those words would be worth another reading before she faced the next day.

When she went to bed, she picked Beau up from the kitchen floor and moved him to the bedroom. Something was off with the cat, and Cheryl wanted him close.

Cheryl woke early and awaited dawn. She cracked eggs into bread to make Egg-in-the-Nest—one food she did know how to cook—made coffee, and calculated an appropriate hour to drop in on Rob and Dianne Thatcher, whose shed had been the source of riverbank debris. Finally, when it seemed like the morning was half spent, she backed her blue Ford out of the driveway and headed to their home.

Rob was outside, which relieved Cheryl of the question whether it was too early to ring the doorbell.

"Good morning." Cheryl pushed her car door closed and walked toward where Rob was sweeping dirt out of the open garage. Behind the garage, toward the back of the lot, was the shed.

Rob leaned on his broom. "Cheryl Cooper, right?"

She nodded.

"Chief Twitchell said we might hear from you."

"I do have a few questions." Cheryl swung her keys around on one finger. "Chief Twitchell said he returned all your stolen items."

"And I told him he shouldn't have bothered."

"So he gave you everything? The papers too?"

Rob tilted his head toward an orange dumpster on the side of the wide driveway. "Everything went straight in there."

"Still, it all belonged to you," Cheryl said. "Someone invaded your property."

"Kids. They did me a favor, getting it out of the shed."

"What do you mean?"

"You saw for yourself it was all junk. My wife is a garage sale fanatic, and she finds stuff in the woods that she thinks she might want for some crafty project. I finally asked her to just keep it all in the shed. I didn't like it taking over the garage."

Cheryl looked past Rob into the garage, which was well kept with nothing to suggest the chaos implied by the condition of the lost items.

"Did you throw away the papers as well?" Cheryl glanced toward the dumpster.

"They were a wet mess, no use to anyone."

"I suppose," Cheryl murmured. "Is your wife home this morning? I'd like to talk to her."

Rob shrugged. "Follow me."

He led her around the side of the house to a back door. Dianne Thatcher was in the kitchen loading the dishwasher. Swaths of blue fabric hung over the back of one kitchen chair, and a sewing machine was set up on one end of the table with a rack of threads nearby. Foam core squares and a glue gun occupied the other end of the table.

"Cheryl." Dianne grabbed a dish towel and wiped her hands. "I'm so sorry. Chief Twitchell told me you were worried about what I'd written on that paper."

"It was a bit surreal to see my own credit card number, given the conditions."

Dianne pulled a chair away from the table and indicated Cheryl should sit.

"I'm terrible at keeping records," she said. "I write things down and stick them away. Half the time I can't find them again myself. Rob is after me about it all the time. Tax season is a nightmare."

"I feel responsible to take good care of my aunt's shop," Cheryl said.

"Please don't stop ordering from me just because I'm disorganized." Dianne sat in a second chair.

"Your table linens sell well," Cheryl said. "People love the handmade touch."

"Every piece is one of a kind."

Cheryl nodded.

"I understand your concern," Dianne said. "My own bank statements were out in the shed. Stupid, I know, in this day and age. The shed wasn't even locked. I'm going to buy a filing cabinet and make a fresh start."

"Of course I still want to carry your items," Cheryl said. "Can I ask you about something else?"

"Certainly."

"Did you have an old oar out in that shed? Maybe one you forgot was there and didn't put on the list?"

Dianne let out a slow exhale. "Now that you bring it up, I think you're right. I'd forgotten all about it. I found it years ago in the woods along the river after the county removed some diseased fallen trees. I thought I might do something interesting with it someday. The paint was faded, of course, but the hues of blue and purple made me think of the Amish dyes, which I've always loved."

Cheryl straightened in her chair. "So you think it was an Amish oar?"

"Who can say? It just made me think of them, and I brought it home."

"Would you want it back if it turned up again?" Cheryl asked.

"Goodness, no. Rob would have my head."

Cheryl stood up. "Thank you. Let's both be more careful with our banking information, and let me know when you have something for the shop."

Cheryl backed out of the Thatcher driveway on to the street heading into the heart of Sugarcreek. She blinked twice at the sight of Levi's buggy rumbling along the road and then carefully passed him before pulling over to wave him down.

Levi reined in his horse and looked down at Cheryl in surprise.

"I just had a curious conversation," she said, stroking the long nose of the horse. "That oar I saw Seth pick up definitely came from the Thatchers' shed. Dianne described it perfectly without any hints from me."

Cheryl went on to recount the conversation.

"Why would an Amish oar be lost in the woods for years?" Cheryl mused. "It's not as if anyone would have taken a boat into the woods."

"I suppose you could if you tried," Levi said. "A shortcut of some sort?"

"Maybe." Cheryl blew out her breath. "I know I should leave it alone. Dianne doesn't want the oar back. Rob dumped everything they got back straight into the trash. I'm the only one who cares, and I don't even have a good reason."

"You saw my daed do something very strange," Levi said softly. "Do not let it go."

Cheryl cocked her head. "Did you hear that?"

"A car is coming." Levi nudged her well off the pavement. "We are standing on a road, after all."

"It's driving too fast." Cheryl stood still as the vibration mounted, lurched, and twisted in another direction.

"It must have turned before it came around the curve," Levi said.

"Turned where?"

"There are some old farm roads that way. No one uses them much, but they're open."

"It's not just any car, Levi. I've heard that one before."

"How can you tell? You did not even see it."

"I don't have to see it. My dad used to help people in our church with their car repairs. I learned to listen to an engine. The way this one accelerates sounds just like the car I heard Monday night at the river." She caught his eye. "Where do those old farm roads lead?"

"You can get to our land that way," he said. "Occasionally we have taken animals to our petting zoo by that route if we were using a trailer and wanted to stay off the main road."

"Is anyone at the zoo today?"

"We do not get a lot of business in the winter, but I am sure Elizabeth is caring for the animals."

"She shouldn't be alone," Cheryl said, alarmed. "The zoo is too far from the house."

"She goes there alone all the time," Levi said. "It is one of her chores, and she loves it."

"But tomorrow is the anniversary, and you should all be careful until the threat has passed."

"What threat?"

Cheryl gulped. While she had told Levi about his father and the oar, she had honored Naomi's wish that she not tell anyone about the note.

"I can't explain right now," she said, "but maybe I'll drive over and say hello to Elizabeth."

"What about the store?"

"I have time before opening."

Her cell phone rang, and Cheryl dug it out of her pocket.

"We wondered if you were coming for your appointment?" said a customer service representative from the bank. "We had you down for eight thirty, and it's nearly nine now."

Cheryl slapped her forehead. "I'm sorry. I got caught up in something."

"We suspended the store's account, but we need signatures and identification on file to open a new one."

"Right. I'll make sure I get there today."

"Anytime that is convenient," the representative said. "I do want to mention that we found two small but suspicious transactions. We'll need you to look at them and let us know whether they are valid. We know you buy from a lot of sources, but we haven't seen these before."

"What kind of transactions?" Cheryl looked up at Levi's watching blue eyes.

"Someone may be testing the account number," the representative said. "Sometimes it happens. If a few small purchases go unnoticed, they try something larger online."

"I will definitely come in. Thank you." Cheryl ended the call.

"Trouble?" Levi said.

"The odds were against it, but it seems as though someone did use the card."

"Then you must go."

"But Elizabeth is alone."

"I will turn around and go home," Levi said. "Promise."

"Watch for a car you don't recognize," Cheryl said, "an old tank of a car, by the sound of it."

"I wish you would tell me what is going on."

"I can't. It's complicated."

Levi held her eyes for a long slow breath, in and out. "Okay, but I hope that when it becomes a little less complicated you will explain."

CHAPTER TEN

The stop at the bank left Cheryl twelve minutes before she would have to unlock the front door of the Swiss Miss and be ready for customers.

Cheryl had not recognized the two suspicious transactions, one of which was in Denmark. Any doubt that changing the account might be an overreaction vanished. She eagerly signed the forms to move the store's funds into an account not connected to the old credit card number anywhere in the cyber world.

Now she ducked into By His Grace, the bookstore down the street from the Swiss Miss. She should have done it three days ago. If she had never seen Seth Miller pick up that old oar, she might have remembered to buy a valentine and get it in the mail on time to arrive by Saturday. Now it would get there late, and Cheryl would never hear the end of it from her brother, Matt. Twenty-three years ago their mother thought it was a sweet idea for her daughter and son to exchange valentines. After all, they were signing valentines for all their classmates. Even at the age of seven, Cheryl rolled her eyes at the idea. Matt was already protesting the idea that he should have to give valentines to any girls. Or boys. Or anyone. They made an instant unspoken pact to give each other the silliest, sappiest cards in the boxed collection.

And they had done it every year since, wherever they were, even though Matt barely contacted her otherwise.

A Valentine's Day display took up four racks just inside the front door. Cards, books, trinkets, photo frames, and posters about the fund-raising banquet on Saturday night.

Cheryl picked up one card. Not sappy enough. Another was not silly enough. The third did not have enough pink for the desired effect. The fourth was too much like one Lance had given Cheryl three years ago. This one she returned to the rack with extra speed.

On the other side of the shelves, someone giggled and conversation emerged.

"I heard one of the winners of the free tickets gave them away," a voice said.

"The lucky dog didn't know what he had," came the response.

"I didn't hear his name, but somebody said he was Amish. They don't hold much with luck."

"Maybe if he won them, it was God's will for him to go."

"I guess he didn't see it that way. He handed them off the next day."

Cheryl slowly returned another rejected card to the rack, her eyes rising to the banquet poster above it.

Every Purchase Enters You for a Free Drawing.

Three Pairs of Tickets Will Be Awarded.

So that was how Levi ended up with a pair of tickets he had no interest in using. Marion Berryhill must have dropped the envelope by the Swiss Miss because she knew the Millers came in often.

But who did Levi give the tickets to?

The conversation drifted away. If the speakers knew who got Levi's tickets, they did not say.

And it didn't matter, Cheryl reminded herself. She had chosen not to buy her own tickets, and Levi didn't ask her in that delicious flitting moment when she thought he might. She hoped whoever was going would have a good time. After flipping through another half-dozen cards, Cheryl chose one. As she paid for it, self-pity washed over her. Despite a five-year engagement, the most she had to look forward to on Valentine's Day was a sappy card contest with her little brother.

At two minutes before ten, Cheryl put the key in the lock and opened the shop. On some mornings, customers loitered on the sidewalk waiting for the shops up and down the street to show signs of being open for business. Today no one seemed determined to make the Swiss Miss the first stop. Cheryl walked through the store, stowed her purse in the back office, and went through the daily ritual of straightening disarrayed items from the previous day.

Standing in front of a selection of candles, Cheryl tossed her dust rag on a shelf and pulled her cell phone from her pocket. Had any of Aunt Mitzi's earlier messages said where she would be at this point in the week? It was midnight in Papua New Guinea, but Aunt Mitzi had never paid much attention to the clock. If she was still at the missionary guesthouse, she might be awake. Mitzi hadn't answered Cheryl's e-mail after the dropped Skype connection, but that was yesterday. Every day seemed to bring a different schedule for the rookie missionary.

Try again, Mitzi had said. *Look deep. It's there somewhere.*

Because of the crackly connection, Cheryl didn't know if her aunt had spoken these phrases in sequence or whether whole sentences separated them.

Look deep where?

What was she looking for?

Cheryl opened a blank e-mail message on her phone and quickly filled the boxes.

> To: Aunt Mitzi
> Subject: Looking for oar
> Hi! Sorry we got interrupted yesterday. If you get this message, let me know what you were trying to tell me at the end. What am I looking for?
> Love, C.

The door opened, and a bevy of browsers entered. Perhaps they were from nearby Berlin or New Philadelphia. The week's milder weather had seemed to draw people ready to be out of the house for a change. Cheryl answered questions while she continued straightening displays. An hour passed, with the shop door opening and closing at regular intervals. Cheryl rang up several small sales, four pieces of fudge, and one cuckoo clock.

In a lull, she pulled her phone from her pocket again. Nothing from Aunt Mitzi. Cheryl reminded herself of the time change. For her own sake, Mitzi should be sleeping. Still, Cheryl couldn't help hoping for a message to arrive. Tomorrow was the anniversary. Glancing at the battery icon on her phone screen, she groaned. Once again she had forgotten to charge it. The phone was not going to last the afternoon.

Cheryl stepped behind the counter and picked up the store's landline. She called the Millers' petting zoo, knowing the only phone on their farm was closest by a few yards to the zoo. She let it ring. Four times. Five. Six. Then it went to the answering machine, and Elizabeth's voice came on with a peppy recording inviting callers to leave a message to make group reservations.

Cheryl hung up. Probably Elizabeth had finished her chores and was safely in the family's home. Hopefully Levi had not left his sister alone. Cheryl now wished she had asked Levi to call her with the news that all was well.

Had he seen the car? Had he seen any unusual detail that might not seem to matter? Levi would not have called, of course, apart from an emergency.

Back in the showroom, Cheryl responded to several "Do you have?" inquiries, set out more fudge, and sold a red vase.

At noon, Lydia arrived.

"Can you stay all afternoon today?" Cheryl said. If Lydia was in the shop and Esther came in as usual, perhaps Cheryl could be away most of the afternoon. She would drive out to the Miller farm and see for herself that everything was well. She might even track down Seth in his barn or his equipment shed, or wherever he might be, and ask him about the note. Maybe she would figure out a way to stop feeling the foreboding of "*or else.*"

"Sorry, but I have to leave right at two," Lydia said. "I promised Mrs. Swartzentruber I would help with the babies while she gets the house ready for her cousin's arrival tomorrow."

Cheryl swallowed her disappointment. "No problem. I'll make sure I'm here at two."

Her phone sounded an alert, and she looked at it immediately. Not Mitzi. The later the hour got in Papua New Guinea, the more Cheryl's hope dimmed for a response before the evening. She ignored the electronic newsletter from a magazine she hadn't read in two years. Before she put her phone away, though, the Low Battery message displayed.

The door opened and two families with small children came in, followed by an older woman browsing alone.

When Esther Miller arrived to work a few hours later, Cheryl followed her into the small office.

"I hope you're having a good day." It was a cheesy way of fishing for information about the Miller household, but Cheryl didn't care.

"I have been out and about most of the day," Esther said as she tucked her bag in a drawer and powered up the desktop computer.

"Oh." Cheryl tried not to sound disappointed. "So you haven't been home?"

Esther shook her head. "I came into town with Daed this morning."

Seth was in town again? That was at least the third time this week—unusual for a man who ran a farm, a maze, and a petting zoo even if winter was not the busy season for any of the businesses.

"How's your mom?" Cheryl asked.

"Quiet," Esther said, her own voice low. "She went out for a long walk right after breakfast."

"Alone?" Tomorrow was the "*or else*" day, but Cheryl still hated the idea of Naomi on her own today.

"Yes." Esther sighed audibly and punched keys. "I offered to go with her, but she said she wanted to pray."

Cheryl sucked in both lips and blew air out her nose.

"I'm trying to finish getting into the accounts," Esther said, "but this thing does not want to cooperate."

"Give it time."

"It crashes every day," Esther said. "It takes so long to do anything! I want to make sure I finish today because I cannot come tomorrow."

"What's happening tomorrow?"

"I am sorry I forgot to tell you. My sister and I made plans," Esther said. "My parents' anniversary is always a good time to have something else to do."

"Will anyone be home with your mother tomorrow?"

"Daed, I suppose, though he will probably spend the whole day in the barn doing stuff that does not need doing."

"And your brothers?"

"I am not sure."

Esther was having a hard enough time with the impending anniversary—enough to prompt her to make distracting plans.

Cheryl didn't want to upset a sixteen-year-old with her own anxieties, but surely Levi would stay close to the farm.

Cheryl moistened her lips and nervously looked at her phone. A dark screen greeted her, the battery's charge fully depleted now.

"I have to run home for my phone charger," she said. Now was the time to go, while both Lydia and Esther were on hand to help customers.

The computer made an encouraging sound.

"Finally," Esther muttered, not looking up.

Cheryl waved across the shop at Lydia. "Be right back."

She only had an hour now if she was going to be back by two. Famished, she would have to squeeze in grabbing some lunch with her errands.

"Lightbulbs," Lydia said.

"I'm sorry?" Cheryl said.

"You keep saying you need to buy lightbulbs for the house. Stop at the hardware store on your way home."

"Good idea. Thanks for the reminder."

How long could it take to buy a package of lightbulbs? Cheryl scooted down the street to the hardware store, where she was not sure which aisle to find the bulbs in. It was a small store, like all the shops on Main Street. Cheryl's impression during her infrequent visits to the store was that most of the customers were townspeople rather than tourists.

She found the bulbs she needed and headed to the checkout counter. She still had forty-six minutes before two o'clock.

And then she saw it.

High on the side wall, above the shelves of batteries, battery-powered small tools, and assorted flashlights.

It was right there, hanging on the wall in an awkward display likely meant to be decorative.

An oar with blue and purple striping.

CHAPTER ELEVEN

The oar was not hanging alone in the display. The fishing rods looked old enough to have belonged to somebody's grandfather, and the long wooden handle of the ax looked precariously like it might separate from the steel head. Plastic vines—not a very good imitation—intertwined the outdoorsy collection, covering parts of the oar.

But Cheryl saw enough. The paint pattern was the same, though not as weathered and faded as the image still fixed in her mind from Monday evening. Now she could discern the colors without a doubt. They were just as she thought—two wide blue stripes, a thin purple one, and the final purple band the widest of them all. She could still picture Seth's grip on the oar and the way his fingers wrapped around the handle.

Instead of proceeding to the counter, Cheryl went up and down the aisles looking for the stout, middle-aged man she knew was the owner. She saw only a few other customers. At the rear of the store, she paused at the opening she knew would lead to the office and storeroom.

"Doug?" she said, hoping the owner was simply occupied with a mundane business task.

But no answer came, and the lights were off. The young clerk at the counter was her only option.

Cheryl set the six-pack of lightbulbs on the counter. "I was admiring the display on the side wall."

Unimpressed, the young man aimed a scanner at the bulbs. *Beep*. "Is that all for today?"

"I wonder if you know where the oar came from."

He shrugged and muttered the total for her purchase.

Cheryl took her time removing a ten-dollar bill from her purse. "How long has it been up there?"

Another shrug. "I never really noticed."

"It looks pretty old." She handed him the money.

"I guess." He punched some numbers on the cash register, the drawer opened, and he started counting change.

"Do you know when Doug will be back?"

"He's out all day." The clerk dropped a handful of coins into Cheryl's palm, followed by limp paper bills. "He'll be back sometime tomorrow. Not sure when."

Cheryl doubted there was any point in suggesting the clerk leave a note asking Doug to call her. Besides, if the oar had anything to do with "*or else,*" sometime tomorrow could be too late.

"I don't need a bag." Cheryl picked up the lightbulbs. "Thank you."

Another customer approached. Cheryl turned from the counter, her eyes catching a glimpse of something familiar at the end of an aisle. She took a few steps.

"Rueben?"

The elderly man looked up. Cheryl wondered why she hadn't seen him earlier when she paced through the store looking for the owner. She moved toward him now.

"Good afternoon," Rueben said.

"Yes, good afternoon," Cheryl answered. "Are you coming by the Swiss Miss today for some checkers?"

Rueben twisted his lips. "I might have to play both sides of the board. I do not think my brother is coming."

"Then it will be a good time to practice new strategies."

Rueben nodded, a twinkle in his eyes.

Cheryl pointed to the display that had caught her eye a few minutes ago. It was large enough to be seen from anywhere in the store, and she frankly wondered why she had never noticed it before.

"That oar is an interesting piece," she said. "Do you know anything about whether the stripes have special meaning?"

"If Ben does not come in to play," Rueben said, "he will not know what hit him the next time."

Cheryl narrowed her eyes slightly. Despite Rueben's age, she had never noticed that he had trouble tracking with a conversation until lately.

"I'm curious about the oar," she said.

"I could quadruple jump if I wanted to," Rueben said.

"I'm sure you could." Cheryl changed the subject. "Is your son still visiting?"

"In fact, maybe I will quintuple jump." Rueben adjusted his hat. "I had better get the old brain cranked up to figure that out."

With agile steps, he marched up the aisle and out the door.

Cheryl buzzed her lips at the odd interchange. Rueben could not have lost his ability for polite conversation in the space of a few days. He didn't want to discuss the oar. Or his son. Or what he might have seen on the riverbank.

Cheryl stepped out into the winter day and hustled home. Thirty-two minutes left.

At home, she expected Beau's usual greeting. He always made his presence known when she came home. Instead, she grimaced at the splotch of cat vomit on the kitchen floor. The food dish was untouched. Had Beau hacked up a fur ball? Cheryl went looking for the cat. She found him asleep on the bathroom floor in a stream of sunlight. His eyes blinked open, but he did not move.

Cheryl scooped him up. "What's the matter, buddy? Not feeling so great today?"

She carried him into the bedroom and picked up her phone charging cord. At the sight of her laptop on the end of the bed, Cheryl decided to take it back to the shop as well. If she did hear from Mitzi before the end of the day and an e-mail exchange started, it would be easier to type on the computer. At the last minute, Cheryl decided to take the cat back with her also. She kept a throw rug there that made a good cat bed in the office. Something told her to keep an eye on Beau today.

Back at the Swiss Miss—two o'clock on the dot—Lydia had her coat handy the minute Cheryl entered.

"What did I miss?" Cheryl said.

"I sold a wheel of cheese," Lydia said. "And a cookbook."

"Well done."

"Rueben stopped in, but he didn't stay long."

"When was that?" Cheryl had seen Rueben in the hardware store only half an hour earlier.

"Maybe fifteen minutes ago." Lydia buttoned her coat. "Is Beau all right?"

"A little droopy," Cheryl said. "I thought maybe I'd keep him in the office for the afternoon."

Lydia picked up something from the counter. "Oh, I almost forgot. I found these on the checkerboard."

"What are they?" Cheryl stepped closer.

"Valentine hearts. I suppose those little kids who were in here earlier left them. I remember they played with the checkers. I left them here to remind myself to wipe off the checkerboard."

"I'll do it," Cheryl said. "You go."

Lydia dropped the candies on the counter again. "Then I will leave them here to remind you."

"Thanks. Kiss the babies for me."

As the door closed behind Lydia, Cheryl picked up the hearts. Although Valentine's Day was only two days away, these were the first candy hearts she'd seen this year. *Be True. Start Now.* They weren't very sticky for being handled by small children. In fact, they were perfectly dry and the messages unsmeared. Cheryl started to drop them in the trash. She would remember to wipe off the checkerboard without this form of reminder. At the last second, though, instead of releasing the hearts into the trash, she closed her hand around them and walked through the shop until she found a tiny purple heart-shaped tin.

It was silly. Cheryl knew that. She shouldn't read too much into a couple of pieces of children's candy. Nevertheless, the message hit home for her. *Be true. Start now.* Wasn't that why she had come to Sugarcreek in the first place—to start fresh and build a new life? Maybe that was the reminder she needed.

Across the street, the afternoon tour bus pulled up. Cheryl snapped the tin shut and tucked it on the shelf under the cash register. Beau meowed, but the timbre of the sound seemed off to Cheryl, and she was glad she'd brought him back with her.

"The tourists are here," Cheryl said to Esther in the office as she set Beau down. She folded the throw rug in half. The cat circled the room before settling on the rug and curling in sleep.

"Do you need me out there?" Esther said.

"How much more do you have to do back here?"

Esther blew out her breath. "Hard to say. The computer crashed again and I had to start over, so I'm not going to finish anyway."

"I'll call somebody." Cheryl tried not to betray her disappointment. Esther wouldn't be in tomorrow. Cheryl would have to finish reviewing the vendors herself. Hopefully there wouldn't be many left.

"This thing is ancient."

Cheryl smiled briefly, wondering if Esther saw the irony in a member of the Amish church pointing out the insufficiency of modern technology.

"I'll try to manage on my own and holler if I need you," Cheryl said. "You do what you can back here."

The door opened, and the first gaggle of tourists burst in.

Beau slept all afternoon. Cheryl had to admit she wasn't sure if this was unusual. She rarely spent an entire afternoon at home with the cat, and when she did, tracking his daytime sleeping patterns was not on her mind. But by the time she closed the shop, Cheryl felt confident she could leave Beau at home long enough to walk on the river.

At her usual parking place, she got out and locked the door. Instead of the direction she normally walked, her gaze turned the other way. Her disjointed conversation with Rueben had played in her mind all afternoon.

Rueben knew something. Cheryl wanted to know what it was.

She began to pace toward the farm where Rueben lived with his daughter. Cheryl had never been there, but Rueben had said it was only a mile or so. Surely it would not be difficult to find the lane that led to the house. Twenty minutes later, yellow lights leaking through the trees heartened her, and she walked with increased purpose. She zigzagged through a stand of trees and found herself not at the main farmhouse, but at the rear of the dawdy haus situated at the back of the lot.

This made Cheryl laugh. No wonder Rueben could slip away unnoticed to walk along the river, leaving his daughter to think he was napping.

It was not yet six o'clock. Would it be impolite to drop in for a visit? The Amish did it all the time, it seemed to Cheryl. They didn't call ahead. They visited. Although she had been in several

Amish homes, she had never seen a dawdy haus, so she was curious. Mostly, though, she wanted to talk to Rueben.

She rounded the small, trim wooden structure and knocked.

"Suppertime already?" Rueben called out.

"Rueben, it's me. Cheryl Cooper."

The door opened, and she looked into his startled eyes.

"You didn't expect to see me here, did you?" she said.

"As a matter of fact, no. Does my daughter know you are here?"

Cheryl laughed. "No. I came from the river. Can we talk?"

Inside, the dawdy haus was spare but inviting. Three comfortable chairs—one the requisite rocker—faced the fireplace in the sitting room. Behind them, a narrow table and two wooden chairs suggested the entrance to a small kitchen. Beside the kitchen was the only bedroom. Wood floors in a warm honey oak color ran seamless and rug-free through the home.

"This is charming," Cheryl said.

"It is more than enough for one old man." Rueben gestured toward a chair.

They sat down, and Cheryl plunged in. "About the oar, Rueben."

"I do not know much about oars these days." Rueben scratched an ear. "I have not been in a boat in twenty years."

"I'm asking about that old oar in the hardware store. You know the one I mean, don't you?"

"I do not even know why I was in that store. I have everything I need right here. If I lack something, I only have to ask and my daughter will provide it."

Cheryl let a beat pass. "I'm sure she felt that way about you when she was young."

"Children are a blessing from the Lord."

"Your children were blessed to have you as a father," Cheryl said. "Rueben, why don't you want to talk about the oar?"

Outside, an engine roared. Cheryl shot out of her chair and rushed to a front window. She knew that sound.

The car was not there. Instead Cheryl heard only the dissipation of the engine and saw the dirty tire tracks left in unmelted snow. She turned around and faced Rueben.

"That was your son's car." She did not ask. She stated.

"Why do the Englisch make such a fuss about cars?" Rueben said. "If I need to go somewhere my horse cannot take me, I will buy a train ticket."

"Rueben."

He stood. "My daughter will be calling me for supper soon."

"Of course." Certain she would not get anything more out of Rueben today, Cheryl moved toward the door. "How much longer will your son be here?"

"Just a few days. Wednesday at the latest."

CHAPTER TWELVE

On Friday morning, Cheryl woke antsy. Anniversary day.

The cat seemed iffy. He was more himself than he'd been the day before, but he hadn't eaten properly in two days. Cheryl checked the litter box for anything suspicious, though she wasn't sure what she ought to be looking for. Nothing appeared unusual.

Cheryl fiddled around the kitchen, eventually making herself a toasted bagel with a smear of cream cheese. If there had been more cheese in the container, she would have indulged. As it was, cream cheese was just one more item for the nonexistent shopping list. While she drank coffee, Cheryl peeled a brown banana and chomped into it. A baker would have known how to use a soft banana in bread, but if Cheryl didn't eat it today she would have to throw it out. Beau stretched across her feet under the table during her second cup of coffee.

As far as Cheryl knew, Naomi had not confronted Seth about the note. Of course, since Naomi had not been into the shop the last two days, Cheryl had no way to know—or even to guess—what had or had not transpired between husband and wife.

If Levi knew anything, he hadn't told Cheryl.

Esther said little, but her face and soft words told Cheryl she was worried about her mother even as she chose to stay out of the way.

Rueben's son creeped Cheryl out, and she hadn't even met him. That malicious-sounding car was his. She was sure of it.

Sighing, Cheryl got up to rinse her plate and coffee mug in the sink. Then she picked up the cat and stroked him for a few minutes, debating whether to take him to the Swiss Miss. He seemed to have had a good night, sleeping at the foot of the bed as he always did. She'd seen no evidence of further vomiting. But he wasn't eating. Cheryl freshened his food and set out a bit of milk. If she got a spare moment today, she would Google cat illnesses.

At eight thirty, Cheryl locked the cottage and set out for the store. Window blinds were going up and lights were going on in the businesses along Main Street. Cheryl wiggled her fingers at Kathy, who owned the Honey Bee Café across from the Swiss Miss. Nearly every day, the wide, inviting front porch in front of the gray café made Cheryl want to pull up a chair and enjoy a hot beverage. Kathy waved Cheryl over as if urging a runner around a baseball diamond to slide into home plate.

"Have you heard?" Kathy said. "Those kids confessed to stealing that stuff from the Thatchers."

"Chief Twitchell told me he talked to them," Cheryl said. She hadn't realized news of the burglary had spread around town.

"Dianne Thatcher came into the café yesterday," Kathy said, as if answering Cheryl's unspoken question. "When she gets flustered, she gets chatty. The parents all made the boys go to her house and apologize."

"That seems only right." Chief Twitchell knew the Thatchers were not the only victims of wrongdoing.

"It was a dare," Kathy said. "They never wanted any of those things. Someone dared them to break in, and they were foolish enough to try."

The shed had not even been locked. No one would have to try very hard to get into it.

"Anyway," Kathy said, "they stashed everything in the rocks upstream. Then we had that cold snap. They didn't count on the weather warming up and thawing ice starting to run down the bank on the way to the river. That jarred everything loose. They took the chief to two other spots where they were hiding what they'd stolen from other garages."

"Well, I hope they learned their lesson." Cheryl was glad to hear Chief Twitchell was following through on his investigation.

"Their parents are mortified."

Cheryl nodded. Her parents would have been more than mortified if she or her brother had ever done anything like what these boys had done. She had never even sneaked out of the house without permission the way so many of her high school friends had done.

"I'll bring you some coffee," Kathy said.

"Thanks, but I've already had my morning quota today."

Cheryl crossed the street again and unlocked the Swiss Miss. She still had nearly an hour before it was time to open for business. A scan of the store reminded her of all the tasks she didn't complete before leaving the day before, but Cheryl turned her eyes from them one after the other.

This was Friday. All Cheryl could think about was the anniversary and the note. "*Or else.*" So instead of wiping shelves, or sorting receipts, or reviewing invoices, or mopping up the streaks of mud yesterday's sloshy weather had brought in, Cheryl stowed her bag, hung her jacket on the back of a chair, and dialed the number for the phone shack at Miller Maze and Petting Zoo.

Of course no one answered. Elizabeth and Esther had their own plans for the day. In the middle of chores, everyone else let the phone ring and listened to messages later. No doubt the sisters had tended the animals early and were on their way.

Cheryl's next call was to Lydia Troyer, who was attached during her rumspringa to her cell phone as tightly as any Englisch teenager Cheryl had ever known.

But Lydia's phone went directly to voice mail, which meant she was probably gabbing with a friend.

Cheryl looked at the time, just after nine. On her usual schedule Lydia would not be in for two or three hours, and Cheryl couldn't wait that long.

She opened a text message and typed. *Something came up. I had to go out. Can you open the shop? I will leave the alley door unlocked.*

If Lydia didn't get the message or couldn't make it into town in time, people who made up the normal light morning traffic would just have to understand. Cheryl took cash from the register to pay Naomi for the goods she'd brought into the shop recently and put it in an envelope. It was as good an excuse as any for driving out to the farm. She unlocked the rear door, donned her jacket, picked up her purse, and locked the front door behind her when she went out. Ten minutes later she was in her car and on her way out to the Miller farm.

Naomi had been stiff during their last exchange. Cheryl couldn't stand the thought of feeling alienated from her a moment later. Levi and Esther would tell her the truth, which meant considerable tension at home on a day that should have been joyous for Seth and Naomi.

Naomi should know she had a friend. That's what Cheryl wanted to tell her. No matter what, she had a friend. And Cheryl would feel better if she could see for herself that everything was fine at the Millers', even if Seth was spending the day alone in the barn.

At a Stop sign, Cheryl paused to verify that she still had Chief Twitchell on speed dial. Just in case.

The sturdy Ford covered the miles between town and the farm smoothly. When Naomi first befriended her, Cheryl had to follow the signs to the petting zoo to find the Miller place. Now she knew the route well. As she had so many times, she followed the creek and approached the covered bridge that would transport her to the farmhouse.

Out of nowhere, an older model green Buick bore down on her. Cheryl slammed on the brakes and swerved to the shoulder. The Buick, its engine screaming obnoxiously, swiped past her. Cheryl yanked the steering wheel farther. Only inches separated them. Gasping, Cheryl leaned away from the door and braced for impact. The Buick's speed rattled Cheryl's small car, but it did not strike her. Instead, it tore across the lanes without stopping, and Cheryl's small Ford skidded to a stop halfway into the ditch.

Shaking, she banged a fist on the steering wheel. What would have happened if she had been within the confines of the covered bridge when that Buick roared across? She could have been killed, and she didn't even get a good look at the driver's face or the license plate.

But she knew who it was. She didn't know his first name, but she knew who it was.

Monday night along the riverbank.

Yesterday on the side of the road with Levi.

Last night outside Rueben's dawdy haus.

The clatter was distinctive. Cheryl had known all along it had to be an older model and a gas guzzler, and she was right. She sat trembling, trying to catch her breath for a few seconds before putting the car in Reverse and gently accelerating. If she gave the engine too much gas, the front tires would dig in and spin in the mud. If she gave too little, the back tires wouldn't get traction on the pavement. Her heart pelting against her ribs and overheating her chest inside her zipped jacket, Cheryl listened to the groan of her own engine and tried to remember every driving lesson her father had ever given her. The Ford inched backward to solid ground.

Cheryl put the car in Drive and accelerated freely now. The Millers were the only family who lived anywhere nearby.

Cheryl prayed she was not already too late.

Chapter Thirteen

Unwilling to spare a second, Cheryl lurched the car to a halt and jumped out of it in one extended motion. She pounded up the front steps of the Miller house and rapped on the door.

"Naomi!" she called. "Levi? Eli? Caleb? Elizabeth?"

Why wasn't she hearing footsteps? The home had no carpet to muffle the sound of movements. All the Miller offspring must be gone, anxious for the awkward day to be over.

Cheryl pivoted to scan the grounds for anything in the yard that looked off, any sign of a disturbance. Everything looked as calm and well kept as it always did. She raced down the steps and around the corner of the house, almost not hearing the front door open. Reversing direction, she looked up to see Naomi standing in the front doorway and clattered up the steps again to stare into her friend's eyes.

"Are you all right?" Cheryl said. Her gaze dropped to Naomi's stocking feet, which made no noise as she stepped back to open the door wider and gestured that Cheryl should enter.

Naomi sucked in her lips. "The morning has been odd, but I am fine enough."

Forcing the pent-up air out of her chest, Cheryl studied Naomi's strained features. "Did you have a visitor this morning?"

"How did you know that?" Naomi said.

"He nearly knocked me off the road." Cheryl stepped into the warmth of the living room. "May I ask who he was?"

Naomi shrugged. "He came to the door a few minutes ago, stared at me long enough to make me uncomfortable, and then said he'd made a mistake. He left without saying why he'd come."

"He didn't do anything?"

"No."

"Did he say anything else?"

"I asked if he was looking for the petting zoo, though no one is there today," Naomi said. "Then I offered to go find Seth, but he shook his head. That's when he left."

"Did he seem angry?"

"Cheryl," Naomi said, "do you think this man had something to do with the note I found in Seth's pocket?"

"Maybe. He sure has an irate way of driving."

"He did look vaguely familiar," Naomi said, "in a long-ago sort of way."

"What do you mean?"

Naomi waved away the subject. "Nothing. I do not know him. I do not know why I said that. I do not know who it was, and I do not want to think about it. Not today."

Cheryl swallowed. If not today, the day of "*or else*," then when? But she knew Naomi well enough to know that pressing her to do something she did not want to do would be a vain effort.

"I brought this." Cheryl extracted the envelope from her pocket. "To pay you."

Naomi took it but immediately set it on the table inside the door. "Is it warm enough outside for a walk?"

"I suppose so," Cheryl said. "Bring a scarf."

Naomi bundled up, and they started down a path Cheryl knew would take them to the petting zoo if they followed the full course.

"Naomi," Cheryl said, "I've been nervous all week about this day. I offended you the last time you were at the Swiss Miss. I tried to tell you what to do, and I shouldn't have. I'm sorry. Please forgive me. I don't want there to be any offense between us."

"I feel the same." Naomi put an arm through Cheryl's elbow. "I was being sensitive about something that happened long ago and really has nothing to do with you. It is just the anniversaries. Sometimes Seth goes to a place where I cannot reach him, and I feel shut out. But it has nothing to do with you, so forgive and forget."

"Anniversaries?" Cheryl tilted her head at Naomi's use of the plural. "Are you having more than one anniversary today?"

"Today is our wedding anniversary," Naomi said. "I do not know what I was thinking getting married four days before the anniversary of Ruth's death. We should have just waited a few more months for a real wedding season. Then I could have had an anniversary that was not always in the shadow of Seth's grief for his first wife."

"I'm sorry," Cheryl murmured.

"At the time I did not realize what it would be like. I was young and in love with a wonderful man. I thought I could cure his grief with new love, but I learned that is not the way of sorrow."

Cheryl squeezed Naomi's hand.

"Two dates every year seem to rattle Seth, the day he married Ruth in November and the day she died in February. For twenty years, I've thought things would get better. I would never ask him to try to forget Ruth, but twenty years is a long time."

They walked in silence. Sounds from the animals began to waft toward them.

"Esther told me she and Elizabeth made plans to see friends," Cheryl said. "Are the boys around today?"

Naomi forced a laugh. "They are mysteriously busy today as well."

Cheryl swallowed irritation at Levi. She had told him enough to know that she was concerned something would happen on this day. Now it almost had, and Levi was nowhere to be seen. When he heard about the stranger at the door—and the Buick speeding recklessly across the bridge—he would be sorry.

"And Seth?" Cheryl said.

"In the barn. I am not sure."

"But he hasn't left the farm?"

"His buggy is here."

Cheryl leaned on a fence railing. "Maybe you shouldn't be alone today."

"You are thinking about the note."

Cheryl nodded. If she had told Levi about the note, he would be here.

"I wanted to ask Seth about it—I still do," Naomi said. "But I just cannot work up the courage when he is so tense already."

"I know you trust him," Cheryl said.

"I do." Naomi pushed off the fence and resumed walking. "I heard some rumors."

"What rumors?" Cheryl smoothly fell into Naomi's pace.

"About how Seth came to marry Ruth. She chose him over another suitor, apparently."

"Who said this?"

"Rueben's daughter. I got the idea there was more to the story than what she was saying."

"Is it so unusual for a woman to date two men and eventually choose one over the other?"

"I suppose not." Naomi plunged her uncovered hands into her coat pockets. "I know Seth loves me, but the way he withdraws has always made me wonder if he loved Ruth more."

"Oh, Naomi." The pain of such a question gashed Cheryl's heart.

"If he worked hard to win her love over another man's affections—"

"That was a long time ago," Cheryl said. "You were a little girl when they got married. No one could have known what the future would bring."

"*Gottes wille*," Naomi murmured.

"You could still ask Seth about the note," Cheryl said softly. "His secret is that he got the note. Yours is that you saw it. Maybe it would help to talk about it. It wouldn't mean you don't trust him."

"Maybe." Naomi sounded noncommittal.

"I saw something curious in the hardware store yesterday." Cheryl backed away from the awkwardness. "There's an old oar as part of a decorative display. It looked just like the one I saw Seth pick up."

"It cannot be the same one," Naomi said. "That oar has been on the wall at the hardware store for years. The tourists like the old-fashioned look."

"I've never noticed it before." Cheryl smelled a whiff of sheep and cow and knew the petting zoo would be around the next bend in the path.

"It is the sort of thing you do not really notice," Naomi said. "It is just supposed to create a feeling—nostalgia about the old racing days, I guess."

"I've heard a little about the races."

"On the river in the summer. The young people would race on Sunday afternoons before their singings. My family looked forward to watching them when we made trips from Dalton to visit our family here."

"Why did the races stop?"

"I am not sure. I was young. I suppose one summer no one wanted to do it anymore."

A sheep baaed, and they entered the zoo. Out of habit, Naomi checked the reservations book in the corner of the small barn.

"We have a school group coming on Monday," Naomi said, "weather permitting."

"That's nice," Cheryl said. "The forecast is clear."

"We can make them some hot chocolate if it is cold."

It was so like Naomi to anticipate how to bring comfort to someone else. While Naomi scanned some other notes tucked in the book, Cheryl surveyed the animals—sheep, pygmy goats, calves, chickens, miniature horses, ducks. Whether locals, tourists, or school groups, children loved seeing the animals up close. Elizabeth's determination to keep the animals clean and well fed was evident.

Cheryl couldn't get the oar out of her head. If the oar had been hanging in the hardware store for years, why was Seth hanging on to its match?

"I should get back," Naomi said. "I left bread rising in the kitchen."

Startled about the time, Cheryl looked at her phone. It was nearly ten, and Lydia had sent no reply text message about getting the Swiss Miss open.

They picked up the pace on the way back to the house and said good-bye standing at Cheryl's car.

"Are you sure you're all right on your own?" Cheryl asked, standing with the car door open.

"I have the bread to look after," Naomi said, "and Seth will come in at lunchtime."

Cheryl held Naomi's eyes. "Talk to him. No one else will be in the house."

Naomi ran her tongue across her upper lip. "I will see if the moment seems right."

Naomi returned to the house, and Cheryl patted her pockets, trying to remember what she'd done with her keys when she rushed to be sure Naomi was safe in the house. Standing there beside her car, she heard the creak of the Miller barn door opening. Seth emerged.

Cheryl waved. Seth hesitated. Cheryl let her car door close, keys still misplaced, and walked toward the barn.

"Happy anniversary," she said.

"Thank you."

"I understand you had a visitor this morning."

"Did we? I've been making repairs in the barn ever since breakfast."

"A driver ran me off the road on my way here."

A glove slid out of Cheryl's pocket. Before she could stoop to retrieve it, Seth picked up the glove.

"Why would someone run you off the road?" Seth handed Cheryl the glove.

"My question is why would someone be so angry leaving your farm?" Cheryl brushed damp dirt off her glove before sliding her hand into it.

Seth said nothing but only met Cheryl's gaze with his own placid expression. Had the driver spoken to Seth before he approached Naomi in the house? She hated to think Seth would lie about not having seen the visitor.

"I saw the other oar in the hardware store," Cheryl said, pulling on her second glove.

"I imagine dozens of people see it every day." Seth took several steps toward the house.

Yes, Cheryl thought, dozens of people saw it every day. But she was the only one who saw Seth pick up its match. She followed Seth.

"Do you know Rueben's son?" she asked.

"Rueben has six sons."

"The one I'm thinking of left about thirty years ago."

"That does not narrow the question. Several of them married into other districts."

"You must be protecting something." Cheryl lengthened her stride to keep up. "Or someone. You must have a good reason for why you picked up that oar at the river."

The door was wide open for him to offer an explanation.

"Well," Seth said, halting his steps, "if you have figured out that much, then perhaps you'll let me do what I need to do."

He resumed his progression toward the house. Cheryl resumed the hunt for her keys.

CHAPTER FOURTEEN

Back in town, Cheryl ducked into the house to check on the cat, who still hadn't touched his food or the milk dish. Otherwise he seemed himself, meowing his disapproval when she set out fresh water before leaving again for the store.

Cheryl flipped the Closed sign to Open only twenty-seven minutes late opening the Swiss Miss. There was no sign of Lydia. Cheryl checked her phone again, but there was neither a text nor a voice message from the girl. This was unlike Lydia, who was taking advantage of every moment of her rumspringa before she likely settled down to baptism and the responsibilities of adult membership in the church without a cell phone.

Visions of a buggy tipped over in a ditch infiltrated Cheryl's mind, and she slapped them away. Feeling anxious about Naomi's anniversary did not mean she should let every alarming thought run free in her brain.

Before Cheryl even got her purse and jacket put away, the shop door opened.

"Good morning." She offered a smile to two women, one of whom she recognized, although her name was slow to take form. Mrs. Cornwall. That sounded right.

"You're late," the stout, gray-haired woman said.

"I'm sorry if I inconvenienced you." Cheryl shoved her items beneath the counter.

"Have you changed your hours?"

"No. Again, I'm sorry. I had to attend to a personal matter."

"You're running a business—your aunt's business. If your store hours begin at ten, then you should be here at ten."

Cheryl pressed her lips together and forced a smile. "Emergencies come up for everybody. What can I help you with?"

"My friend is visiting from out of town. We just want to look around."

"Can I help you find something in particular?"

"Oh no. We're not planning to buy anything. I just wanted her to see how darling the shop is."

Cheryl swallowed her reply. Mrs. Cornwall was the one who pointed out Cheryl was running a *business*. The Swiss Miss was not some sort of public museum.

"Well," she said, "just let me know if you need something."

In an effort to bide her time waiting for them to leave, Cheryl chose the aisle farthest from Mrs. Cornwall to begin her daily straightening and dusting regimen.

Several sets of customers came and went. Cheryl had long ago observed that the Swiss Miss seemed to be the sort of shop people enjoyed visiting together to discover surprises and unusual gift ideas. Though she ordered from the same vendors on a regular basis, many items were handcrafted, like Dianne Thatcher's linens, so the inventory varied with each delivery. Nearly every day something new arrived. Part of the store's charm was that customers never knew what they might find. Ben and Rueben Vogel popped in for a quick game of checkers, which always drew the attention of visiting children. By eleven thirty, the store was thinning out. People would move instead to the cafés around town, looking for lunch.

"Hello again."

Cheryl looked up to see the owner of the energetic voice, Kathy from the Honey Bee Café.

"Twice in one morning," Cheryl said.

Kathy tapped a finger against her temple. "After I saw you, I had a brilliant idea."

"Oh?"

"I know just the person you should go to the banquet with tomorrow night."

"I'm not planning to go." Cheryl nudged the big hand of one of the cuckoo clocks, uncertain whether it was keeping proper time. She might have to take it out of the display. "I sent in a donation already."

"Oh, but tomorrow is Valentine's Day. It's a good excuse for a night out, and someday you can say you met the love of your life at the banquet."

Cheryl raised her eyebrows.

"I can set you up. Just say the word. You'll love him, and he already has tickets."

"*Mmm*," Cheryl said, "tickets but no date."

The only thing worse than not being in a relationship on Valentine's Day was somebody pitying her at the last minute and setting her up with somebody else who was also dateless and therefore just as pitiable.

"I know what you're thinking," Kathy said, "but give him a chance. He's a wonderful man."

"I'm sure he is," Cheryl said, "but I'm not much for being set up." She'd been set up with Lance six years ago. When they broke up, she'd promised herself no more blind dates. If Levi had invited her to the banquet in that exquisite moment when she thought he might, she would have gone, but she wasn't interested in matchmaking.

"Don't you even want to know who he is?" Kathy set her bottom lip in a pout.

"I'm sure he's lovely, but I'm going to decline." Cheryl moved behind the counter to scrounge for fresh boxes of buttercream fudge.

"But it's not some dubious stranger. It's somebody you probably already know."

Cheryl was unpersuaded. If she knew the man, then why didn't he ask her himself? Besides, she couldn't think of any man in town she'd want to go to the banquet with.

Except Levi, and he hadn't asked her. And he wouldn't ask her, because he'd given away his tickets. And he wasn't interested in marriage. And if he were, he wouldn't be looking for a woman who wasn't even Amish.

"Sorry, I don't think so," Cheryl said.

"Think about it. If you change your mind, let me know."

"I know where to find you." Cheryl arranged the fudge where the afternoon tourists would be sure to find it.

As Kathy exited, she held the door open for Rachel Swartzentruber, who was struggling to get a two-seater stroller through the door.

Cheryl grinned. The twins! Cheryl paced to the front of the store and leaned over the boys.

"It feels like I haven't seen them in ages." Cheryl marveled at the babies. One was sleeping, a blanket tucked around him. The other's eyes were wide open and curious. Cheryl gave him a silly grin, and his arms flapped in response.

"You can visit any time you want," Rachel said. "Just drive out. I do not even have to know you are coming."

"Since he's awake, can I hold him?"

Rachel chuckled at her flapping infant. "I think John would like that."

Cheryl unfastened the safety belt and carefully extracted the tiny boy. His hand went immediately to her spiky red hair, as it always did. It was so unlike his mother's brown hair fastened in a bun and hidden under a prayer kapp. Cheryl supposed that when he was older, she wouldn't like to have him pulling her hair, but right now she giggled at his curiosity.

"I have been to my mother-in-law's," Rachel said, shrugging a backpack off her shoulders. "She sent some mini loaves of bread. She thought you might like to sell them when the bus comes this afternoon."

Rachel unwrapped a towel, and the fragrance of fresh bread filled Cheryl's nostrils.

"I'll sell them if I don't gobble them down myself first," Cheryl said. If any one food was responsible for the fifteen pounds Cheryl never seemed to be able to shed, it was homemade bread. "They smell wonderful!"

"Also, my husband is making a couple of wooden doll strollers." Rachel stroked her son's cheek in Cheryl's arms. "He wonders if you would carry them on commission."

"Of course! Amish toys always sell well." Amish crafts would be perfect in the remodeled turret room.

"Good. I will tell him." Rachel's attention now went to her sleeping son. "When they were newborns, I managed to keep them on the same schedule. Now it is getting harder and harder."

"It must be hard for you to get out and about." Cheryl inhaled the sweet scent of the baby's head.

"It is difficult to do alone," Rachel said. "The stroller is a blessing. I try to coordinate with where my husband is going. And his mother is a big help."

Cheryl returned the baby to his stroller and took the bread from Rachel's arms. "She was sweet to send the bread."

"She was out to visit Rueben Vogel's daughter yesterday." Pushing the stroller, Rachel followed Cheryl toward the front of the store. "Did you know Rueben's son was back in town?"

Cheryl's eyes flicked up from the counter as she arranged bread. "I did hear that."

"I never knew him, of course," Rachel said. "He was gone long before I was born. People in our church do not know why he left in the first place, much less why he would be back after thirty years."

"Did she see him?" Cheryl began to calculate when she might go introduce herself to Rueben's daughter.

Rachel shook her head. "My mother-in-law says that after all these years she probably would not even recognize him if he crossed the street right in front of her. I guess he does not look much like Rueben."

"Perhaps he took after his mother," Cheryl said.

"I should get going. My husband will be waiting." Rachel maneuvered the stroller to turn it around and reached for the wakeful twin.

As Rachel left, Cheryl pressed her lips out, wondering about Rueben's son. After thirty years, how many people would recognize him? Rachel's mother-in-law was likely not alone. Thirty years was the difference between young adulthood and middle age.

Just before noon, Lydia rushed through the door. "I am so sorry! I just now saw your message."

"It's all right," Cheryl said. "Everything worked out."

"I was visiting one of my old school friends. Her parents are very conservative. They do not ever want a phone to ring in their house, not even for someone on rumspringa. I wanted to respect their wishes, so I turned off my phone. I only remembered to turn it on again a few minutes ago."

"No harm."

"I know Esther's not here. Do you need to go out?"

"I'll just run over to the Honey Bee and be right back."

A few minutes later, Cheryl settled in the store's office with an egg salad sandwich and a cup of split pea soup to tackle the final handful of vendors who routinely charged the shop's credit card. She blew across the top of her soup, wishing Levi would happen by. Naomi hadn't said what the boys were up to, just that they were all off the farm. The best Cheryl could hope for was that Seth would come to his senses and stay close to his wife—at least physically. He should know more than anyone else what the mysterious note meant. Maybe Rueben's son was driving the strange car, and obviously he was angry about something, but that didn't mean he'd written the note. Circumstantial, Chief Twitchell would say. It could have been anyone. Only two people could know for sure—the note's writer and Seth.

The afternoon tour bus arrived, and passengers gathered their bearings on the sidewalk before most of them opted to start with the Swiss Miss.

"I am back," the note had said. "How could you steal someone's life and walk away? I will be there on the anniversary. Make sure you are, or else."

Coming into town with a crowd could be the perfect cover. Leaving Lydia to work the register, Cheryl weaved between displays scrutinizing the movements of tourists.

It would have helped to know what she was looking for.

Her examination descended on one man who looked to be in his fifties and separated himself from the main group early on. He seemed not to focus on any items in the store, instead moving in an odd way as if he was nervous.

Maybe he was nervous. Maybe he had something in mind today. Maybe he hadn't gotten off that tour bus. Who knew where he'd come from?

Cheryl approached him. "Can I help you find anything?"

"No thanks."

She followed him a few more steps. "If you need something, just let me know."

"I don't need anything. Leave me alone."

Cheryl stepped back, startled.

"I'm sorry," he said. "Sorry, sorry, sorry."

A woman, younger, hurried up the aisle. "Dad, are you all right?"

"Sorry, sorry, sorry."

The woman turned to Cheryl. "I apologize if my father alarmed you. I thought he was ready for an outing, but perhaps it's too soon."

"It's all right," Cheryl said. After all, the man hadn't actually done anything.

"Dad, would you rather sit on the bus for a few minutes?"

He nodded, and his daughter guided him out of the store.

Cheryl's chest burned at the conclusion she'd jumped to. With admiration, she watched the woman's patience as she guided her father to the refuge of the bus, where the driver, Howard Knisley, had his nose in a book.

Someone tapped her shoulder. "Excuse me. I've always wanted a cuckoo clock. They remind me of my grandmother's house. I wonder which clock you think is best."

Cheryl walked with the customer to the clock display and discussed the features of the various models. Gradually the crowd thinned. Lydia gathered her things and left as well. At five, Cheryl locked up the store, but she stayed nearly another hour to tally receipts, put cash in the safe, and clean the floor thoroughly.

Beau was sleeping in the kitchen when Cheryl got home but woke when she dropped her keys on the counter. Cheryl picked him up before inspecting his food dish.

"Good boy," she said. "You ate something."

He stared into her eyes. Cheryl tried to sort out if his gaze carried a message.

Darkness was not far off. Cheryl had missed her chance to get to the river to walk today, but she had something else in mind anyway.

"Let's go for a ride," she said to the cat as she grabbed an apple to snack on.

By the time Cheryl reached the Miller farm for the second time that day, the evening had fully descended. She turned off the headlights and eased the car to the edge of the front yard before cutting the engine. The house was lit with activity. Cheryl supposed that Levi, Caleb, Eli, Elizabeth, and Esther had made their way home. Only Sarah, Seth's married daughter, was missing. Cheryl sat with Beau in her lap, watching the house and munching on crackers. Over the next three hours, lights went off one room at a time as the household found repose. The front door opened, and Cheryl saw the beam of a flashlight. She straightened behind the steering wheel, ready to start the car and follow if necessary. But the light progressed no farther than the front porch. In its illumination, Cheryl could see that it was Seth who had emerged and now held vigil in the cold.

The flashlight snapped off. Cheryl turned up the collar of her jacket.

CHAPTER FIFTEEN

Cheryl roused, stiff from cold and startled that she had fallen asleep in her car. In her lap under her gloved hands, Beau meowed at her sudden movement.

She had not come to the Miller farm with a plan. Only when she saw Seth come out and sit on the steps did Cheryl hunker down to survey his movements. They had been few. A crescent moon and stars illuminated the abysmal darkness and provided enough light to make out Seth's shape. Whether it also revealed Cheryl's small car to Seth, she didn't care.

Cheryl breathed in and out with deliberation. Her phone had said 11:21 the last time she looked at it. Now it displayed 1:14. In between the two time readings, midnight had come and gone. The anniversary had ended.

And Seth and his flashlight had ceased their vigil.

Had he too waited for the end of a day laden with tense perplexity? And had he gone into the house, or had he gone somewhere else? No lamps beamed from within the house, which gave every appearance of being a slumbering haven for its occupants. Most likely even Seth was sound asleep beside Naomi.

Beau climbed up to one shoulder. Cheryl rubbed her eyes and turned the key in the ignition.

"We'll go home," she said to the cat. "I guess Naomi was right. Whatever that note meant, Seth took care of it." She might have to swallow her pride and apologize for doubting Seth. *Demut*, the Amish called it. Humility.

Bleary-eyed, Cheryl arrived at the Swiss Miss seven hours later. She had been ignoring the stack of papers with questions written on yellow sticky notes that Esther kept adding to the pile as she learned to work on the books, and Valentine's Day was likely to be busy for every shop on Main Street. Cheryl couldn't afford to lollygag in bed no matter how little she had slept. She straightened the displays as usual, checked the back room to be sure any saleable items even distantly related to Valentine's Day had been taken to the store shelves, and tore open a package of red and pink balloons. By the time Cheryl had puffed her cheeks and inflated seven, she decided that was adequate. She rustled through a junk draw in the office for string and tied the balloons in two displays, one at the cash register and one among the wooden toys near the store window. Then she turned to Esther's paperwork, promising herself that if she got through the questions, she would reward herself with coffee from the Honey Bee Café before business hours began.

When the shop door opened, Cheryl thought she had lost track of time—which hardly seemed possible with a row of cuckoo clocks on sentry duty. It was not yet nine thirty. Cheryl left the desk and glanced into the store.

"Levi," Cheryl said. "Is everything all right?"

Levi tilted his head. "Why would it not be?"

Cheryl moved toward him. "I know yesterday was a strenuous day for your parents."

He nodded. "But it is over."

"Good."

Levi scratched an ear. "I am not very *goot* at being subtle, so I am going to say it straight out."

"Say what?"

"You were out on the farm last night."

Adrenaline shot through Cheryl's chest.

"My bedroom window is on the front of the house," Levi said. "I looked out, and the moon was catching something, so I looked closer."

Cheryl tugged a spike of hair at the back of her head. "I admit I was there."

"It was very late. May I ask why?"

She told him about the old Buick barreling off the farm right after a stranger had come to the front door.

"I tried to talk to your father," she said. "I wanted to find a way to ask him to please stay close to Naomi."

"He was home all day."

"He was nowhere in sight when that man came to the door."

Levi shuffled his feet. "Well, as I said, the day is over. Whatever has been making you so nervous did not happen. Hopefully we can all move on."

"Hopefully." Cheryl met Levi's gaze. "Aren't you worried at all that something *could* have happened?"

"But nothing did. The Bible tells us not to worry about tomorrow. I am certainly not going to worry about yesterday."

Levi was starting to sound as odd as his father.

"No, I suppose not," Cheryl said. Surely Levi would not be so quick to move on if he knew about the note. Cheryl braced herself to break Naomi's confidence. "Levi—"

The shop door opened, and Kathy bustled in from across the street. "Oh, Levi. If I'd realized you were here, I would have brought another coffee." Steam rose through the slit of the lid on a takeout cup as she set it on the counter.

"I was just leaving," he said. "I am sure we all have a busy day."

Cheryl nodded. As Levi paced out of the shop, Kathy slid the coffee toward Cheryl.

"I just wanted to give you one last chance to change your mind about that date," Kathy said. "I would hate for him to ask someone else."

"So you're trying to bribe me with coffee?" Cheryl picked up the cup and inhaled the aroma.

"Is it working?"

Cheryl sipped and welcomed the warmth trickling down her throat. "I know you mean well, but I don't think so. Can I still keep the coffee?"

Kathy swatted Cheryl's arm. "You're a stubborn one."

"That's what my mother always said."

"Okay, I give up."

As Kathy scuttled out of the shop, Cheryl surveyed the row of cuckoo clocks, two of which were due to chirp their announcements that another quarter hour had passed. In another fifteen minutes, the business day would begin.

Foot traffic surged and waned along Main Street all morning. As Cheryl predicted, business in the Swiss Miss was brisk. Townspeople and tourists alike came in for last-minute gifts and decorations, whether for romantic relationships, friendships, or family members. During lulls, Cheryl checked her phone. News from Aunt Mitzi would be welcome. But Mitzi usually stayed only a day or two at a time in a location with Internet access, so Cheryl supposed the days-long silence meant her aunt was in a remote region again. Cheryl had no way to know when Mitzi might return to the city. It could be weeks.

Weeks.

Cheryl missed her aunt. Mitzi would have had some advice about Seth. She might even have said something that made sense of the note in Seth's pocket.

Look deep.

Deep where? Was Cheryl supposed to look deep literally—in the river? Or did Mitzi merely use the phrase as a figure of speech? In that case, Cheryl needed to think more deeply.

The tour bus was seven minutes late, but when Cheryl saw the number of passengers—including lots of couples—she imagined getting everyone boarded and settled had taken some extra time. The bus was especially full for a winter excursion. A banner on the side of the bus in large red lettering said, Valentine's Day Special. Passengers streamed out of the bus. On most Saturdays, Cheryl was alone in the store. Today, though, she'd made sure Esther and Lydia could split the afternoon hours.

"Here they come," Cheryl said.

"We will sell them everything we have," Esther said.

"That's the spirit."

The door opened, and the afternoon rush began. Cheryl and Esther took turns behind the counter while the other answered questions around the store. The cash register was in steady use. At midafternoon when Lydia arrived to relieve Esther, Cheryl wished she had asked them both to stay the entire day. The door opened and closed all afternoon, giving Cheryl little time to think about anything but the task at hand. Ben and Rueben came in to play checkers, but Cheryl was too busy to do more than whiz by them and wave. Heart necklaces, sentimental mugs, chocolates, carved wooden heart-shaped boxes, red-trimmed tablecloths—Lydia and Cheryl rang it up and bagged it up all afternoon. It would take Cheryl twice as long as usual to tally the day's receipts.

Finally, toward five o'clock, the influx of customers waned. One couple barely into their twenties remained, the young woman lingering at the rack of silver lockets but in the end carrying only a mug to the counter.

"Happy Valentine's Day," Cheryl said, handing the woman a bag and change. She'd been forcing the greeting through her lips all day. This should be the last time.

"It's a lucky one for us," the woman said. "We just found out a few hours ago that we get to go to the banquet tonight. Can you believe it? Somebody gave us free tickets. We wanted to go, but we couldn't afford it."

"That's wonderful for you." Cheryl smiled.

Apparently Levi was not the only ticket winner choosing not to attend—or perhaps Levi's tickets had made their way into the hands of this eager young couple. What did it matter? In a few minutes Cheryl could close the store, lock up the contents of the till, go home, and forget all about Valentine's Day.

"Are you sure it is all right if I leave?" Lydia asked when they were at last alone in the store.

"Absolutely. Thanks for coming in. I'll finish up and see you on Monday."

Cheryl tallied the day's receipts, stored the cash in the safe, and made a quick tour through the store looking for any task that could not wait until Monday morning. She didn't see the hearts until she straightened the display of photo frames. But there they were.

Two little candies.

Cheryl picked them up. They had the dry feel of candy straight from the box. *Do Good. I'm Sure.*

She went to the cash register, reached into the shelf beneath, and pulled out the tiny tin she had stashed two days earlier. She set the new hearts beside the ones Lydia had found on the checkerboard. *Be True. Start Now. Do Good. I'm Sure.* It was silly, but somehow finding more hearts on this day, when she was on the verge of giving up wondering about anniversaries and oars and odd behavior, felt like encouragement.

It *was* silly. Still, Cheryl snapped the lid in place and put the tin back under the cash register. On the street, activity was thinning out. On most Saturday nights, a couple of restaurants in town might lure some casual budget-conscious diners. Today the banquet would be the big draw, pulling people off of Main Street to a venue on the outskirts of town. As she reached for the light switch and turned the Open sign to Closed, Cheryl heard the *clip-clop* of a horse and buggy and peered out to see who it might be.

It was Levi's buggy, with Sugar pulling. Surely he had not been in town all day. Besides, he was not headed in the direction of home. Esther had said he had plans for the evening that didn't involve the banquet. With a pang, Cheryl mentally replayed the moment when she'd thought he was about to invite her to the event. Whatever Levi was doing tonight, it was sure to be more exciting than her evening at home alone with her cat.

A gust of cold air blew through the openings where the insulation had turned brittle and cracked, stirring a sensation of imminent snow. The weekend's warming trend had reversed and declined all week. After last night's surveillance of the Miller home, a couple of logs in the fireplace and an evening at home might be just what Cheryl needed.

Look deep.

Mitzi couldn't mean something as obvious as the basement, could she? The shop's dank, unfinished basement was used for a few boxes of overflow stock, but for the most part Cheryl was unsure what else was down there. The old crates had never piqued her interest before.

It was unlikely Mitzi meant the lower level, but what did Cheryl have to lose by looking? It would only take a few minutes to determine whether it was worth the effort to look more thoroughly. In the office, she reached up and unlatched the sliding miniature bolt that kept the door closed well above the reach of any curious child who might wander into the office and tug on the door. Aunt Mitzi was nothing if not vigilant about safety. By the time Cheryl reached the bottom of the stairs, the door had fallen closed behind her just as she expected. She waved her hand in the dark to find and pull the chain that would turn on the single lightbulb.

Above her Cheryl heard footsteps thumping awkwardly across the floor. *We're closed.* She'd hardly had a moment to sit down all day. She would not be ungracious, but a customer lingering after business hours might test her patience. Besides, she had turned off the main lights upstairs and flipped the sign, making it obvious the Swiss Miss was closed.

The floor above her creaked. Someone was in the office.

Cheryl started up the stairs. "Hello?"

The bolt slid into place. The heavy footsteps retreated.

Chapter Sixteen

Cheryl scrambled up the steps and twisted the doorknob. It turned, but the top of the door held firm at the bolt.

Cheryl banged an open palm against the door. "Who's there?"

Steps thudded across the polished wood floor above, and the bell jangled as the front door closed.

"Hello!" Cheryl banged again.

It was too late. Whoever was there had gone.

Cheryl was certain the store was empty when she came downstairs. She didn't remember hearing the bell, but it was easy enough to be lost in her own thoughts and not to notice a sound that repeated dozens of times a day.

She made a face for no one to see and huffed aggravation. All she wanted was to get home to her fire and her cat.

This was no accident. Someone deliberately closed the door and slid the bolt into place. Lydia and Esther knew to keep the door locked, but they were gone. Esther left hours ago, and Cheryl had seen Lydia gather her coat and bag.

Someone was watching. Someone knew Cheryl was alone in the shop. She pressed her back against the door and slid down to the top stair. Why had she not paid more attention to the odd sensation that someone was following her earlier in the week?

Surely this was not Seth's doing. Even his odd behavior of the last few days would not lead him to lock Cheryl in the basement.

Life would be simpler if Cheryl had not seen Seth pick up that oar, or if she had not persisted in walking on the river path in the early evenings. No one but Naomi knew Cheryl had seen the note in Seth's pocket, so why would someone want to hurt her?

The pieces of Cheryl's week were random, unconnected. She couldn't tie the oar to the note. She couldn't tie footsteps following her on the path to Seth or the oar. The only suspicion that made any sense was that Rueben's son was driving that monster Buick with its noisy engine and that he was the stranger who visited the Miller farm. But why? As hard as she might try, Rueben would not be coerced into confirming anything.

Cheryl huffed again and pulled her cell phone from her pocket. If she were someone to leave her phone in her purse or coat pocket, she would really be in a pickle. As it was, she only needed to call someone. The contact list in her phone was full of numbers of people who ran businesses on Main Street. Somebody would still be around.

Kathy across the street at the Honey Bee was Cheryl's first thought. Cheryl made the call. The number went straight to voice mail. Either Kathy was on the phone or she had it turned off while she worked in the restaurant. Cheryl opted not to leave a message and tried the restaurant's number. No answer. Kathy must have closed early to get ready for the banquet.

Marion Berryhill was just down the street at By His Grace. Cheryl tried both the store number and the home number for the

Berryhills. No answer. Ray and Marion were primary organizers for the banquet. If anyone had reason to be at the venue early, it was them.

"Sugar and grits," Cheryl muttered, scrolling through the numbers on her phone. Her Southern mother's expression came in handy at frustrating moments.

Cheryl did not know Jacob Hoffman at Hoffman's Furniture very well, but for some reason she had an entry for him in her phone list. He would have a phone in his shop and at home, and perhaps a cell phone. The number Cheryl had could be any one of the three. It didn't matter which, as long as he answered.

No answer.

Agnes Winslow at Sugarcreek Sisters Quilt Shoppe. No answer.

Gail Murray at Buttons 'n Bows. No answer.

Greta Yoder at Yoder's Corner. No answer.

Had phone service for all over Sugarcreek gone out? Half the town would be preparing for the big Valentine's Day banquet, but what happened to people being attached at the hip to their cell phones?

Cheryl's finger hovered over the number listed for Chief Twitchell. Would rescuing her from her own basement come under the category of "to protect and serve"? Wasn't it part of small-town charm to be able to call the police chief for any need at all? No. She might need whatever credibility she had left with Chief Twitchell for a bigger problem, something that involved an actual crime. She could hear him now, saying that he had nothing to investigate in this instance of alleged foul play—no clues, no evidence, no suspects. He would give her that look that said, *Why did you bother me?*

Instead, Cheryl selected the number for the phone shack on the Miller farm. It was unlikely anyone would answer at suppertime on a Saturday night, but Cheryl was desperate.

"Come on, come on, come on," she murmured.

The number rang six times. Just as Cheryl resolved that on this occasion she would leave a message, the ringing ceased.

"Hello? Miller Maze and Petting Zoo."

"Elizabeth?"

"Yes."

"This is Cheryl."

"Oh. Hi."

"Is everything all right?" If something happened to the Millers while Cheryl was locked in a basement, she would never forgive herself for not getting to the bottom of things sooner.

"It is suppertime. I am not supposed to be out here, but I wanted to check on one of the goats that has been sick."

"Sorry," Cheryl said, "but I'm relieved you answered." She explained her dilemma.

"I'll be there as soon as I am able," Elizabeth said. "I will have to tell Dacd."

"I don't want to get you in trouble."

"I will not be in trouble. I will just have to explain. It might take an hour."

"Whatever it takes," Cheryl said. "The front door is open. Just come through to the office. I can't thank you enough."

She clicked off.

An hour.

The damp basement was noticeably colder than the shop upstairs or the office where Cheryl's jacket hung on the back of the desk chair. Discovering an old blanket would be nice right about now. Not especially hopeful, Cheryl stood up and went down the stairs for the second time. Perhaps the lightbulb would put off some heat.

At the base of the stairs, Cheryl paused to do ten clumsy jumping jacks in an effort to persuade herself she could keep warm. She might as well look around. After all, that's what she came down to do in the first place. If she kept moving, her mind might not fixate on the chill seeping through her skin and settling into her bones.

In the months since arriving in Sugarcreek, Cheryl hadn't paid much attention to the basement. Occasionally, she carried a box down for temporary storage and left it at the bottom of the stairs without venturing farther in. Someday Aunt Mitzi would return, and her belongings would be where she left them. Now, however, Cheryl began to lift lids of boxes and remove whatever was stacked on top of a crate to see what it obscured underneath. She found a canvas drop cloth so old it was brittle to the touch, an oil lamp with a broken handle, books that looked like castoffs from an antiques shop. When she uncovered nostalgic milk tins, she wondered if the Amish had ever used them. If so, they would automatically be worth more. Whether or not she could sell them, they might clean up enough to add a nice touch to the crafty turret room. When she dragged a crate away from the wall and a mouse darted over her toes, Cheryl nearly fell over backward on to a pair of old suitcases.

She put a hand over her chest while she recovered her breath and her posture, unsure whether she should worry about where the mouse was or pretend she hadn't seen it.

Nothing looked relevant to a mysterious oar or Seth's annual mood swings or the car that Rueben's son drove. But how would she know what was relevant if she had no clue what she was looking for? Wasn't that the point of looking deeper?

Cheryl shivered and did ten more jumping jacks.

Above her, the bare lightbulb flickered.

"Oh no you don't," Cheryl said.

The light went out.

Chapter Seventeen

Sitting on an old hard-sided suitcase after all, Cheryl shuddered in the dark. As soon as she was released from this dungeon, she would hang a sweater on a nail at the top of the stairs. She knew just the one, a ratty brown cardigan that had belonged to her Uncle Ralph. He used to wear it for yard work. If she ever got trapped here again—which she fully intended *not* to do—at least she could take comfort in something warm and familiar.

Cheryl looked at the time on her cell phone and then made herself count to five hundred before looking again. If Elizabeth was right and it would take her about an hour to get there, Cheryl faced at least thirty more minutes of captivity.

She turned on the flashlight app on her phone and swept the basement with its light. If only someone would invent an app that put off heat. In the security of the lightbulb's illumination, Cheryl hadn't thought to look for a window. In the back of her mind was the image of two basement windows that she routinely walked past on the side of the old house-turned-store. How hard could it be to break a window?

A faint scratching sound convinced her to try. The mouse was on the loose.

The windows were set high. Climbing up, rather than breaking glass, might be the greater challenge. The image of her five-foot, six-inch frame, with its extra fifteen pounds, wriggling through one of the narrow windows was unpleasant. On the other hand, it wouldn't hurt to investigate. She just needed something to stand on. If she could get a grip on the precarious windowsill, she could do a pull-up to the glass and slam her elbow through it.

Right. Who was she kidding? She hadn't done a pull-up since gym class in the ninth grade, and she only got half credit for the one she eked out then. Besides, there was nothing to stand on. Even sitting on the suitcase was making it cave in slightly. After she hung a sweater on a nail, she would tuck a ladder under the stairs. *She* intended never to get caught in this situation again, but someone else might. Lacking a ladder, maybe she could climb something else. Sweeping the basement again in her phone's light, Cheryl spied an old wooden chair. She dragged it to the wall, positioned it under a window, turned an empty metal crate upside down in the seat, and hiked up one leg. The basement ceiling was low enough that she might have a chance of reaching a window.

The chair wiggled beneath her weight. Cheryl refused to believe her desperate plan was fallible. It might be too late to call Elizabeth and tell her not to come, but at least Cheryl could wait for her upstairs in light and warmth.

And without a mouse crawling across her feet in the dark.

Cheryl braced herself with one arm against the wall. She would have to put away her phone and use both hands to steady herself on top of the crate.

Even if she'd admitted her doubts about the chair's ability to hold her weight, Cheryl hadn't counted on the crate sliding against the wood. The crate slipped out from under one foot and crashed to the floor. The chair was not far behind it. Cheryl managed to slow her own tumble but landed on her back.

The wind knocked out of her, Cheryl sat up and counted to five hundred one more time, wondering if a mouse's eyes would shine in the dark.

Suppose somebody did mean to lock her in the basement. Why? What was she being kept from?

Beau.

What kind of monster would use an innocent cat to send a sinister message? If anything happened to Beau, all sense of graciousness would explode out of Cheryl's head.

Noise above her made Cheryl tilt her head up even in the dark. This time the footsteps sounded more like shuffling than thudding. She staggered to the base of the stairs and with one hand on the wall climbed the steps. Right after she hung a sweater and stowed a ladder, she would install a railing.

"Hello!" she called.

When she reached the door, Cheryl made a fist and rapped with fury. "I'm in here!"

The footsteps took more solid form. Elizabeth had not come alone.

Unless it wasn't Elizabeth at all. Cheryl heard voices but could not make out words. She kept one hand fisted to swing if necessary.

That self-defense class her brother had goaded her into taking years ago might yet pay off.

The bolt creaked out of its cradle. The door opened.

Cheryl stared into Naomi's wide brown eyes. Behind Naomi stood Seth.

"Where's Elizabeth?" Cheryl said.

"Whatever you think of me lately," Seth said, "I have more sense as a father than to send my daughter out alone at night into who knows what."

"Who on earth would lock you in the basement?" Naomi stepped back so Cheryl could emerge into the office.

"That's what I'd like to know." Cheryl glared at Seth. She couldn't help it.

"You cannot think Seth had anything to do with this," Naomi said.

"Maybe not directly," Cheryl mumbled.

"And not indirectly either," Naomi said.

His hands in his pockets, Seth met Cheryl's eyes without expression.

"What are you doing with that oar?" Cheryl asked.

Seth glanced at Naomi.

"That's right," Cheryl said. "She knows. I told her what I saw." *You should have told her. You should have told her about the note. Maybe if you had, we wouldn't be here now.*

"It has nothing to do with this," Seth said.

"How do I know that?"

"Because I am telling you." Seth's voice did not rise.

"Stop it, you two," Naomi said. "Cheryl, I am sure it was frightening to get locked in the basement, but you are out now. And Seth had nothing to do with it. So what if he picked up an old oar? You are making too much of this."

Cheryl pressed her fingertips into her eye sockets. "I'm sorry. It's been a long week."

Naomi took Cheryl's jacket off the back of the chair and handed it to her. "Would you like us to deliver you home?"

"I'll walk, thank you." She could use the air. Cheryl donned her jacket and found her purse. "Thank you for coming to my rescue. Both of you. It was kind of you."

"Of course we would come," Naomi said. "You must know how fond we are of you—both of us."

Cheryl nodded, though at the moment she was less convinced of Seth's sentiment than Naomi's. Her basement ruminations had persuaded her of one thing: Seth had something to do with the oar, and Seth had something to do with the note. Those two items were not randomly unrelated, no matter what Naomi wanted to believe. Cheryl forced herself to breathe normally as she thanked the Millers once again for coming and said good night. Their buggy clattered down the street as she turned her key in the lock. Maybe a security system wouldn't be a bad investment.

Chief Twitchell waved from a few doors down. "Mindin' your own business these days?"

Cheryl stifled her response, saying instead, "You're working late on a Saturday night."

"Crime has no schedule," he said. "I just finished up a call you might be interested in."

"Oh?"

"Not much I can do right now with the bank closed, but we may have tracked down that activity on your credit card."

"That's good news!" Finally something was going right.

"Come see me next week. We'll sort it out."

Cheryl nodded. Chief Twitchell waved again before crossing the street.

The first snowflake Cheryl was aware of landed on her nose. The temperature had dropped steeply from the daytime high. One isolated flake quickly turned into steady precipitation. She had always liked snow, even in the deepest winter freezes. A fire, a cup of hot chocolate, a book, and a cat made for a cozy indoor evening while the ground turned white outside. Cheryl had all the requisite elements waiting for her only four blocks away.

But snow on Valentine's Day seemed to turn the knife of envy in her chest. If she were watching a Hallmark movie, of course it would snow on Valentine's Day evening. The hero and heroine would walk hand in hand, oblivious to the temperatures, pausing under a streetlight for a kiss. Her hat would fall off, but she wouldn't care. They wouldn't even be wearing suitable jackets. They never did in films. Whatever tensions had come between them earlier in the movie would fade away in the strength of their love.

Of course Cheryl knew it wasn't always like that. Maybe even never. After all, look what happened to her and Lance. Still, snow on Valentine's Day added up to romance, and Cheryl wasn't in the mood for it tonight. She would go home and watch golf reruns on ESPN if that's what it took to get Valentine's Day out of her head.

She headed into the second segment of her four-block walk home.

And she had that creepy feeling again.

Someone was behind her.

She slowed. He slowed.

She sped up. He sped up.

At least it seemed that way to her.

At the next intersection, she made her decision.

Chapter Eighteen

Cheryl whirled and braced her feet shoulder-width apart, her hands out of her pockets and ready for rapid deployment.

"Why are you following me?"

The man halted immediately. "I'm sorry?"

"This isn't the first time. I don't have to be a detective to know that someone's been following me. It stops now."

He raised his eyebrows and shoulders in tandem. "I'm sorry if someone has been following you, but I assure you it isn't me."

"You've been behind me for the last two blocks." Cheryl gripped the strap of her purse. She could swing it right at his head.

"I'm just walking down the sidewalk, the same as you." He looked over her shoulder and down the street.

Cheryl refused to turn and follow his gaze. She was too smart to fall for such a ploy. "What kind of car do you drive?"

"Excuse me?"

"What kind of car do you drive?"

"An old beater that has seen me through college, veterinary school, and my first job."

"A Buick?"

"A Chevy." The man gestured across the street. "Look, if you'd like, I'll walk on the other side of the street, or I'll walk ahead of you where you can keep your eye on me."

Cheryl narrowed her eyes at him.

"I just moved to Sugarcreek a few weeks ago," he said. "I'm Brandon. I'd offer to shake your hand, but I'm afraid you might rip my arm out of its socket."

Cheryl said nothing.

"Would you mind if I went ahead?" he said. "It's cold just standing here."

"I'm sorry. I've been rude," Cheryl said without moving. "I'm Cheryl."

"Something spooked you." Brandon stepped to one side. "I hope your evening improves."

"I'm sorry to have held you up."

"No problem. I normally try to park closer, but today finding a space seemed next to impossible."

Cheryl nodded. "Valentine's Day. All the shops have been busy."

"Everybody running around getting ready for the banquet probably made things even worse."

"Are you going?" Cheryl wished she could swallow back the words as soon as they left her mouth. Why should she care? He was a stranger. And he *might* have been following her.

He laughed. "No. Levi Miller gave me a pair of tickets, but it didn't work out to use them."

"You know Levi?"

"I'm a veterinarian. I treated a horse on the Miller farm a couple of weeks ago," Brandon said. "Do you know them?"

"Pretty well, actually." She spoke with confidence she did not feel at the moment.

"They seem nice."

"They are." Around them the snow thickened. "Why didn't you go?"

"I barely know anyone in town yet. Somebody tried to set me up on a blind date, but that didn't work out. I don't blame the poor woman. Blind dates are not my favorite either."

Heat rose through Cheryl's neck. "Oh." She chewed one corner of her mouth.

"Are you all right?"

"I'm pretty sure that poor woman was me."

Brandon lifted his chin with the hint of a smile.

"Kathy Snyder at the Honey Bee?" Cheryl said.

"That's right. She spoke very highly of you."

"And you as well." Cheryl watched Brandon's face as snow melted into the wavy brown hair brushing his ears and collar. He wore no hat, and red tinged his ears and nose from the cold, but gentleness crinkled his eyes. Sincerity. Winsomeness. A pleasing scent of aftershave rose from his navy jacket, and he suppressed a shudder. He really was cold. In that moment Cheryl had a hard time seeing how she could have suspected this mild man of anything sinister. This whole week had made her jumpy.

Vague regret oozed through her chest. He'd been willing. She was the one who put the kibosh on Kathy's scheme. Yet here they were, together at the start of the evening regardless of her refusal to cooperate earlier in the day. Maybe God was smiling from heaven at the pleasure of His sovereignty. Cheryl had prayed often enough that God would give her another chance at love—with the right man. Cheryl wanted no confusion on that question.

"Kathy said I didn't need a date," Brandon said. "I might meet somebody there, she said. But considering it's Valentine's Day, that just seemed a little too…"

"Desperate?" Cheryl supplied. "Pitiful?"

Brandon laughed again. "Something like that. Anyway, I left the tickets with her a couple of hours ago. I hope she found someone who could use them at the last minute."

"A young couple," Cheryl said. "Maybe twenty years old. They were in my store just before closing."

"You have a store in town?"

Cheryl pointed down the block. "The Swiss Miss. My aunt owns it, but she asked me to run it while she's out of the country."

"I'll have to stop in."

"Please do."

"Do you mind if we keep moving? I'm from Florida. This weather is about to do me in."

Cheryl turned around and resumed forward motion. "Don't they need vets in Florida?"

"I had the opportunity to buy a practice," Brandon said. "A college friend's parents were selling out and moving someplace warm."

"Florida?"

"Arizona." Brandon dug his hands deeper into his pockets. "I've never lived north of Atlanta. Maybe I shouldn't have moved to Ohio in the middle of winter."

"It gets better. Besides, I like the snow."

"I shall aspire to do the same."

The slight Southern twang in Brandon's voice had been lost to Cheryl's ears while she was busy assessing the level of threat he represented. It lilted, songlike, now.

"Did you always want to be a veterinarian?" Cheryl asked.

"My sisters and I maintained a monagerie of animals," Brandon said. "My parents were quite indulgent on that matter, so I suppose my path was set early on."

In another half a block, they would be in front of her house. Normally Cheryl was grateful for the short pedestrian commute to work. Now after shrugging off her angry-bear persona and turning back into the nice person she liked to believe she usually was, a few more blocks of conversation would have been welcome. She slowed her steps as they reached her driveway.

"This is me."

Brandon glanced at the bungalow. "It looks charming."

"Even more so on the inside."

He waved a finger down the block. "My car is just up there."

"I'm sorry again for practically attacking you," Cheryl said.

"All is forgotten."

Cheryl considered inviting Brandon in for hot chocolate. It seemed the least she could do after having accosted and delayed him. The red on his ears and nose had spread across his cheeks. But

Levi's face waved through her mind, and she reminded herself that Brandon the vet technically was still in the category of Perfect Stranger.

"I have a cat," she said.

He smiled. "Lucky cat."

"Maybe I'll bring him to see you. He's not himself lately."

"Any time."

"I'm not sure how to tell if he's really sick."

"Follow your instinct," Brandon said.

"Anything I should watch for?"

"Changes in habit."

"He doesn't always eat."

"Watch the litter box. People know their own pets best, but I'll be happy to have a look if you're worried."

"Thank you."

Cheryl walked a few steps up her driveway before turning to watch Brandon's receding back. In the next block he crossed the street, pulled keys from his pocket, and got in an old brown Chevy parked under a streetlight. Cheryl hustled inside before Brandon had a chance to drive past her house and catch her gawking.

CHAPTER NINETEEN

An indistinct sensation of her own breath rising and falling wove in and out of Cheryl's consciousness. How long ago had she pulled the quilt off the back of the sofa? Twenty minutes or two hours? Either way, Cheryl had quickly descended into resolute slumber in the middle of the day, her favorite part of an unscheduled Sunday afternoon. Beau curled against her ribs in his own sleep. Cheryl's brain reluctantly returned from its abandonment to an after-church nap, but her eyelids protested against the notion that they should open.

Visions of the morning worship crisscrossed. The musicians at their instruments. The pastor in the pulpit. Light streaming through windows. And Brandon sitting three rows ahead of Cheryl just across the aisle. She tried not to stare, but at least half a dozen times her gaze drifted toward Brandon. Mostly she saw the back of his head, at most a profile if he happened to turn for a moment. Had he attended her church before this? She'd never noticed, never heard his name. But he had the confidence to come alone, and she liked that.

On the sofa, Cheryl opened her eyes and inventoried what she could be doing with the afternoon. Catch up on paperwork from the shop. Mop the kitchen floor before embarrassment ensued during a neighbor's drop-in visit. Laundry. Google cat illnesses.

None of it seemed worthy. If she didn't get up soon, though, she would be awake far too late in the evening.

Cheryl scratched the top of Beau's head. Did cats get fevers? Did he have a headache? How would she know if his illness, mild so far, was silently worsening?

"Trust your instincts," Brandon had said last night.

He was right. Cheryl already knew Beau had not been himself the last few days. If she watched him, she would know if he was worse and she would take him to see Brandon.

Brandon who? Cheryl didn't even get the veterinarian's last name.

Trust your instincts. Good advice for more than cat health. If Cheryl's instincts were not so persistent, she would have given up on the oar mystery days ago.

But she hadn't.

And she wouldn't.

She wasn't merely being stubborn. Something was going on with Seth, and it was enough to make Naomi insecure about her husband's love.

Her cell phone's tune jolted her reluctant eyes open at last. When she startled and reached for the end table, Beau meowed his protest.

"Mom," the screen said.

Cheryl answered the call. "Hi, Momma."

"Hello, beautiful one."

Her mother's cheery voice quelled Cheryl's preoccupation. "How are you, Momma?"

"This is the day the Lord has made."

"Let us rejoice and be glad in it." Cheryl gave the familiar refrain that Ginny Cooper had coaxed out of her children since they were toddlers.

"Church was wonderful this morning," Ginny said. "Mrs. Tudor is getting over her pneumonia. The neighbor's adorable grandchildren brought me a plate of cookies as soon as I got home from church. The weather is lovely. People are wrong when they say all it does is rain in Seattle. It's a delightful day."

Cheryl smiled while Beau resettled himself on her chest. "It's beautiful here too."

"What are you up to?"

"More like *down* to. Napping. But I'm about to get up and make myself useful."

"It's Sunday. Usefulness is not a requirement. How's the cottage?"

"I love it more all the time."

"It's still hard for me to picture you living in the middle of Mitzi's things. She was always one to keep piles of stuff 'just in case.'"

"I confess I still find a surprise every now and then when I open a drawer or a closet, but she made a good effort to pack up anything truly personal and put it in the basement." Cheryl's gaze went to her Bible on the coffee table, open again to the verse Mitzi had left for her.

"My guess is she still has every note or card Ralph ever gave her," Ginny said. "And my goodness. All his photos."

Something clicked. Uncle Ralph had been an avid amateur photographer. During Cheryl's childhood visits, he took her out looking for views to capture on film. Everyone said he could have been a professional instead of slaving as an accountant. Cheryl supposed he had eventually made the switch to a digital camera.

"None of his pictures are out," Cheryl said. "Aunt Mitzi must have packed them away."

"I'm sure she wanted you to feel free to do your own decorating."

"I always liked his old pictures."

"They must be around somewhere."

"In the basement, I suppose."

"I doubt Mitzi would mind if you looked for them."

"Maybe I will," Cheryl murmured.

A doorbell chimed at the other end of the call.

"I'd better get the door," Cheryl's mother said.

"Maybe the neighbors made you brownies now," Cheryl said.

"One can always hope."

They ended the call, and Cheryl gently extricated herself from Beau. In the kitchen, she downed a glass of cold water. She should have thought of her uncle's photos before this. Where were they, and was it too much to hope they might contain what Cheryl was looking for?

Cheryl had only been down to the cottage's basement once since her arrival, to stow the empty suitcases and flattened boxes that had accommodated her own move to Sugarcreek. Confident that Uncle Ralph's photos were not in any of the closets or cupboards on the ground floor—Cheryl would have encountered them by now—she opened a door at one end of the kitchen, groped for a light switch, and gripped the railing on her way down the decades-old wooden stairs. At their base, she glanced around. At least Uncle Ralph had electrified the basement, and Cheryl had more to rely on than one bare bulb.

Some of the boxes were labeled: Dishes. Magazines for Crafts. Extra Bedding. Miscellaneous Yarn. Ralph's Sweaters. Small Tools. Paint Supplies. Many were closed only by folded flaps tucked under each other. Some were sealed with packing tape. The stacks of boxes had more to do with similar size than organized content.

Cheryl chose one unlabeled and unsealed carton to open. Mugs wrapped in place mats. She moved to another. Empty three-ring binders. She chose a third. At least three dozen egg cartons, no doubt intended for something crafty.

For the second time in half an hour, Cheryl's cell phone disturbed the silence, this time with an alert that she had received an e-mail.

From Aunt Mitzi.

A quick glance revealed it was longer than just a few lines. Cheryl sprinted upstairs to read more comfortably on her laptop screen.

My darling Cheryl,

What a disappointment that our last attempt to Skype was unsuccessful. Inevitably I feel like there is so much I'd like to tell you and not enough time, especially when we never know if we'll be cut off. The latest news on this end is that the translator for our evangelism team has fallen ill. He's a delightful young man who grew up in Daru and learned very good English as a teenager in Port Moresby. His knack for several of the indigenous languages is remarkable. We've just brought him to the missionary guesthouse, where the doctor says he's quite sick and needs someone to look after him for a few weeks. We believe he has an aunt or a cousin in Port Moresby who may take him in while he recovers, but in the meantime, I agreed to stay here for a few unexpected days while all that is sorted out. It doesn't seem fair to expect the couple who run the guesthouse to take on the responsibility of his care.

When we Skyped, I suspect I heard more of your questions than you heard of my answers. I only meant to say that while I don't know much—or anything at all—about why the summer races on the river stopped, it always seemed odd to me that they came to an end as abruptly as they did. I think you're right to suspect there's a story that few people know.

My recollection is that while many people enjoyed watching the races, the group of Amish men who did the rowing were a tight bunch of friends who had grown up together. Everyone's oars were painted differently, which struck me as odd considering how careful the Amish are about vanity even now, but I suppose when young people are on rumspringa it's difficult to predict what they will want to try out. Your uncle Ralph took a few pictures, I believe, though I have no idea what ever happened to them. He was such a perfectionist that he would destroy pictures he didn't feel were up to snuff.

Of course, we don't want anyone to get hurt by digging up the past, but if there is a chance that someone would benefit from the truth, then it's worth the effort, isn't it? I hope you will keep on looking, but with gentleness and discretion. I do love Seth and Naomi and want only what's best for them.

I hear my charge coughing again, so I'll sign off and go tend to him. He keeps me up all hours. Perhaps I'll have a chance to Skype again, though at the moment I can't say just when.

Love, Aunt Mitzi

Cheryl read the message again before closing the laptop. It had to be more than a coincidence that her mother reminded her of Uncle Ralph's photos and a few minutes later Aunt Mitzi suggested he might even have taken photos of the river racing.

God's will, the Amish would say. They left nothing to coincidence, and maybe they were right. Perhaps it was worth another foray into the basement boxes.

Cheryl's eyes rose to the picture window, where winter light streamed in a shaft. While she was reading, Beau had found it and now stretched out on a coiled rag rug in the warmth.

The basement would still be there later in the evening or tomorrow. At this time of year, the shop's six-days-a-week schedule left Cheryl few opportunities to walk along the river in daylight. Beau looked content for now. Cheryl grabbed her jacket and gloves and drove out to the river. She parked in her usual spot and started down her usual path. Surely the time of day would feel less unsettling. Cheryl had no intention of forsaking her late-afternoon walks, but each day that sunset was delayed by even two minutes would bring relief.

No swinging headlights in the dark.

No unseen footfalls behind her on the path.

No gunning motors.

No junk thrown across the riverbank.

Cheryl wanted only to experience the peace that had drawn her to this habit in the first place.

She paused to take her phone out of her pocket. Perhaps even Uncle Ralph would be surprised at the quality of a smartphone photo these days. It was the only camera Cheryl had, and she remembered Aunt Mitzi's jolly plea to "send pictures" of the winter beauty. Cheryl snapped three in various directions to send once she returned to the cottage and took time to write a reply message.

As Cheryl returned her phone to her pocket, a twig snapped behind her and she whirled.

Nothing. No one. It must have been an animal.

Cheryl puffed her cheeks and exhaled. This was ridiculous. She couldn't be skittish every time she heard a noise. She stepped off the path to lean against a tree and soak in the view. Water lapped the edge of the riverbed. A lone bird called. Somewhere out of sight, the voices of children rose in laughter, followed by a cautious mother calling them away from the water's boundary. On the road beyond the path an occasional car passed in no hurry.

Absolutely nothing sinister.

In fact, all these sounds should have been part of the peaceful setting. Cheryl thought she had left city fears behind with Lance. If she could rewind to six days ago and avoid the scene that marred the river's peace—make it never have happened—she would.

But she couldn't.

As it was, she would always pass that spot just ahead and wonder what the truth was.

There was still another anniversary to get through on Tuesday. Cheryl still had one day to figure out what the oar had to do with the note—and why her best friend suspected that the death of her husband's first wife marred the peace of their marriage.

CHAPTER TWENTY

The choking gurgle came first and then the infusing odor. Cheryl rolled over in her bed on Monday morning. "*Eww,* Beau, what's going on?"

The mess that had escaped the cat and soiled the bedspread brought Cheryl to full wakefulness. She threw back the blankets, scooped up Beau, and carried him to the bathroom for further inspection. Porcelain, tile, and litter box were a better environment for the animal's illness than carpet, bedding, and clothing. Cheryl set Beau in the kitty litter, where he vomited again and trembled.

"Poor buddy." If Cheryl had not decided the night before to sleep in, she might not have even been home to witness this crisis. "We're going to find that vet."

Cheryl pulled khakis and a pink polo shirt from the closet and dressed quickly. Hopping on one foot while she tugged a sock and shoe on to the other, she checked on Beau. She had gotten the cat to the litter box just in time. In all their years together she had not seen Beau shake like this.

"I'm moving as fast as I can," Cheryl said. Both feet were appropriately clad now, and she donned yesterday's sweater because it conveniently hung from the hook on the bathroom door. Cheryl glanced at herself in the mirror. The advantage of her willful, spiked hair was that running her fingers through it while she crossed the bedroom could pass for combing.

Cheryl yanked the bedding off the mattress and headed for the laundry room off the kitchen, grateful for her aunt's large capacity washer and dryer. On the way back to the bedroom, she grabbed her phone. Thumbs hovering over the options, Cheryl thought what to do next.

It was already almost eight thirty. She did not know Brandon's last name or the name of another veterinarian. Without Brandon's name or the name of the practice he had taken over, how would she find his office? And what about the store?

She put the phone on the Speaker setting and dialed Lydia's cell phone number. Out of respect for how the Amish generally felt about telephones, Cheryl tried not to be frivolous with calls to the teenagers who carried phones. But this was important. While the phone rang, she pulled a rag towel out of the narrow linen closet and approached Beau to wipe him off before picking him up.

"Hello."

"Lydia, it's me, Cheryl."

"*Guder mariye.*"

"Not such a good morning so far," Cheryl said. "Beau is sick and making a mess of everything. I need to get to the vet's, and I don't know how long it might take. Can you open the store today?"

"I think so."

"I'll leave the key under the mat at my house, if you don't mind swinging by here first."

"No problem."

"Thanks. I'll owe you big time. I'll get there as soon as I can."

Cheryl ended the call, wrapped the towel around Beau, and decided to grab another for good measure.

If only her keys were somewhere in sight. Cheryl made three rounds through the rooms of the small cottage before spying the keys peeking out from under the magazine she had been reading last night. She managed to get her jacket on without setting Beau down. Once she had him situated on the floor of the passenger side, she twisted the store key off the ring to leave it for Lydia.

Then sitting behind the wheel with the engine running, Cheryl huddled over her phone to figure out where she was going. She opened an Internet search bar and entered *Veterinarian Brandon Sugarcreek Ohio.*

No promising results.

Veterinarians Sugarcreek Ohio.

This brought up a list of wide-ranging addresses. Some Cheryl recognized as being in other towns. Others showed street names she didn't recognize. None showed a vet with the first name of Brandon. He was probably too new to town to have a listing, or perhaps he hadn't changed the name of the practice.

Somebody had to know Brandon's last name.

Cheryl dialed Kathy Snyder's number. If she was trying to set Cheryl up on a date, surely she knew the man's last name. After four rings came the buoyant invitation to leave a message.

That wouldn't do Beau any good right now.

Cheryl tried the Berryhills at the bookstore.

No answer.

Cheryl ended the attempted call with an irritated puff. This was as bad as being locked in the store's basement on the night of the banquet. Why did no one ever answer the phone when she needed help?

The rap on her car window made her gasp. Relieved at the face she saw, Cheryl let out her breath and fingered the button that would lower the glass.

"Levi."

"Is everything all right?" he said. "I saw you in the car with the motor running. It seemed odd that you were not moving."

Cheryl explained the dilemma.

"Dr. Richardson," Levi said. "Brandon Richardson. He did a good job with Methuselah."

"Do you know his address?"

"No, but I know where his office is."

"Terrific. Can you give me some directions? The intersection? The name of the place?"

"It is a little tricky to find," Levi said. "I should just go with you."

Cheryl glanced toward the street, expecting to see a horse and buggy in front of her house. Nothing was there. "Where's your rig?"

"Daed has it. He brought me to town so I could go to the library."

"Library?"

"It is a long story," Levi said. "What matters now is Beau. It will be fastest to go in your car."

Cheryl nodded and pushed the Unlock button. Levi circled the vehicle and opened the passenger door.

"Watch out," Cheryl said. "He's there on the floor."

Gently, Levi stooped to gather the cat in his arms before arranging himself in the seat and fumbling for the seat belt. Cheryl's shoulders relaxed. She was not alone.

"Which way?" she asked.

Levi pointed. "Out to the highway and then down about three miles."

"Wouldn't it be more convenient if he was right in town?" Cheryl backed out of the driveway.

"He does a lot of work on the farms. He is in the office in the mornings and makes rounds in the afternoon unless someone comes in with an emergency."

"Like my poor Beau."

At the sound of his name, the cat opened one eye for a couple of seconds.

"How long has he been like this?" Levi said.

"He's been a bit off for a few days. Not eating as much as usual. Sleeping more than usual. It just got dramatic this morning."

"Dr. Richardson will fix him right up."

"I hope so."

A few minutes later, Levi said, "Slow down here. There is a right turn just after the curve. It is easy to go past it."

Cheryl slowed and made the turn. "Thank you for coming with me."

"Uh-oh." Levi lifted the cat and made sure to hold the towel under Beau's face.

The mess wasn't as bad this time, and Levi managed to contain it.

Cheryl eased into a parking spot. "I don't see any other cars."

"It is early," Levi said. He opened the passenger door. "Maybe some air is a good idea."

Cheryl nodded. "Do you want me to hold him?"

"I have him."

Cheryl watched Levi's placid grasp on Beau. A lot of her friends in Columbus would have been put off by a pet being sick in the car. Cheryl guessed this was not anything close to the worst animal illness Levi had seen on a farm in the last thirty years. He was unflapped, and his calm had spread to her the moment he got in the car.

Cheryl dropped her keys in her pocket. "Can I ask you about something?"

"Of course."

"Why do you suppose your father never wanted his children to be out on the river?"

Levi shook his head. "Something happened, I suppose. Maybe an accident when he was young. Daed has never talked about it."

"But he used to row, didn't he? I've heard about the rowing races in the summers."

"That was a long time ago. Before I was born."

"So you've never seen one of the races?"

"No. Some of the older men at church have suggested the young men should take it up again."

"Will they?"

"I do not know. I am not so young myself."

Levi's comment sent a pinch of pain through Cheryl. They were the same age. Sometimes feeling like an old maid invaded her emotions, but she had never thought of Levi in those terms. But thirty was a late age to take up a new sport, she supposed.

"Did the races stop all of a sudden?" Cheryl said. "Or did they peter out because people lost interest?"

Levi shrugged. "I do not really know. You would have to ask someone older."

"Someone your father's age?"

"Perhaps. But I do not advise asking him right now."

Cheryl watched a white Toyota pull into the lot.

"You are still thinking about the oar," Levi said.

"I can't get it off my mind. I'm convinced it has something to do with the note."

"What note? You mentioned a note last week."

"Did I?" Cheryl's hands broke out in sweat. "I shouldn't have said that."

"But you did say it."

"I take it back." A young woman sat in the Toyota talking on a phone.

"I cannot help you if I do not know what you are talking about."

Cheryl met Levi's eyes. "Naomi asked me not to tell anyone."

"She received a note?"

"No." Cheryl couldn't figure out how to backpedal. Why couldn't she learn to think before she spoke? All her life, her brain behaved as if every thought that flitted through demanded to be articulated.

"She wrote a note?" Levi asked.

"No."

Levi stroked Beau's head, thinking. "She found a note."

Cheryl sucked in a deep breath.

"What did it say?" Levi asked.

"Nothing about an oar," Cheryl said. "That's all me."

Levi thought further. "So why the urgency to find the oar?"

"Gut instinct." Cheryl held steady under Levi's gaze, simultaneously hoping he would let it go and that he would press further.

"When you are ready, you will tell me," he said finally. "In the meantime, if I see the oar, I will tell you."

"Thank you."

A car door slammed, and the young woman left the Toyota and turned a key in the clinic door.

"It is not Dr. Richardson yet," Levi said, "but you can start on the paperwork."

CHAPTER TWENTY-ONE

A few days," Cheryl said in response to the receptionist's inquiry about the length of Beau's illness. The young woman fastened a name tag to her shirt. *Tammy.*

"Your first time here?" Tammy said.

Cheryl nodded. "I've only been in town a few months. But I did meet Brandon—Dr. Richardson—recently."

"We're all still getting used to him." Tammy slid a clipboard across the counter toward Cheryl. "But he's wonderful with the animals. He'll take good care of your cat."

"Is he here?"

"Not yet. It shouldn't be long. Let me know if you have questions on the forms."

Clipboard in hand, Cheryl pivoted. Levi was settled in an armless maroon chair cradling Beau in his lap. Cheryl sat next to him, gripped the pen attached by chain to the clipboard, and began filling in the blank lines.

"He stopped shaking," Levi said.

"Is that good or bad?"

"He is awake. I would think that is a good sign."

Cheryl paused her administrative task to look at Beau's eyes. They were open, but they looked cloudy to her.

She turned back to the forms. "I'd better finish this." Infections. Shots. Neutered. Cheryl checked the relevant boxes, which were not many. Beau had always been a healthy animal. At the bottom of the third page, she signed her name.

The door opened, raw air whooshed in, and Brandon Richardson stood in the waiting room.

"Good morning." Brandon shrugged out of his coat and hung it, haphazard, on a hook. "I take it your cat has not improved since Saturday night."

"Much worse this morning." Cheryl described the latest manifestations of Beau's illness.

Levi and Cheryl stood up, and he turned the cat toward Brandon.

Brandon softly cupped Beau's chin to hold his head up. "How's Methuselah?"

"He is doing well," Levi said. "My father is glad to have him available for work again."

"I think he'll live up to his name."

"If Gott wills," Levi said.

"I didn't get to use those banquet tickets you gave me after all," Brandon said as he took Beau into his arms. "Cheryl tells me they went to good use, though. No food went to waste."

"I am glad someone could use them."

"I would have been glad to go." Brandon winked at Cheryl. "If I'd known Cheryl was the person Kathy was trying to set me up with on Saturday, I might have taken myself to the Swiss Miss to plead my case."

Cheryl blanched.

"I did not realize the two of you had met," Levi said.

"Saturday night," Brandon said. "We had a lovely impromptu romantic walk in the snow."

Cheryl's foot began to jiggle. "We ran into each other on the street."

"Best part of my day," Brandon said.

Cheryl flushed, a melding of embarrassment and curiosity. "Then you must have had a drab day."

"Seeing you again so soon certainly brightens my week."

"I don't want to take up your whole day," Cheryl said, gesturing toward the cat. "You probably have an appointment schedule."

Behind them, Tammy cleared her throat. "He certainly does."

"Then let's get to it," Brandon said. "Come on back."

Cheryl looked at Levi.

"You go on," Levi said. "You do not need me."

Glancing over her shoulder one last time at Levi, Cheryl followed Brandon into an exam room.

Brandon laid Beau on an examination table and held him still with an experienced spread of his fingers.

"Tell me what happened," he said. "How did things go from bad to worse?"

Cheryl would have to do something about the disgusting litter box in the bathroom. Hopefully getting the bedding in the washer immediately would assuage the assault it had sustained from the cat that morning. She gave Brandon the details.

"He's been droopy for days," she said. "Then this morning—bam! Full out sick."

Brandon turned the cat's face toward him and held a small light above his eyes. "I'm glad you felt you could call on me. I was sincere in my invitation the other night to bring him in."

"It was Levi who knew where to find you. It's lucky he happened by at the right moment."

"God's will, wouldn't he say?"

"Yes." Cheryl's breath faltered. "I suppose so."

"I don't know much about the Amish, but I hear them say that quite a bit."

Cheryl nodded.

"So if it was God's will for Levi to happen by, then it must be God's will for us to see each other again." Brandon lifted a playful pair of brown eyes toward Cheryl's face.

Cheryl shifted her weight. She would be kidding herself if she said her chest didn't warm at the way Brandon's eyes caught the light and shone with inquiry and expectancy.

Brandon pressed his lips together for a moment while his fingers palpated the cat's abdomen. "Nothing seems enlarged, but he does seem lethargic even for a cat."

"Even for a cat?"

"You should see what it's like to hold a puppy still for an exam. Or a bunny. Or a piglet."

"A piglet?"

"On some of the farms."

"That's right. Levi mentioned you make rounds."

"Maybe if you moved to a farm I'd have a good excuse to come see you."

"I'm at the Swiss Miss six days a week."

"Is that an invitation?"

Maybe. Maybe not. "Feel free to drop in. We carry some nice things."

"You come highly recommended."

Did he mean her or the shop? Cheryl fumbled. "Well... if you have a chance."

"I can make the chance."

Part of Cheryl wanted to fix a time and part of her wanted to bolt.

"Is Beau all right?" she said.

Brandon picked up the cat and held him against his chest. "I'd like to keep him overnight. We could make sure he's properly hydrated, perhaps give him something for his digestion. We can see how he is tomorrow and go from there."

"Who would look after him?"

"I have overnight staff. When I bought the practice I also inherited a kennel out back. We keep the sick animals separate from the healthy ones, of course. The point is that there's always someone here looking after them. If something happens, I'm just a phone call away."

"Please call me if you decide you have to do anything more than hydration."

"Of course."

Cheryl approached Brandon to scratch Beau's neck. The cat still smelled sick, but Brandon's scrubbed scent and light cologne fluttered in on Cheryl's breath.

"We'll take good care of Beau." In the nearness, Brandon spoke softly.

Tammy rapped on the open door. "Dr. Richardson, there's a phone call for you. Mr. Hardison says his cow took a turn for the worse overnight. Line two."

Cheryl moistened her lips and stepped back. "I should go."

Cheryl followed Tammy back to the reception area. It was empty.

"What happened to Levi—Mr. Miller?"

Tammy shrugged. "He stepped out a few minutes ago."

"Will he be back?"

"Didn't say."

Cheryl zipped her jacket and pushed the door open. Levi couldn't have gone far. They were several miles out of town, and not much else was around. Maybe he just needed some air. She paced across the front of the building and looked down one side and then the other.

No Levi.

"Sugar and grits," Cheryl said.

How long had she been in the exam room with Brandon? It was hard to calculate how much of a head start Levi had. Cheryl walked along one side of the building toward the kennel in the back. A company of dogs romped and chased.

No Levi.

She scanned the surrounding area for a few minutes before deciding to return to her car and drive toward town.

And there he was, walking on the side of the road. Cheryl slowed and stopped just past him. She swung the driver's door open.

"What happened, Levi?"

His stride closed the yards between them with what looked like reluctance.

"I did not want to be in the way," Levi said.

"In the way of what?" Cheryl hadn't noticed anyone else in the waiting room. Someone sitting in the chairs wouldn't disturb Tammy's phone calls or paperwork.

Levi stopped at the side of the car without answering.

"Levi?"

He looked over her shoulder and then brought his eyes back to meet hers. "Brandon Richardson is a nice man."

"Nice enough."

"Maybe you should have gone to the banquet with him."

"I didn't know he was the one Kathy was trying to set me up with," Cheryl said. "Besides, I don't really know him."

"He seems to like you."

"Levi, he's going to take care of my sick cat." Cheryl banished the memory of light in Brandon's eyes. She wouldn't trade her friendship with Levi for big eyes and curly hair.

"But he likes you," Levi said.

"He doesn't know me." *Not like you know me.*

"He would like to get to know you," Levi said. "I can tell. If he invites you out, you should accept."

Now this was getting weird. Levi was offering dating advice?

"I suppose I'll cross that bridge if I come to it," Cheryl said. "But I don't want things to get strange between you and me."

"Why should they get strange?"

Well, for one, you walked off and left me without saying anything.

"They just might," Cheryl said. "It's been a hard week with the strain between Naomi and me. I don't want anything like that to happen to you and me because you thought...for nothing... something is happening."

"I understand."

What a noncommittal thing to say under the circumstances. What did he understand?

"Levi," Cheryl said, "I consider you my friend." *Even my* good *friend.*

"And you are mine."

Cheryl swallowed hard. Levi felt so out of reach.

"I barely know Brandon," she said. "I didn't even know his last name until an hour ago."

"I pray you will be happy however this new friendship develops."

"Levi." But Cheryl didn't know how to continue the sentence. She gestured to the car. "Let me take you wherever you're going. Back to town?"

He nodded. "The library."

Cheryl had forgotten all about the task that brought Levi into town that morning. They settled into the car.

Cheryl pulled out into the traffic lane. "I've never heard you mention using the library before."

"I do from time to time, when I have a particular topic to learn about."

"What's the topic this time?"

He waved her off. "Nothing too interesting."

Levi certainly had his mysteries. It seemed like a harmless question to answer. Cheryl didn't press it. They rode in silence for a minute.

"Do you dread tomorrow?" she asked.

"Dread?"

"It's the anniversary of your mother's death, isn't it?" Cheryl accelerated slightly, her foot on the pedal matching the slight surge in her pulse.

"That is right."

"You were pretty little, weren't you?"

"Not quite five."

"Would I be nosy if I asked what you remember?"

He shrugged. "Only vague impressions. My *dawdy* took Caleb and me out to the dawdy haus. A couple of women came. Only when I was older did I realize one of them had been the midwife."

"I can't imagine losing my mother even now. It must have been a shock to you and Caleb."

"I did not know my mother was with child, so I was surprised when it was all over and my mother was gone and my sister Sarah was in the cradle. Caleb remembers even less than I do."

Sadness eddied in Cheryl's gut. Three small motherless children with no more than gray outlines for memories. They deserved more. She breathed a prayer of gratitude that Naomi had come into their lives and taken on a ready-made family at an age when Cheryl and her college friends were wondering when the next party would happen.

Cheryl watched the odometer, calculating how much more time she would have Levi captive in the car. She let her foot off the gas to buy herself an extra ninety seconds.

"I have one more nosy question," she said.

"What is it?"

"Has anything bad ever happened on the anniversary of your mother's death?"

"Bad in what way?"

"Something...dramatic."

"Other than my daed's moods?"

Cheryl nodded. "Something that actually *happened*."

"Does your question have anything to do with the oar and the note you will not tell me about?"

"*Can't* tell you about."

Levi was quiet. After one more turn, Main Street would be within view.

"Gott keeps us," Levi said. "No matter what, Gott keeps us."

Chapter Twenty-Two

Cheryl exhaled relief when she arrived at the Swiss Miss and everything appeared just as it should. The morning Annie's Amish Tours bus was parked on the street, having already disgorged its flow of curious lookers. Cheryl slapped a window, startling Howard Knisley to lift his head out of the latest suspense novel he was reading in between transportation duties.

He scowled. She grinned. His eyes returned to the book.

Inside the shop, Lydia rang up a sale with characteristic efficiency and bagged four items while at the same time explaining to another shopper how to operate a cuckoo clock. Did Lydia's parents know what a jewel of responsibility they had in her? Even if she experimented with worldly freedoms by wearing jeans and carrying a cell phone, she was trustworthy, courteous, and easy-mannered. When the time came that Lydia stopped working at the Swiss Miss, the regular customers would miss her. So would Cheryl.

Cheryl touched Lydia lightly on the shoulder as she walked past to deposit her jacket and purse in the office. Her lack of breakfast and morning coffee was catching up with her system, but Lydia had already done Cheryl a huge favor. Instead of coffee from the Honey Bee, Cheryl set up the hesitant drip pot she occasionally resorted to in the office. The pot was at least half as old as she was and showed its age. While she waited for it to produce brown liquid, she crammed a handful of crackers in her mouth. She was as ready as she was ever going to be.

"Do you need a break?" she said to Lydia at the counter as soon as she swallowed sufficiently.

"I am fine," Lydia said, straightening a display of Naomi Miller's strawberry jams at the end of the counter. "How is Beau?"

"Dehydrated, we think. They kept him for observation."

"Poor kitty. And poor Cheryl. It's hard when a pet is suffering."

Trustworthy, courteous, easy-mannered, and sympathetic. Aunt Mitzi knew how to hire the right people.

"Thanks," Cheryl said, her throat unexpectedly thick.

The bell above the door jangled. Kathy Snyder rustled in. She raised a covered cup in one hand.

"Coffee?"

Cheryl nearly leaped over the counter. Kathy laughed and placed the beverage between Cheryl's grateful, waiting, and outstretched hands.

"Don't slap me for saying this," Kathy said, "but you missed a lovely banquet. The food was scrumptious. Fancy schmancy. Not like eating at the café."

"I like your food," Cheryl said before slugging hot coffee.

"I do too, but this was another category altogether."

"Who catered?"

"A restaurant in Berlin. I'll get the name. We'll drive over so you can taste the deliciousness for yourself."

"I'm game." Cheryl swallowed coffee again, convincing herself the caffeine was kicking in already.

"I'd better scoot. The lunch rush, you know. It starts earlier and earlier."

On her way out, Kathy held the door open for Marion Berryhill, who entered with her baby sleeping on her shoulder.

"I ran into Levi at the library," Marion said. "He told me about Beau."

Did he possibly tell you what he was researching? Cheryl did not dare ask. "Dr. Richardson doesn't seem too worried."

"Then I'm sure you shouldn't be either." Marion kissed her baby's head. "I see you've got a bit of Valentine's merchandise left. So do we. Ray is busy packing it up right now."

"It's on my list for today," Cheryl said. It would be a relief to get all the relentless reminders of romantic love put away for another year. She could close the boxes and close her heart and get on with what her life was rather than what she wished it would be.

"Goodness, those decorations at the banquet were incredible," Marion said. "Such a romantic ambiance!"

Cheryl shrugged one shoulder.

"Oh, that's right," Marion said. "You couldn't make it."

Didn't make it, not *couldn't.* Cheryl offered no response.

"I just dropped in to ask about Beau," Marion said. "If I'm lucky, I can tuck this sleepy baby in the crib for a good long nap and help Ray get some work done."

"Thanks for dropping in."

Cheryl surveyed the vestiges of Valentine's Day in the Swiss Miss. One business day made an enormous difference in the relevance of what was on the shelves. If her morning had gone as planned, she would have had most of it marked down or cleared away by now, ready to entice customers with St. Patrick's Day for the next few weeks.

Lydia rang up several small sales. Cheryl grabbed price signs, red stickers, and a marker in preparation for the task of discerning which red heart-shaped paraphernalia might still sell if sufficiently reduced. Overall she'd done a reasonable job at estimating the holiday selection. The final numbers would tell the whole story, but even if she had to dispose of what remained, Cheryl felt certain the Valentine's effort had been profitable.

The last of the morning bus customers drifted out, and Cheryl welcomed the respite. She hadn't noticed when Ben and Rueben had come in and taken their seats at the checkers table. She glanced up at the sinewy brothers a few times while she scrawled *Valentine's Day 75% Off* on several price signs and taped them to shelves before affixing red stickers to the pertinent items.

The shop's door swung open again, admitting a blast of cold air with a pair of middle-aged women.

"That was the best Valentine's banquet I've ever been to," one of them said.

Cheryl kept her head down. No one was likely to be seeking out Valentine's goods two days after the date. Only an irresistible bargain would bring an impulse sale. Yet half the people who came in the store couldn't talk about anything but the banquet Cheryl had missed.

Not *missed*, she reminded herself. *Chose not to attend.*

"Have you ever laughed so hard in your life?" the second woman said. "That comedy entertainment took the dour expression right off my husband's face. He's already said he would go again if someone brought that duo back to town."

"It was worth every penny of the donation price and more."

Cheryl slapped on a half-dozen stickers. She'd heard as much about the banquet as she could tolerate at that moment. Was it too soon to take refuge in the office and call to check on Beau?

Probably. Definitely.

In the lull between customers, Cheryl took a dust rag and began looking for the worst spots. Nothing deterred sales more than a dirty store. Along the way, she straightened a few items, drifting toward the checkerboard as she worked. Once there she paused for a few minutes to watch the silent game. When she arrived in Sugarcreek, the brothers played without speaking because Rueben felt obliged to shun the brother who had left the Amish church. Eventually he'd been relieved of that position by the church leaders, but long habits die hard. While both brothers would speak to Cheryl, she rarely heard them speak to each other.

Rueben made his move. Ben took his time responding. While Rueben waited, nary a muscle twitched. Cheryl stared at the board, trying to figure out the strategy each player pursued and how many moves later they would collide in a way that forced defeat.

Cheryl and her brother, Matt, had played checkers as children—but they could hardly wait to clobber each other with the next move. Neither had the patience to look deeper into the game and see the path the immediate move might create. Perhaps if they had stuck with it for many decades, as the Vogel brothers had, they might have been wiser. There was something sweet about watching Ben and Rueben play, something calming. Inevitably when Cheryl watched, her own heart rate slowed.

The next time the door opened, it was Esther, her cheeks flushed with cold.

"Did you walk?" Cheryl asked.

"It is a sunny day, and it is not so far."

Cheryl did not know many people outside her Amish friends who would refer to two miles as "not so far." Esther did it all the time.

"I am glad you got out of the basement," Esther said. "How awful to be trapped down there."

"Who was trapped in the basement?" Lydia's voice broke in.

"Cheryl. Saturday evening. Did you not hear?"

Cheryl watched Lydia's face redden.

"After closing time?" Lydia said.

"That's right," Cheryl said.

"I thought maybe you were just taking the trash out to the alley," Lydia said. "I am so sorry."

"What are you talking about?" Cheryl put down her dust rag. "You were gone."

"I came back. I left a book on the desk in the office. When I tried the front door and it was still unlocked, I came in to get it. Then I noticed the bolt was open on the basement door."

"And you locked it."

Lydia nodded. "As a course of habit, I'm afraid I might have."

"But it sounded like somebody bigger," Cheryl said. "Heavy steps."

"My feet were hurting because I borrowed my sister's boots. They were too tight, so I untied them."

"And that made it hard to walk," Esther said.

Lydia nodded again. "I am so, so sorry."

"You had no way to know I was down there," Cheryl said.

"I should have called down the stairs. I was in a rush and not really thinking straight."

"It's not your fault," Cheryl said. "And everything worked out. Esther's parents came in and let me out. No harm done."

Cheryl would spare Lydia the memory of her heart pounding, and the mouse, and the fall off the milk crate. Certainly she would not repeat the tense words she had with Seth. Even now remembering Saturday night made her heart speed up. It had been an honest mistake, and there was no reason to wonder who would want her out of the way or why.

If she had left the store earlier or later than she did, she wouldn't have run into Brandon Richardson on the street. She wouldn't have known what to do for Beau. She would have missed the warmth in Brandon's brown eyes.

Cheryl pushed the thought of Brandon's face out of her mind. He was taking care of Beau. That's all there was to it.

Beau.

Cheryl didn't care if she was a nag. She wanted to know how Beau was. She slipped into the office and took the card Tammy had given her out of her jacket pocket before picking up the phone to dial.

Tammy answered, and Cheryl identified herself.

"I just wondered how Beau is doing."

"Dr. Richardson isn't here," Tammy said, "but I know he looked in on Beau before he left. Don't worry. We'll call you if anything happens."

Cheryl hung up the phone and blew out her breath. Tammy could probably get more work done if anxious pet owners would simply trust the veterinary practice. Cheryl also knew she would call again before the day was over, no matter how much Tammy reassured her.

She looked at the time. Even though she had arrived late that morning at the Swiss Miss, she had a window when both girls were in the shop. All she needed was thirty minutes—or less. When she came to work this morning, straight from the vet's office, she'd parked on Main Street in front of the shop. She wouldn't even lose time running home for the car. Driving out to the Millers', making sure that nothing strange was happening on the afternoon before the anniversary of Ruth's death, and getting back in the shop could be accomplished before the girls had time to miss her. Maybe she could even run into the Honey Bee to pick up a sandwich. Then Lydia could go, and Cheryl would be around for the afternoon tour bus.

Cheryl had her jacket on and her purse over her shoulder when she heard the crash. She scrambled out to the main room.

"What happened?"

Both girls were racing toward the end of one aisle.

"It is Mrs. Cornwall," Lydia called out.

Cheryl joined the investigation. "Mrs. Cornwall, are you all right?"

"Don't you people ever clean the floor?" Mrs. Cornwall glared from the floor. "All it takes is a drop of snow melting off of a boot and somebody can break an ankle."

Cheryl stifled a grimace. Of all the people who could get hurt in the store, Mrs. Cornwall had the most potential to stir up a nightmare.

"Did you hurt your ankle?" Cheryl squatted to help Mrs. Cornwall sit up. "Lydia, run across the street and ask Kathy for some ice."

Lydia was out the door. Cheryl yanked off her jacket to wad up beneath Mrs. Cornwall's ankle. Where had Aunt Mitzi filed the insurance policy? How much liability did the store have?

"Shall I call your husband?" Cheryl asked. "Or someone else?"

"I'm hardly in any condition to walk out of here on my own two feet," Mrs. Cornwall snapped.

"I will look up the number," Esther said, hustling toward the office.

"Do you think I don't know my own phone number?" Mrs. Cornwall shouted. "I can assure you I know my lawyer's number as well."

"Esther is just trying to help," Cheryl said.

"She could have *helped* by keeping the floor dry." Mrs. Cornwall huffed but supplied her home phone number.

Lydia returned with ice in a sealed plastic bag.

"Perhaps we could help you to the office," Cheryl said. "It will be more comfortable to wait there."

It took all three of them to lift Mrs. Cornwall off the floor—where Cheryl didn't see a hint of a puddle—and help her hobble to the office to sit in the desk chair. While Esther made a call, Cheryl gingerly lifted the injured foot to a second chair, arranged it on a pillow, and wrapped the ice around it as best she could.

Esther hung up the phone. "Mr. Cornwall said he can be here in fifteen minutes."

Cheryl sent the girls out to the main room while she offered Mrs. Cornwall a glass of water. The clock on the office wall ticked off every excruciating second. Fifteen minutes passed, then twenty. Finally, at minute twenty-six, Mr. Cornwall arrived. The girls followed him back into the office.

"I stopped to borrow a pair of crutches," he said.

"I don't know how to use those things." His wife pushed away the offering.

"You can at least try," he said.

Cheryl's patience—inspired by liability issues more than true compassion, if she told the truth—was rapidly waning. She did not envy Mr. Cornwall's task.

"We will help you," Esther said. "We will make sure you get out to the car safely."

"That's right," Lydia said. "We are young. Lean on us. You do not have to put your foot down at all."

"We could sue you for this." Mrs. Cornwall scowled but accepted assistance.

Cheryl let out a long, controlled breath as she watched the girls support Mrs. Cornwall through the store and out the door. As they maneuvered her into the waiting car, the mail carrier arrived.

He reached into his pouch and handed Cheryl a rubber-banded stack of mail. "What happened here?"

"Minor accident," Cheryl said, hoping Mrs. Cornwall would see it that way once her ankle stopped throbbing.

"Could happen to anyone." He pointed at the mail Cheryl now held. "There's a letter from your aunt in there."

"Thank you!"

Finally something would brighten Cheryl's day. She couldn't leave now. Lydia had already stayed most of an hour longer than she planned. But a letter from Mitzi would take Cheryl's mind off of what might or might not be happening on the Miller farm. Before the carrier was out of the store, Cheryl had ripped the edge off the letter.

My darling Cheryl,

It's hard to say when this letter will actually leave Papua New Guinea, much less when it will arrive in Sugarcreek. We may even have e-mailed or talked on Skype by the time this old-fashioned missive reaches you. But you know how I am about letters. They may be a dying art in the twenty-first century, but I think there's nothing like a personal letter that has not been through a computer or cyberspace to share one heart with another.

As I write, I suppose you are getting ready for Valentine's Day. Do you and Matt still send each other those silly cards? I hope so. I don't imagine I will get my hands on a Valentine, silly or otherwise, to send to you, but I hope you will receive this as my Valentine. I'm sending a letter to Matt at the same time so you can both know you are on my heart.

Last year at this time you were an engaged woman, no doubt hoping you would not see another Valentine's Day in your single state. But unless you've been withholding some deliciously good news, this Valentine's Day may be hard. So my message to you is simple but profound. I pray that you are not discouraged. I pray that you cling to the certainty that your life can be full of meaning and significance regardless of your marital status. I pray that you will know this year, above all years, how deeply God Himself loves you, and that there is no greater love. I pray that you believe with conviction that you are ready and able to do whatever God asks you to do with your life, and in the process plumb the depths of love that you can share with people who need it most.

I do not fail to pray for you each day.

By now you are probably hoping for signs of spring. What did Punxsutawney Phil have to say on the matter?

The river is glorious in spring—as it is in every season, actually. And summer is delightful. This year you get to experience it all. Find someone to take you out in a rowboat. You won't regret it.

The girls tumbled back into the store, and Cheryl folded the half-read letter. The travelogue portion of what Aunt Mitzi was seeing and experiencing in the faraway country she had dreamed of for four decades would have to wait. That was the beauty of Aunt Mitzi's letters—she lingered over them, filling them with details that had always made Cheryl feel she was sitting right next to her aunt as she read them. She had a long evening ahead of her without even Beau's company. Savoring the letter would more than fill the hours at the end of Cheryl's day.

Cheryl released Lydia and sent Esther on her way as soon as the busiest part of the afternoon rush had passed. By the late afternoon, she was alone in the store. The discount signs had worked. Valentine's Day was a fading memory of good sales. Once again, Cheryl walked through the store straightening and cleaning. She swept thoroughly and made sure not a drop of slush remained on the polished wood floor.

She nearly didn't see the hearts on the shelf that had held Valentine's Day merchandise.

Three hearts.

My Pal.

It's Love.

Choose Me.

Three, not two, lined up in a straight line. This was not a child dropping candy. This was a message.

But from whom? And why three this time?

Cheryl retrieved the heart-shaped tin where she had kept the previous sets of hearts. She dropped the newest messages into the collection.

This time, though, instead of tucking the tin away under the counter, she pushed it into the pocket of her khakis.

CHAPTER TWENTY-THREE

The day's cash was tallied and locked in the office safe fifteen minutes after closing. Straightening and sweeping had eased the drama of Mrs. Cornwall's fall. Only a small box had been required for removing the last vestiges of the Valentine's display. The final reminder of the irregular day was Cheryl's growling stomach, which was no longer satisfied with the dry crackers in the office. She needed a proper meal, and theoretically it was now just minutes away.

When the bell on the door chimed, Cheryl chided herself for not locking the door on the stroke of five. When she looked up, though, the sight brought relief.

Naomi and Elizabeth bustled in from the cold—and Naomi turned the sign to Closed.

"I know we are late," Naomi said. "Seth dropped us at Mrs. Lehman's hours ago, and we rode into town with her this afternoon."

"Where is she now?" Cheryl glanced out the window.

"Long gone," Cheryl said. "Elizabeth and I have been next door at the quilt shop planning our next projects. Caleb will fetch us any minute now."

"I'm always glad to see you!" Cheryl offered Naomi a quick hug. Her mind eased at the sight of mother and daughter looking as if they'd had a perfectly normal day. Even if she had driven out to the farm as she'd hoped, she might not have found Naomi home. The sick cat, Mrs. Cornwall's fall—none of it mattered now. Naomi had filled her day with visits and pleasure.

Tomorrow would be the day that mattered.

"It is all my doing," Elizabeth said. "I said we should stop in and invite you to supper. I thought you might like to see the quilt I have been working on. It is nearly finished."

"The last time I saw it," Cheryl said, "it was a pile of triangles and squares."

"Maam says I have to finish this one before I can start another."

"It is only sensible," Naomi said.

"Please come and see how far I've gotten," Elizabeth said. "It will be fun to show you, and you know you love Maam's bread."

Cheryl's mouth salivated at the mention of the bread. Picturing it slathered in home-churned butter, she glanced at Naomi. "Are you sure it's no trouble?"

"None. I left a stew in the oven, and I made the rolls yesterday. It is a simple offering, and we would love to have you."

Either Naomi was as peaceful as she seemed or she was putting on a good show for her daughter. Elizabeth never knew the woman her father mourned, but she was old enough to know the significance of the next day's date. Perhaps Naomi and Elizabeth had gone out visiting because tension was already thick at the Miller house. What would Seth think of a dinner guest?

"Please?" Elizabeth's dark eyes pleaded.

"I would be delighted." If Cheryl went to the farm, she could see for herself that everything was all right, and perhaps she and Naomi could snatch a few minutes of private conversation about the following day.

"I hear the buggy." Elizabeth stepped to the store's front window. "Caleb just pulled up."

"Come in an hour," Naomi said to Cheryl. "All will be ready."

Naomi and Elizabeth slipped out. Cheryl scooted to the office for her jacket and bag. She wouldn't have time for a walk along the river, but she had time to go home, freshen up, grab a snack to tide her over, and squeeze in a phone call to check on Beau.

Precisely one hour after Naomi's departure from the store, Cheryl approached the covered bridge. Before entering, she pulled to the side of the road, stopped, and lowered the car window to listen. All she wanted to hear was babbling water under the bridge—certainly no sound of a belligerent engine. Exhaling, she wiped sweat from her palms. She might never be able to drive across the bridge again without feeling her heart pound at how close she had come to being trapped within it with a reckless driver coming straight toward her. After inhaling and releasing several deep breaths, she raised the window and proceeded with caution.

The pasture was clear, the animals already in their warm stalls for the night. Lights gleaming from within the house wrapped it in a flush of warmth and welcome. The family would gather for supper and devotions, and it was unlikely anyone would go out again except to tend the livestock.

It was a normal evening at the Miller house on the eve of "*or else.*"

Cheryl left the car and approached the house. Before she could lift her hand to knock, Elizabeth opened the door.

"I am so glad you came!"

"It smells wonderful!" Cheryl inhaled deeply. The fragrance of seasoned stew in the oven all afternoon made Cheryl's quick bites of cheese and raisins half an hour ago seem wildly insufficient.

"When I make stew, it never smells as good as Maam's," Elizabeth said, closing the door against the dropping temperatures. "Maybe someday when I get married she will tell me her secret."

Cheryl's stomach gurgled in anticipation. As inept a cook as she was, she imagined she was literate enough to follow a recipe for stew, but she also knew Naomi did not cook with recipes. Whatever her secret, it would never find its way to paper.

"I'd like to be helpful," Cheryl said. "Is your maam in the kitchen?"

"Go on through," Elizabeth said. "Maam says everything is almost ready. We will have to look at the quilt after supper."

"We'll have plenty of time." Cheryl kicked off her slushy shoes and hung her jacket on the rack beside the door before padding into the kitchen.

"You are here!" Naomi's face brightened.

Cheryl searched her friend's expression but found herself unable to judge what lay behind it.

"Can I do anything?" Cheryl said. The table already was set. Pitchers of water and milk stood like sentries.

"Keep me company." Naomi rapidly sliced a cucumber and scooped the result into a bowl of lettuce.

Cheryl settled into a chair. "Is everything... I just wondered..."

"You are thinking about tomorrow, aren't you?" Naomi carved the core out of a tomato.

"Yes. The anniversary in the note must be tomorrow."

Naomi drizzled a creamy dressing into the salad. "Gottes wille."

God's will. The Amish often said this as easily as Cheryl's friends in Columbus would say, "Hi, how are you?" They expressed no angst about what God's will might be. It just was. Cheryl rarely knew what to say in response.

"That's true," she said, "but—"

Elizabeth swooped into the room. "I told the boys everything is nearly ready."

Naomi handed her daughter the salad and pointed Cheryl to a basket of rolls before opening the oven to remove the crock of stew. The three of them lined the food up in the center of the table. Family members emerged from their quiet corners of the house and took their places. From his place at one end, Seth bowed his head, and around him the family did the same. Cheryl closed her eyes and formed mental words of gratitude and grace. She was never certain how long a silent prayer before a meal should last and forced herself not to peek at anyone else.

Finally she sensed the release of movement on both sides of her and opened her eyes. Naomi ladled stew into a bowl and handed it to Eli, who passed it down the table until it reached Seth. One by one the Millers received their steaming supper. Seated between Elizabeth and Esther on one side of the table, Cheryl was directly across from Levi, who sat between Caleb and Eli. His blue eyes met her gaze, and he offered a passing smile of encouragement as he started the bread basket on its lap around the table.

Cheryl stirred her stew to cool it a bit and buttered a roll, determined to be polite and eat no more than one despite her certainty that she could eat a dozen. She savored the flavors melding in her mouth as she listened to table conversation.

Seth mentioned he had some new ideas about rotating crops in the spring planting to keep the soil nourished. Eli said he had taken advantage of the clear weather to make some fence repairs. Caleb had spent the day mucking stalls. Esther told the story of Mrs. Cornwall's fall. Naomi reported on her visit to Mrs. Lehman.

It was routine conversation that could have happened on any evening of the year at the Miller house. Cheryl glanced at Seth as often as she could without being perceived as staring. He lacked the teasing tone Cheryl often heard him use with his children, but he was far from terse. When his children spoke, he listened. Some measure of subdued demeanor on this date was understandable even twenty-five years after losing his first wife.

"*Or else.*"

For the sake of his family, Cheryl decided, Seth restrained from exhibiting any concern about what the next day might bring. Had he also surrendered the words of the note to God's will? Was Cheryl the only one who could not keep from borrowing worry from tomorrow?

"I understand we had quite a few visitors at the petting zoo this morning." Seth took a roll and then passed the basket to Esther beside him, starting its second turn around the table.

Elizabeth nodded her dark head with enthusiasm. "A school group. One little girl was ready to ask her mother for a pet goat."

Chuckles circled the table. Cheryl pitied the poor mother who was having that conversation over her dinner.

"Another man was there too," Elizabeth said. "At first I thought he was with the class, but after a while I realized no one seemed to know him."

"A man alone?" Cheryl blurted the question.

Elizabeth nodded.

"It happens sometimes," Naomi said. "People who come alone are usually full of questions about the animals."

"Not this man," Elizabeth said. "His questions were about us."

Seth's eyebrows lifted, though the rhythm of his butter knife did not waver.

I've been trying to tell you! Cheryl wanted to shout.

Levi caught her eye but spoke to Elizabeth. "What kind of questions?"

Elizabeth shrugged. "How many brothers and sisters I have. How I like church. What do we really think about rumspringa."

"Many people ask those questions," Naomi said.

"I'm used to it from the Englisch," Elizabeth said. "This man was dressed like the Englisch, but something about the way he spoke made me think he was Plain."

"Probably just German," Seth said.

"What kind of car did he drive?" Cheryl asked.

Elizabeth laughed. "I do not know such things. It was old."

"Green?"

"I think so."

"It's nothing," Seth said.

Cheryl squirmed, looking for Levi's eyes once again.

But instead of lingering on the subject of the strange visitor, Levi asked about Beau, and the conversation moved on.

When the bowls and plates were scraped and stacked in the middle of the table, Seth reached for his thick Bible and cleared his throat.

"Our devotion tonight," he said, "comes from Isaiah 26:3. 'Thou wilt keep him in perfect peace, whose mind is stayed on thee: because he trusteth in thee.' Many times in our lives, others would assail our peace. You are all old enough to have had these experiences. You must make judgments about who you trust. Stresses and fears might consume your minds. In these times we must listen to Isaiah. When we stay our minds on Gott Himself, then we will have peace—and not only peace, but *perfect* peace. This peace does not come from trying to manipulate or connive for a result we have set our hearts on. This peace comes only from trusting in Gott. It is Gott who keeps us in peace, not ourselves. We would do well to remember this the next time—and every time—we encounter a situation that may distress us. Where is our trust? Where we find trust, we also find peace."

Heads nodded around the table. Even Cheryl murmured her *Amen* of agreement. Yet she heard a warning in the words that she doubted any of Seth's children heard. Perhaps he had even chosen the verse for the evening devotion especially for Cheryl to hear.

Esther stood and picked up a stack of plates. Naomi nimbly grabbed four glasses within her reach.

"Elizabeth," Naomi said, "you should take Cheryl to see the quilt before it gets any later. Esther and I will clean up."

Cheryl scooted her chair back. While she was interested in Elizabeth's quilt, she also wished she could follow Naomi into the kitchen and urge her once again to talk to Seth about the note. What if this man who visited the petting zoo was its writer? And she wished she could have a private conversation with Levi. Confidential or not, she was going to tell him about that note. But instead of either of these options, Cheryl followed Elizabeth up the stairs.

Elizabeth had spread her unfinished quilt of blues and browns and greens across her bed. Cheryl gasped when she saw it. If she practiced for twenty years she would never produce the flawless stitching that Elizabeth had achieved by age eighteen.

"What's the pattern called?" Cheryl dared to finger one corner of the quilt top.

"Tree of life. I hope I will have it for the rest of my life to remind me of Gottes care."

"It's beautiful, Elizabeth. You should be proud."

Elizabeth put one hand to her mouth. "Oh no. Demut. Humility is our way."

"Of course. Then you can be humbly grateful for the talent God gave you."

"I think it is okay if I agree to that. Whatever we have comes from Gott."

"I hope you'll show it to me again once you finish quilting and have the binding on."

"You can see it any time you visit." Elizabeth folded the quilt in half and then quarters. "I suppose we should go back downstairs."

The front room was quiet when they reached it. Seth poked at the flames in the fireplace. Eli looked bored and jiggled one knee on the brightly colored rag rug covering the polished wood floor. In a recliner, Caleb had his head back in his chair half asleep. On the sofa, one arm resting on a dark blue and white quilted pillow, Levi had a book in his lap but his eyes were not moving.

"I should help with the dishes," Elizabeth said.

"I'll go with you." Cheryl turned her feet toward the kitchen.

"You are our guest," Elizabeth countered. "You sit and enjoy the evening."

Before Cheryl could protest further, Elizabeth disappeared through the door to the kitchen, leaving Cheryl standing at the bottom of the stairs staring at the Miller men. Tentative, she stood beside a rocker. Levi looked up in unspoken question.

"Thank you all for your hospitality," Cheryl said without sitting. "I've had a long day. Perhaps I'll say good night now."

Seth nodded. "I hope you have good news on your cat tomorrow."

"Thank you."

Levi stood. "I will get a flashlight and walk you out."

They went into the kitchen together. Cheryl said good-bye to Naomi and the girls while Levi opened a drawer and removed a long light.

"I will get my coat and go out with you," Elizabeth said.

Cheryl glanced at Levi, forcing her eyes not to linger. Naomi saved her from forming a tactful response.

"Levi already has the light out," Naomi said. "He can walk Cheryl out. I need you to help finish up in here."

Now Cheryl caught Naomi's eyes. "Thank you again. For everything."

Naomi gave a nod a quarter of an inch deep and turned back to scrubbing the stew pot.

Cheryl slipped into her jacket and shoes, and she and Levi descended the front steps in tandem.

"You did not have to walk me out," she said.

"I know. I had to talk to you alone."

Adrenaline surged. "What happened?"

"I saw that oar this afternoon." Instead of heading toward Cheryl's car, Levi aimed the light at the equipment shed. "Just a few hours ago I saw Daed go into the shed with it and come out with empty hands."

"So it has been here all this time—a whole week?"

Levi set a brisk pace. "I cannot say. I only know what I saw today. I went back later on my own just to be sure."

Cheryl raced ahead in the yellow beam of illumination and tugged on the shed's door.

It stuck.

Levi came up behind her, reached around her, and pulled. For a moment Cheryl let herself imagine what it might be like to have his arms around her. The door gave.

They stepped in, and the door fell closed behind them. Levi swept the light past an old plow, over two buggy wheels, around a collection of garden hoes and rakes.

He inhaled sharply.

"What's wrong?"

"It is gone."

"It can't be! You saw it yourself."

Levi aimed the light straight into a corner. "It was right there, propped up."

"Maybe it fell over or dropped behind something."

"He moved it," Levi whispered.

"But why?" Cheryl's hopes capsized.

Levi remained silent.

"That note," Cheryl said softly, her reluctance worn down. "It's about tomorrow. Something is going to happen tomorrow, and your daed knows what it is."

"Are you at last going to tell me about the mysterious note?"

They both jumped when the door creaked. Cheryl grabbed Levi's arm and spun toward the door.

Seth raised a battery-powered lantern, exposing them. "I think it is time for Cheryl to be on her way."

Chapter Twenty-Four

Cheryl would not have imagined the absence of a cat at the foot of her bed would interfere with her sleep. But it had. Twice she woke in darkness and vaguely wondered where Beau had gone. Then she remembered. Then the effort it took not to call Brandon's overnight staff and inquire about Beau made her too wakeful for an easy return to sleep. She drowsed, briefly reaching a stage of sleep that allowed dreams of farmland and rowing oars and Seth's scowling face. Gone was the twinkle in his eye Cheryl had come to expect when he teased her with a straight face. It was lost in a river, struck by an oar.

Morning light carried relief.

After double-checking both her e-mails and the text messages on her phone, Cheryl took comfort in the adage that no news about Beau was good news. She could at least wait until normal business hours before pestering the veterinary employees.

What had Seth done with that oar the night before? And what was he going to do with it today as he remembered both his daughter Sarah's birth and losing her mother?

This would be a good day for Levi to find justification for a trip into town. It wasn't as if he lived miles and miles away like some of the Amish. The Miller farm was an easy distance from town by buggy or on foot. Cheryl showered, dressed, breakfasted, and strode down Main Street with eyes and ears alert for the clatter of horse hoofs and the swaying box of a buggy. But she heard only drifts of voices and shop owners greeting each other as they unlocked doors and turned on lights.

In the Swiss Miss, Cheryl tossed her jacket on the back of the desk chair and jammed her purse out of sight before picking up the stack of papers from the desk and transferring them out to the counter. If she perched on the stool while she sorted and read, she could glance up from time to time to see who was passing by.

Eventually she made herself wait at least twenty seconds before lifting her eyes with the next hopeful glance.

Levi did not come. When the door opened and the bell jangled, it was Mr. Cornwall.

Cheryl's gut skidded against her abdomen wall as she popped off her stool. "How's your wife?"

"Dramatic as always."

Cheryl laid down her pen. "But her ankle—"

"Her ankle will give her plenty of opportunity to be waited on, but the urgent care doctor didn't even refer her to an orthopedist. Pain meds for a few days if she wants them. Ice and elevate. That's about it."

"I'm glad to hear that."

Mr. Cornwall shifted his balance. "I came in to thank you for looking after her and to let you know that no matter what threats she might have made, you have nothing to worry about."

"That's a relief." Pulsing adrenaline subsided in Cheryl's chest. At least she would not have to explain to her aunt that the shop had been sued.

"It was an accident. Nobody's fault."

"Thank you for saying that."

"Now, if you've got any of that buttercream fudge from Heini's, I'd like to take her a piece or two."

"On the house!" Cheryl swiftly wrapped three creamy sweet squares and arranged them in a small paper bag. "Please let Mrs. Cornwall know we all hope she recovers quickly."

Mr. Cornwall folded the top of the bag down several times and carefully put it in his jacket pocket. As he left, a UPS delivery truck pulled up in front of the store. Anticipation clamored through Cheryl. The driver dropped out of his seat, opened the back of the truck, let down a ramp, and disappeared inside. Cheryl propped open the front door, ignoring the immediate plunge in temperature inside. A moment later, the driver emerged with a large box strapped on to a dolly.

Yes! The new shelves for the turret room had arrived. Cheryl showed the way to the small curved room, signed for the delivery, and thanked the man profusely. She had ordered the shelves weeks ago. The heavy cardboard wrapped around them was closed with the longest, thickest staples Cheryl had ever seen. Only leveraging a long flat screwdriver would do the job of loosening them.

Cheryl was rummaging under the counter when Esther and Naomi came in.

"What's wrong?" Esther asked.

"The shelves are here!" Cheryl popped her head up and pulled open a drawer. "I can't find the screwdriver."

"I needed it last week and couldn't find it then either," Esther said.

"Sugar and grits," Cheryl said. "I guess I'll have to buy another."

"I know I am early," Esther said, dropping her coat off her shoulders, "but Maam was coming into town, so I figured to walk with her."

Esther rounded the counter and went into the office. Cheryl's glance went to Naomi's empty hands.

"I am here to buy today," Naomi said, "not sell."

"But you bring me some of my best-selling items," Cheryl said.

"I will be back later this week." Naomi pointed at the fudge. "Seth does not like to admit he thinks someone else's fudge is better than mine, but I know he likes those buttercreams. I thought I would take him a few."

Only four fudge squares remained. Cheryl started wrapping them.

"He will not want to talk," Naomi said, "but I want to show him in some way that I know this is a painful day for him."

And for you. Did Seth ever think about how his moods around this date every year affected the wife he was blessed to have *now*?

"Has he said anything about the note?" Cheryl slid the fudge into a bag.

Naomi shook her head.

"Naomi," Cheryl said. Something could happen—perhaps something preventable if Seth and Naomi would just talk about it.

"Gottes wille," Naomi whispered. "I trust Seth, and I trust God."

"Well," Cheryl said, "I'm glad to see you."

"How is Beau?" Naomi took the fudge from Cheryl and offered a five-dollar bill.

Cheryl waved away the money. Naomi's goods were the attraction for a good part of the local traffic into the shop as well as tourist sales. The least Cheryl could do was give her a few pieces of candy.

"I'm not sure how Beau is," Cheryl said. "I didn't hear anything overnight."

"Then he must be doing well. You should call to be sure."

Cheryl glanced at the row of cuckoo clocks. It was nearly ten now, surely late enough for the veterinary practice to be in full swing for the day. She pulled her cell phone from her back pocket.

"Maybe I will," she said.

A minute later she brightened. "Really? I can come get him? *Hmm*... I'm not sure when I can get there."

Esther stood behind the cash register and leaned into Cheryl's shoulder with her own. "Go. I can handle things here."

Cheryl spoke into the phone. "I guess I'm coming now. I'll see you in a few minutes."

"I will go with you," Naomi said. "Just to be sure everything is all right. Then maybe you can swing by the farm to drop me off."

"Gladly." Surely Naomi's day was already full. Gratitude splashed through Cheryl at the simple gesture of friendship—and the chance to keep Naomi within her sight for at least part of the day. "We'll have to walk to the cottage to get my car."

"What is four blocks after I have come two miles?"

Cheryl ducked into the office for her jacket and purse before stepping into the sunlight with Naomi. They walked about a block before Naomi's steps slowed.

"What's the matter?" Cheryl tried to follow Naomi's gaze.

"That man across the street," Naomi said. "He's the man who came to the farm by mistake on Friday."

"Are you sure?"

"Yes. He stood right there on my porch and looked me full in the face."

He was familiar to Cheryl too. From the top of the lane leading on to the Miller property, Cheryl hadn't seen his face clearly on the day he appeared at Naomi's door, but it wasn't his face that gave him away now. She'd heard that gait before—uneven, with one boot thicker than the other.

"I supposed he was a lost tourist," Naomi said. "I guess he had a long weekend in Sugarcreek if he was here Friday and is still here on Tuesday."

Or he's not a tourist.

"He's headed to the hardware store," Cheryl said.

Naomi chuckled. "Anyone's allowed."

Cheryl's pace picked up.

"Where are you going?" Naomi asked.

"To the hardware store."

The man pushed open the door and entered the store.

"Cheryl, do not be silly," Naomi said.

There was nothing silly about it. This man was no lost tourist. Cheryl pushed into the shop and scanned the aisles. The man was studying a display of door knobs.

The tug on her arm nearly took Cheryl off balance.

"I must insist we leave," Naomi said. "If that man is someone other than a tourist on a long weekend, I do not want you tangling with him."

"You know something," Cheryl said. On the day the man went to the farm, Naomi had said he looked vaguely familiar.

"No, I do not," Naomi said. "Focus on what matters. We are going to get Beau, remember?"

Beau was safe where he was, something Cheryl couldn't say with certainty about Naomi. Or Seth. But she humored Naomi and turned away from the hardware store.

Tammy greeted them both by name when they reached Brandon's office.

"The tech's notes said Beau had a good night," Tammy said. "Dr. Richardson is having one last look at him now before we release him."

"Can I see him?" Cheryl asked.

"You can both go on back. Room Two."

Brandon turned and smiled as Cheryl and Naomi entered the exam room. He had Beau in his arms.

"Here's your mama now," he said.

"Is everything all right?" Cheryl reached for her cat.

"Perfect. He responded well to rehydrating and has perked up quite a bit from yesterday."

Cheryl could see that. Beau was trying to climb to his favorite spot on her shoulder, and his eyes were bright.

"Has he eaten?"

"Last night and again this morning," Brandon said. "If it happens again, I'd like to see him to be sure we can't find a reason for the symptoms, but you're free to take him home and keep an eye on him there."

"Thank you so much."

"My pleasure. I'm sorry your cat had to get sick to bring us together, but I'm glad for the excuse to see you two days in a row."

Cheryl's neck warmed.

"Why don't we have coffee one afternoon?" Brandon said. "I could come by the Swiss Miss, and we could pop across the street to the Honey Bee. Kathy would be tickled."

Now what Cheryl felt was a full-on blush. It was just coffee, and she liked Brandon—even apart from his care of her pet. Why shouldn't she agree to a casual meeting? But the main reason for her blush stood beside her, trying to get Beau to look at her. Brandon seemed unperturbed that anyone should witness his flirting or invitation, but it wasn't that simple for Cheryl. Not when she was standing beside Levi's mother. Yesterday Levi had been with her, and now Naomi. When she felt the way she did about Levi, thinking about whether to accept even a casual date with another man was too awkward to sort out in front of Levi's stepmother.

"I'm pretty busy right now," Cheryl said. "Maybe some other time."

"Next week?" Brandon said.

"I'll have to see." Cheryl avoided his eyes. "Do I check out with Tammy?"

"She'll have your paperwork ready."

"Thank you again." Still Cheryl did not meet his gaze. "See you around."

"I hope so."

Naomi held Beau while Cheryl paid the charges and received written instructions for care and follow-up.

"Thanks for coming with me," Cheryl said in the car. Beau settled on Naomi's lap. "Are you sure you don't need to go back to town?"

Naomi tapped the bag of fudge. "I got what I went for."

"You walked all the way into town for a few pieces of chocolate?"

"If it will make Seth's day easier, it will be worth it. I wanted to be sure I had them in time for lunch."

And what about your day? Cheryl doubted Seth knew Naomi sometimes wondered if he'd loved Ruth more. It wasn't the sort of thing Naomi would tell him.

On the farm, Cheryl took comfort in seeing all three Miller sons working close to the house. The barn door was open wide as Caleb and Eli carried feed and supplies in. Levi was nearby nailing shingles on the roof of the hen house.

"Oh, good," Naomi said. "I've been hoping someone would work on that hole in the roof before it got any worse."

Cheryl put the car in Park. "Thanks again for coming."

"Thanks again for the fudge." Naomi transferred the cat to Cheryl's lap. "I am so glad Beau seems to be all right."

"Me too."

Naomi picked up the bag of candy and opened the passenger door. As she disappeared into the house, Cheryl tried to persuade Beau to make himself comfortable on the passenger seat or the floor. Driving with him sprawled across her shoulders didn't seem safe. She glanced up a few times to follow Levi's movements. For a moment no one else was in the farm yard. Levi sauntered over.

Cheryl lowered her car window. "Any sign of the oar?"

Levi shook his head. "Not for want of looking. I am scrounging up one excuse after another to be in the outbuildings."

"Where's your father?"

Levi shrugged. "No one is sure. We all hope he will get back to normal after today."

There was more to the day than Levi realized. "The note."

"Are you ready to tell me?"

Cheryl moistened her lips. She would have told him last night if Seth hadn't interrupted them.

"Naomi found it," she said. "It sounded threatening, and it had to do with an anniversary."

"And since their wedding anniversary passed...," Levi said.

Cheryl nodded. "Keep an eye on Naomi today."

"I will try. But I know she wants to do some visiting after lunch. And she often walks alone."

"I wish she wouldn't be by herself."

"It is not my place to tell her what to do or when to be worried."

222 | Sugarcreek Amish Mysteries

Cheryl sighed. He was right.

Levi pointed at the cat. "He seems better."

"He is! I'll have to watch him for a few days." Cheryl glanced at the settled cat. "I'd better get back to the store."

The afternoon passed with no remarkable events. No one sliding around on the store floor. No difficult customers. No surprise messages from the bank. No fresh gossip. Even the checkerboard went untouched all afternoon. As the day waned, each time the door opened the air gusting in seemed to drop several biting degrees. Getting ready to carry Beau home—she'd kept him in the office all day where she could check on him— Cheryl reached into her jacket pockets for her gloves.

She found only one.

She dug into the depths again. Still only one.

Aunt Mitzi had given her those gloves, and they weren't cheap. Cheryl groaned, realizing she'd probably lost the errant glove on Sunday, the last time she'd worn the pair for part of the time while she walked along the river. She pulled on one glove now and arranged the exposed hand under the cat for warmth. Once she had Beau settled at home, Cheryl grabbed the biggest flashlight she'd come across in the cottage and backed her car out of the driveway for the second time that day.

It was a long shot, but Cheryl had to try. She walked slowly along her usual route, pausing every few steps to illumine the edges of the path. Looking for a dark glove in damp, muddy soil in the falling evening seemed an impossible combination. Still Cheryl persisted.

She reached the farthest point she had traversed on Sunday with no sight of the glove. After two days, it could be trampled into the mud or picked up by another walker or dragged away by a small animal.

Cheryl shut off the beam of light and turned her back to the river, instead staring into the woods. What secrets did they hold? These woods were where Mrs. Thatcher found that old oar years ago. If she hadn't taken it home, and if her shed hadn't been burgled, Seth would never have found the oar. If Cheryl hadn't taken up a new habit of evening walks, she would never have seen Seth. Would the Amish say this was all God's will? Would her own pastor agree? If they were right, Cheryl would sure like to see the purpose in it all.

The day was ending. Seth's and Naomi's wedding anniversary had passed without incident—except for the stranger at the door who had done nothing—and now the anniversary of the death of Seth's first wife was closing, also without incident.

But the oar.

Seth had picked it up, hidden it, and now moved it.

It meant something.

Behind Cheryl, the sound of the water deviated.

Swish. Whoosh. Swish. Whoosh.

The sound was smooth, fluid, almost in rhythm with the flow of the river.

Almost.

But it wasn't the flow of the river. In the last few weeks she'd spent untold hours hearing the river's voice.

Swish. Whoosh.

Slight as it was, this was a disturbance.

Someone was on the river. Rowing.

Cheryl rotated to peer into the darkness, gripping the flashlight in her hand. If she aimed it out on the water she might see who was out there—or confirm what she suspected. She hesitated. If she directed the beam indirectly, and only for a second or two, perhaps that would be enough for her to discern something without exposing herself.

She crouched behind a rank of bushes, looking through the winter-bare branches, and aligned her eyes with her best guess of where the sound was coming from before flashing the light on and off.

Seth was on the water.

And he wasn't alone.

CHAPTER TWENTY-FIVE

The flashlight fell from Cheryl's shocked grasp with a soft thud on to squishy ground beneath her feet.

She held still.

The distance between her and the rowboat was sufficient to reassure her that the occupants could not have heard the dropping light or the gasp that fled her throat. After a week of intuition that *something* was going on but no tangible proof, the vindication was sweet.

Levi and Naomi both had said that Seth hated the water so much he wouldn't even allow his children to enjoy the recreation it offered. Yet there he was in a rowboat under cover of darkness. Cheryl's fingers went to the lump her cell phone formed in her pocket. She could call Chief Twitchell.

And say what?

That two men were out in a boat?

That one of them had received a secret threatening note? That the other had probably written the note? That Seth might have been forced to row out to the middle of the river?

Pure speculation.

Swish. Whoosh. Swish. Whoosh. The sounds grew more distant.

Cheryl's eyes watered with the effort of boring her gaze through thickening darkness. The rowing rhythm ceased, leaving only gentle lapping and gurgling of a slow-moving river.

The sounds of peace.

Except they weren't.

Against the blackness, a lantern flickered—the sort some of the Amish still used even though flashlights were easier. Around the edges of its glow, shadows huddled, the light between them. Cheryl could perceive no indication of an argument or maliciousness. No raised voices wafting on night air. No sudden movements. No disruption to the nocturnal river whispers. Just two men in a boat having a private conversation, even if it was an odd time of year to choose the river as the setting for their discussion.

Cheryl's calves began to burn. All the walking she did was insufficient preparation for hunching behind a bush indefinitely. She unfolded her form. If she couldn't see them, how could they see her? And what if they did? She was no threat.

If Beau weren't home alone in uncertain health, Cheryl might have held vigil until the *swish* and *whoosh* began again and brought the men into view. Her curiosity would be satisfied if nothing else. But she wasn't taking any chances with the cat, not on his first night home. Naomi trusted her husband. Cheryl would have to try to do the same.

Beau was glad to see her—as glad as any cat ever was. Cheryl's brother liked to say she would have been better off with a puppy who would jump up and down at the sight of her rather than a cat that may or may not move its tail a quarter of an inch to acknowledge her presence. Cheryl preferred to believe she knew the moods of her own pet, and it meant something when Beau walked in tight circles underfoot. She was glad to see Beau had eaten while she was out and deposited the proof of his improved digestion in the litter box. For herself, Cheryl opened a can of minestrone soup and heated it. The previous night's erratic sleep left her exhausted, and she crawled into bed early with Beau nearby. Cheryl closed the bedroom door to make sure he would not wander off and be sick somewhere else in the house.

She startled awake when Beau meowed. He pounced from his spot at the foot of the bed onto her chest and licked her face—like a puppy, Matt would say. The red lights of the bedside clock glowed that it was a few minutes after midnight.

"Let's go back to sleep," she muttered, nudging Beau off her chest and onto the bed.

Instead of settling, he leaped to the nightstand.

"Careful!" Cheryl sat up, ready to catch the lamp if the cat knocked against it. "What are you doing?"

Beau meowed.

Cheryl's cell phone beside the clock pinged. She reached for it.

Five e-mail messages.

All from Aunt Mitzi in the last hour. Cheryl had slept through the previous alert sounds and would have missed the last one as well if it weren't for Beau.

"Come here, you scrumptious thing!" With Beau against her chest, Cheryl read the messages one after the other. All had the same thrust.

I'm available to Skype. Thought I would see if you were awake.

Cheryl threw back the blankets and raced out to the living room where she'd left her laptop. She opened Skype, clicked her aunt's contact entry, and within a minute was grinning at Mitzi's beaming face.

"Hello, sleepyhead," Mitzi said.

"You're a sight for sore eyes."

"We have a good, strong signal here today. Did you get my letter?"

"Yesterday. It was perfect timing after a tough day."

Cheryl filled her aunt in on recent events—including Seth's mysterious cloaked river jaunt.

"That doesn't sound like the Seth I've known for so long," Aunt Mitzi said. "You're right to think something is going on that would make him behave so oddly."

"What did you mean when you told me to 'look deep'?"

"I was talking about your uncle's photos. They're in crates in the basement. I know it's not climate-controlled and I probably shouldn't keep them down there, but I wanted to make sure they weren't in your way."

"You think there are photos that will help me figure things out?"

"Maybe," Mitzi said. "He was never without a camera within reach, as you well know. It got so no one really paid attention to what he was shooting. He never exploited anyone, never tried to profit off of someone's image without permission. Those crates hold decades of photos. Some are labeled, but many aren't. That was going to be his retirement project. He always dreamed of doing a book."

"I'm sorry he didn't get to do it," Cheryl said.

"How could we know he wouldn't have a retirement?" Mitzi's voice grew soft. "Anyway, the photos belong to me now, and I'm telling you to go through them. Don't just look at the ones on top. Look deep because they're not very organized and what you need might be at the bottom of the pile. The Amish trusted him not to violate the way they felt about photographs. He didn't sell or reproduce them. They hardly noticed Ralph was there most of the time. He kept his distance with that monster telephoto lens he was so pleased with."

"Why didn't I ever know Uncle Ralph took pictures of the Amish?"

"He didn't show them to anyone. That's why they let him take them."

"What am I looking for?"

"That's something I can't tell you. I can only suggest that your uncle would have one of the best photographic records of Sugarcreek of anyone in the county. I can't think of anyone who took more pictures than he did or had such uninhibited access to the Amish families. You're on your own to look for the clue the pictures might hold."

"It's worth a shot," Cheryl said. She hoped she would not read in the morning paper that a man's body had washed up in the river outside Sugarcreek. It was too late to stop whatever might have happened between Seth and the author of the note, but it wasn't too late to explain it—and perhaps break the annual cycle of Seth's moods.

"Look at absolutely anything you find down there," Mitzi said. "Don't hesitate. Look deep in those piles. Then e-mail me what you find. I can't wait to find out what the mystery is."

"I might not solve it," Cheryl said.

"If determination counts, you will." Mitzi put two fingers to her lips and threw Cheryl a kiss. "I have to go, but I should be able to get e-mail for another day or two."

They disconnected, and Cheryl pulled the cat into her lap. "You're my hero. Thanks for waking me up."

It was now nearly one in the morning, and Cheryl was wide awake. She wouldn't get back to sleep for hours, if at all. Coffee couldn't possibly hurt, and it might give her brain the boost she needed to recognize what she was looking for. Beau followed Cheryl into the kitchen, where she flipped on the lights and started the coffeepot. It had just begun to gurgle when Cheryl abruptly froze her movements.

What was that?

A creak. Footfalls? Outside the front door.

Cheryl scooped up the cat, moved swiftly through the cottage, and closed Beau into the bedroom. Then she inched toward the front door.

Another creak. Somebody was definitely out there—close to the house—in the middle of the night.

Cheryl eased open the closet door, reached into the back left corner, and extracted her uncle's old baseball bat. Uncle Ralph was the one who taught Cheryl how to keep her eye on the ball as a pitch arrived. She had a good swing. If she had to use it, she would. She moved to the front window, beside the door, and used one finger to displace the edge of the drapes and peered out. The porch looked empty, and she heard nothing.

She flipped the switch to the porch light and yanked open the front door. With both hands gripping the bat, she stepped outside.

No one was there.

She stepped away from the house, down the front steps, scanning the yard.

No one.

Whoever had been there was gone. If anyone had been there at all. Cheryl raised her eyes to the night sky, picking out a couple of constellations while she waited for her heart rate to return to normal. Only when she turned back to the house did she see the pink and yellow hearts on the old metal milk box Aunt Mitzi had kept outside the door for four decades.

Cheryl picked them up.

Love Bug.

Be a Sport.

This was getting creepy. It was one thing to find conversation hearts around the store where dozens of people went in and out on any given day. It was another to find them in the middle of the night only inches away from her front door.

If she'd had any doubts that the hearts were a message, the latest contributions to the collection removed them. Inside the cottage, Cheryl retrieved the heart-shaped tin and laid the hearts out in the order in which she'd found them.

Be True. Start Now. Do Good. I'm Sure. My Pal. It's Love. Choose Me. Love Bug. Be a Sport.

They meant something. But what?

Love. Friendship. Sports. A choice.

The answer was somewhere—maybe in Uncle Ralph's photos.

Cheryl let Beau out of the bedroom, filled the largest coffee mug in the kitchen, and went down the basement stairs.

CHAPTER TWENTY-SIX

B eau had chosen a crate and sprawled across it within the first
minute in the basement. After sifting through four other
stacked containers, Cheryl finally nudged the cat from his resting
spot and unlatched the purple crate. Inside were six covered boxes.
One at a time, Cheryl opened them and flipped through photos.
As she lifted the last box out, she had just about convinced herself
to give up the hunt for the night and attempt to sleep for a couple
of hours before heading to the shop.

But after she looked in the sixth box, sleep was out of the
question. Beau raised his head and meowed, and Cheryl replaced
the lid on the crate and carried a single box upstairs. While a fresh
pot of coffee dripped, Cheryl spread the results of her nocturnal
gleaning along the counters under the bright lights of the kitchen.
Some were as small as three-by-five, but most were eight-by-ten, and
many were framed closely enough to yield ample details. Coffee in
hand, she started in one corner of the room and worked her way
around, studying the prints and choosing a few to transfer to the
table. These she arranged in four rows. Moving them around like
puzzle pieces, she eventually settled on a sequence that seemed to tell
a story.

A story with Amish characters.

A story of conflict, anguish, and triumph.

A story of oars. And not just any oars.

Cheryl's eyes blurred with the effort of inspecting the final eight photos for the umpteenth time. She would look as many times as it took until she no longer discerned fresh details.

No more glances she hadn't noticed before.

No more unseen figures slouching against the trees.

No more puzzling.

No more secrets of the river.

Cheryl tapped one finger on a small face in the third photo in her lineup. This was the person who should see these photos next.

Naomi.

Would she even recognize herself? Cheryl almost hadn't.

Some of the other faces seemed familiar as well, but it was so long ago. Unchanged Amish clothing styles were no help in pinpointing the era, but the occasional Englisch person in the pictures suggested the era of Cheryl's birth. She'd seen those hairstyles and shirt prints in her baby pictures, sported by her parents and the various relatives who passed her around.

Thirty years ago.

It might be overwhelming to take the seventeen photos tiled across the table in neat rows. Cheryl picked out one and then another, finally settling on five. In the small second bedroom that also functioned as a home office, Cheryl rummaged for a nine-by-twelve manila envelope and slid the selected photos inside. For extra protection, she tucked the envelope in a lightweight shoulder bag. Risking a crease or a tear after all these years was unacceptable.

While her impulse was to drive straight out to the Miller farm, Cheryl tended to her normal morning routine. She dressed, tidied the kitchen, made the bed, checked that Beau had food and water. But today when she left the house, she put her head through the strap of the extra bag and wore it across her body. And when she got to the Swiss Miss, she opened a file drawer and secured the bag away from potential mishaps.

She reviewed invoices, filed paperwork, and straightened shelves. Then she carried two boxes of St. Patrick's items out of a corner of the office into the store and flipped the sign on the shop door from Closed to Open. When customers arrived, she answered questions about the cuckoo clocks, called Heini's to order more buttercream fudge, greeted browsers with the same enthusiasm she extended to paying customers, rang up incidental sales, and cleaned fingerprints off a display case. Until at least one of the girls came in, Cheryl couldn't leave the shop, so she might as well be productive. Every time the bell jangled, she glanced up hoping it was Esther or Lydia.

After ringing up several sales in a row, Cheryl looked up to greet the next customer approaching the counter.

"Dr. Richardson," she said.

"What happened to 'Brandon'?"

"Brandon. How are you?"

"I'm well. And you?"

"Fine, thank you." She could not begin to explain the jumble of emotions she felt about this anniversary day, nor what she had spent her night doing when presumably he was sleeping.

He made a quarter turn and scanned the store. "It looks like you have a solid business here."

"All my aunt's doing," Cheryl said. "I'm trying to be a good steward for the day she returns."

"I'm sure she will say, 'Well done, good and faithful servant.'"

Cheryl blushed. "Thank you."

Brandon cleared his throat. "I may have been pushy the last couple of days. I didn't mean to make you uncomfortable."

Cheryl ran one finger along the edge of the cash register. "Things are complicated right now."

"I'm anxious to make friends, I suppose. I hope I can still count you among them."

"Yes, absolutely." Cheryl avoided his eyes, lest she should want to fall into them. "I know what it's like to be new to town. Everybody needs friends."

"How's Beau?"

Now she looked at Brandon's face. "Much better! Thank you so much."

"Good. I'm glad to hear it. Bring him in any time."

"You are officially his veterinarian."

"At your service." He smiled.

"I'll see you again, I'm sure."

"I hope so."

As the door closed behind him, Cheryl pushed out her breath. Brandon Richardson had the same kind heart as Levi Miller.

Birds burst out of the cuckoo clocks with the announcement of eleven o'clock. Amid the clatter, Cheryl almost didn't hear the bell above the door jangle. Esther came in—with Naomi right behind her.

"Three days in a row!" Cheryl greeted them with glee. Naomi's presence in town would make things even easier than if Cheryl tried to get away to drive out to the farm.

"Shocking, I know." Naomi laughed and set a basket on the counter.

Cheryl's chest tightened. Fatigue etched Naomi's face.

Esther unbuttoned her coat. "Maam stayed up late baking last night."

"But it wasn't your usual baking day," Cheryl said, peeking in the basket.

"I was in the mood." Naomi's voice caught, contradicting her words.

"Esther," Cheryl said, "I'd love to duck across the street for some coffee with your maam. Do you think you can find the trays and put the baked goods out?"

"Of course." Esther stepped away.

"Do you have time, Naomi?" Cheryl said.

"I suppose. We came in one of the buggies today."

"Great!" Cheryl turned to Esther again. "If you need me, just call. I can be right back."

"I will be fine. Go."

"Let me grab my coat." Cheryl sidestepped past Esther into the office, pulled out the file drawer, removed the strapped bag, and snatched her jacket off the hook.

Naomi and Cheryl stepped out into a biting wind.

"I have a feeling the urge to bake was not the only reason you were up late," Cheryl said.

Naomi offered no response as they hustled across the street.

"Look who's here." Kathy Snyder grinned from where she was wiping a table. "I was just wondering if I should run over with some coffee if I got a break."

"For a change, I'm coming to you," Cheryl said.

"Always welcome. And you've brought Naomi. What's the Miller news these days?"

While Naomi gave a polite but evasive answer, Cheryl glanced around the Honey Bee Café. Few of the tables were occupied. They must have hit a lull between morning coffee drinkers and the lunch crowd.

"Is it all right if we sit at that back corner table?" Cheryl pointed.

"Anywhere you like," Kathy said, "but that's such a small table."

"It's away from the door," Cheryl said, though she had never minded being near the door before. In fact, normally if she visited the café during the day she preferred to keep the Swiss Miss within sight. Today she wanted to minimize interruptions.

Kathy led them across the café. "We have a new sandwich on the menu."

"Kaffee for me, please," Naomi said, pulling a chair away from the table.

"That should do it for me too," Cheryl said.

"Any chance you've changed your mind about Brandon Richardson?" Kathy winked. "He's such a nice man. I could still set you up."

Cheryl coughed and swallowed. "I'll think about it." The response seemed the quickest way to curtail that strand of conversation. When a party of six came through the café door, Cheryl breathed relief at the distraction they would provide for Kathy.

"I'll be right back with coffee." Kathy pivoted toward the door to greet the customers.

Cheryl sat with the bag in her lap. "So now both anniversaries are over."

Naomi nodded.

Cheryl let a moment pass in silence before saying, "I really want to know how you are, Naomi."

"Tired as a field horse after harvest."

"Did you stay up baking because you were waiting for Seth to come home?"

Naomi's eyes widened.

"Someone was out on the river in a boat last night," Cheryl said. "I'm pretty sure one of the people I saw was Seth. But that was at suppertime."

"On the river? In a boat?"

Cheryl nodded.

"Seth hates the water."

"I know."

"Seth never came home for supper." Naomi's face twisted in restraint. "Levi led the devotions, the girls cleaned up, and still he wasn't home."

"You must have been worried sick."

"The Bible tells us, 'Be careful for nothing; but in every thing by prayer and supplication with thanksgiving let your requests be made known unto God.' Somehow last night I could not help myself. I confess I worried. It is not like Seth to stay out that late, and now he has done it twice. Even after he got home, he went straight to bed without saying where he'd been. By then I had to stay up and wait for the breads to come out of the oven."

"He didn't say anything at all?"

"He apologized for missing supper. What in the world would he have been doing in a boat?"

"If we knew that, we might understand about the oar."

Kathy appeared with two mugs of coffee. Cheryl offered a smile that she hoped expressed gratitude without inviting conversation. Another duo came through the door. Naomi opened a packet of sugar and drizzled it into her coffee. Cheryl pushed her mug to the side.

"I want to show you something," she said. "Photos."

Naomi stirred her coffee. "Photos of what?"

"I'm hoping you can tell me." Cheryl opened the manila envelope and removed three of the five photos. One by one she laid them in front of Naomi.

Naomi gasped. "Where did you get these?"

"My Uncle Ralph took them. It's the old river races, right?"

"I was little," Naomi said. "My memories are fuzzy, but I think so."

Naomi's eyes moved up and down and back and forth as she absorbed the pictures. One photo showed a cluster of eight rowboats with young men gripping the oars. Others showed the bystanders cheering them on.

Cheryl pointed to a girl at the edge of one picture. "This one looks a lot like Esther, but younger. Is It you?"

Naomi pulled the photo closer. "My goodness, I have never seen a photo of myself as a child."

"Never?"

Naomi shook her head. "We do not take photos. They might lead to pride. But that does look like the face I remember from the bathroom mirror."

"How old do you think you were?"

Naomi leaned over the image. "Eight? Nine?"

Cheryl did mental calculations. "So Seth would have been eighteen or nineteen?"

"That's right."

"How old was he when he married Ruth?"

"Not yet twenty." Naomi turned her mug around and ran a finger down the handle. "What is this about, Cheryl?"

"Who else do you recognize?" Cheryl dodged Naomi's question.

Naomi drew in a slow breath and pushed it out. "Let's see. These are some of the Vogel children, I think."

"Ben and Rueben?"

Naomi shook her head. "Wrong generation. Rueben's children. I forget how many he had. Quite a few."

"Who else?"

"So many people came to those races," Naomi said. "My mother thought they were a frivolous waste of time, but my father thought they were good clean fun and looked forward to them when we visited Sugarcreek in the summertime."

A thought piqued Cheryl's curiosity. "Is your father in the crowd?"

Naomi hunted through the sea of faces. Cheryl knew the instant she recognized her father. Tears overflowed Naomi's eyes.

"I have never seen a photo of him either," Naomi said. "How young he looked!"

Cheryl waited while memories surfaced for Naomi.

"I think I remember this day." Naomi wiped her tears with the back of one hand. "It was one of the last times they raced."

Cheryl waited again, watching Naomi's face as names began to come back to her. Swartzentrubers. Troyers. Lehmans. Kaufmans. Hershberger cousins. Hilty brothers. Stutzmans. Grabers.

Finally Naomi settled a finger on one of the rowers. "That looks like Seth."

Cheryl swallowed. "I thought so too."

"In all the years we have been man and wife, he has hated the river." Naomi raised her eyes to meet Cheryl's. "Now you are showing me a picture of him rowing more than thirty years ago and telling me he was out on the water last night."

Nodding, Cheryl held her hands still and waited for Naomi's eyes to have their fill of the photos.

"I remember how many people used to enjoy watching the races," Naomi said. "I guess I never thought much about who was actually racing."

"Look at the oars," Cheryl said softly.

Naomi peered. "You think it is the same."

Her ringing cell phone startled Cheryl. Esther needed help.

CHAPTER TWENTY-SEVEN

The glut of customers thinned, but not before the passage of a swift hour thick with purchases.

"Wow," Cheryl said when she and Esther were alone in the shop again. "What's in the drinking water to make everybody decide to buy something today?"

"You are not complaining, are you?" Esther tilted her head to inspect Cheryl's expression.

"Certainly not." Cheryl removed a wad of bills from the cash register drawer and sifted through them with one thumb. "This is too much cash to keep on hand. I'm going to get yesterday's receipts from the safe and run to the bank. Will you be all right?"

"That missing screwdriver never turned up," Esther said.

"Right. While I'm out I'll get a new one."

"Did my maam go home?"

"I'm not sure." Cheryl filled out a deposit slip and dropped the bills into a zippered blue bank bag. "She didn't say."

"I know she might visit someone. I just do not remember who. I told her I would walk home."

On the sidewalk, Cheryl looked around for Naomi's buggy. One parked down the street was identical to the one the Millers drove, but the horses were wrong. Cheryl chuckled. Who would have thought that an assistant bank manager from Columbus would pay attention to the distinguishing marks of rural horses or black box buggies? But she'd gotten quite good at it, recognizing rigs as easily as her old friends recognized cars.

She dispatched her errand at the bank and paced with purpose to the hardware store. The lost screwdriver was as old as the hills. Perhaps it was time for a whole new set for the odd jobs that came up around the shop. She tugged on the door and went inside. One fluorescent light was blinking. Cheryl blinked back as she oriented herself and headed down the aisle along the wall where she had seen the small battery-powered tools when she came in for lightbulbs a few days earlier. Maybe she would get herself a power screwdriver and save on elbow grease.

Cheryl glanced up at the decorative display above the array of tools and batteries, expecting to see the oar she had taken months to notice.

It was there.

And so was its twin.

Cheryl braced her feet and tilted her head for a more thorough inspection. Most of the nostalgic arrangement was unaltered, but now two oars crisscrossed. One was more faded than the other, but the stripes were the same purple and blue—two wide bands of blue then a thinner one and a final wide swath of purple.

A voice penetrated Cheryl's concentration—Doug, the owner of the hardware store. Just the person she needed to see. He was talking with a customer in the next aisle about grit measurements of sandpaper. Cheryl strode up the aisle, around the endcap display, and toward the rack where the two men stood. How long could it take to choose sandpaper? She could wait.

Finally, the customer lumbered toward the counter to pay for his selection and Doug turned toward Cheryl with a raised eyebrow.

"There are two oars now," Cheryl blurted out. "Where did you get the second oar?"

"It's quite something, isn't it?" Doug said. "After all these years of that oar hanging on the wall, suddenly its mate turns up."

"Yes, quite something. I'm curious to know how it happened."

Doug shrugged. "I came into the store this morning about seven, as I always do. There it was, propped up against the back door."

"You didn't see who left it?"

"Nope. Wish I did. I'd like to say thanks."

"How odd."

"There was a note," Doug said.

Cheryl's eyes grew large against her will. "What did it say?"

"A pair belongs together."

Cheryl echoed the phrase softly and then said, "Thanks, Doug. I've got to go."

"What did you come in for?"

"Another time." Cheryl was halfway up the aisle. The screwdrivers could wait.

Outside the hardware store, she began pacing up the sidewalk without lifting her gaze.

"Whoa!"

Her nose was inches from the badge on Chief Twitchell's uniform. He caught her by the elbows.

"You okay?" he said.

"I...yes...I'm fine," Cheryl said. "Thinking about something. I'm sorry."

"You didn't come to see me," Chief Twitchell said. "About that paperwork."

Cheryl pressed a hand to her forehead. "It's been an abnormal week so far. My cat was sick...and other things."

"Well, we have someone in custody to question. Pretty sure we got your guy. We just need you to verify some information."

Cheryl nodded. "I'll try to remember to come in."

"I have time now," the chief said.

"Um...I have to do something else. Maybe tomorrow?"

"Suit yourself, then. I've done my job, and the bank's done theirs."

Cheryl hustled back toward the Swiss Miss. Lydia was not scheduled to come in, but Cheryl had to find a way to be out of the store again today. Esther was busy with a customer when Cheryl reached the shop. Walking past a couple admiring the cuckoo clocks, Cheryl avoided eye contact. Instead, she pulled her phone from her pocket and tapped in Lydia's phone number.

"Something's come up," Cheryl explained when the girl answered. "I could really use your help in the shop."

"You have been out a lot lately," Lydia said.

"I know. But things will get back to normal soon. Can you help today?"

"Well, I was looking forward to a day off."

Cheryl's foot began to tap. "Please, Lydia. It's important."

"Okay. But my daed is out with the buggy, so it might be a little while."

"As soon as you can."

"I will figure something out."

Cheryl ended the call and shoved the phone into a pocket. She might as well get out of her coat and do something productive while she waited for Lydia. Wandering past a glassware display, she redistributed the items to fill in the gaps left by purchases that morning.

And there they were. Two hearts.

Puppy Love. Forever.

Cheryl picked them up and closed her fist around the candy. Had they been there when she left for the bank? Or had the person leaving hearts been in the store while she was out? She couldn't be sure. The morning had been unusually busy. Many of the usuals had dropped in at some point—Marion Berryhill, Gail Murray, Kathy Snyder, Rueben and Ben Vogel. But Cheryl had been out of the shop so much of the day already.

The hearts had been coming for a week—and whoever left them knew where Cheryl lived. Somebody in town, right under her nose, was trying to give her a message.

Later Cheryl would ask Esther if she could remember who else had been in that day. For now, though, first things first.

Seth Miller.

The couple looking at cuckoo clocks lifted beckoning hands, and Cheryl could not avoid them any longer. The happy result of the distraction was that they bought one. Cheryl left Esther to complete the sale and went into the cramped office.

She had to talk to Seth. If her suspicions were right, the topic was too tender for Naomi, which was why Cheryl had withheld the fifth photo from her friend.

But Seth would not agree to speak to her if she simply showed up on the family farm. Besides, Cheryl couldn't risk going out to the Millers' and Naomi coming home and stumbling into the conversation.

She needed help. A coconspirator.

Levi.

Who did not carry a phone.

Cheryl glanced out to the main room, wondering if Esther knew what her brother's plans were today. Or her sister's.

Cheryl's best bet was Elizabeth. If she was out at the petting zoo, she might hear the phone, and if she wasn't busy with customers she would gladly answer.

The phone rang five times. Then came that blessed silent space, that moment of someone lifting the phone and moving it close to offer a greeting.

"Guder mariye. Miller Maze and Petting Zoo."

Giddy relief threatened to undo Cheryl. She forced herself to speak with even ordinariness.

"Good morning, Elizabeth. I hope you are well."

"Very well, thank you."

"I wonder if you might have time to give Levi a message."

"I can try," Elizabeth said. "I do not have any visitors at the zoo right now."

"Would you ask him to call me?"

Elizabeth hesitated. "Levi does not like to use the telephone."

"I know. But it's important. Tell him it's important."

"I will do my best."

Cheryl gave her cell phone number. With her ears attuned to monitor sounds from the store, Cheryl held her phone in one hand. With the other she entered numbers into spreadsheets on the computer screen. Sales totals. Payroll hours. Reorder numbers. Three times she got up and minded the cash register for a few minutes while Esther helped other customers. This would have been a good day for business to be slow, but instead the opposite seemed to be happening. Five times Cheryl checked her phone to make sure she hadn't missed a call. At last Lydia arrived. Cheryl pulled Esther into the office and asked if she could stay longer, promising to drive her home if necessary. Esther's dark eyes clouded with questions, but she agreed.

Cheryl's phone rang.

"This is Levi."

Cheryl let herself sink into the office chair. "I need a big favor."

"How can I help you?"

"Bring your father into town and meet me at Yoder's Corner."

Silence.

"What will I tell him about why?" Levi finally said.

Cheryl had not considered the question. "I found a couple of things."

Levi waited.

"First," Cheryl said, "the missing oar turned up in the hardware store. Second, thirty-year-old photos turned up in my aunt's basement."

"Photos?"

"Of your parents, if my suspicions are right."

More silence.

"Maam took the buggy," Levi said.

"I know, but you have another one, don't you?"

"Caleb has it."

Cheryl groaned. "Isn't there an old one, or a cart, or a wagon? Something?"

"Couldn't you come here?"

"What if Naomi comes home? She shouldn't hear us. Not yet."

"It sounds like you believe you have gotten to the bottom of things."

"I'm close," Cheryl said. "I just need help with this last bit."

"I suppose we could use the open cart I sometimes use to get to my Saturday evening tutoring group, if the weather is mild enough."

The details in Levi's statement jarred Cheryl.

"Tutoring group?"

"Seventh and eighth grade Amish boys. It is their last chance to learn algebra. But I have to use the library to make sure I get it right myself. They have some old textbooks."

"That's where you were on the night of the banquet," Cheryl murmured. "Tutoring."

"Of course. On Saturdays the boys work all day on the farms. Their parents agreed to let me help them after the chores are finished and supper is over. They have to meet standards or the whole school could be endangered with the state."

"Tutoring. I had no idea!"

"It would be prideful to make anything of it. I am only trying to help the church boys. I would not disappoint them for something like an Englisch banquet."

"Of course not."

Levi sighed into the phone. "I will see what I can do about my father."

"Yoder's Corner in an hour?"

"If I cannot convince him, I will come alone," Levi said.

CHAPTER TWENTY-EIGHT

Forty-five minutes later, the alarm Cheryl had set on her phone went off, reminding her it was time to leave. Not that she needed reminding. She'd hardly taken her eyes off the clock, and a couple of the cuckoos announced the time every fifteen minutes.

"Leaving now?" Lydia said when the alarm sounded.

"Yes. Thanks again for coming in."

"How long should I count on staying?"

"Not sure. But I won't be far—just down at Yoder's Corner."

Cheryl planned to arrive early at the restaurant and stake out a table. There she would use the spare minutes to calmly review what she would say to Seth. How she would show him the photos. How she would watch his face when he saw them. She jostled out of the Swiss Miss on to the sidewalk along Main Street and turned her feet toward Yoder's Corner. She hadn't gotten far, though, when a gaggle of bags and boxes came up along one side of her. Peeking through an opening, Cheryl could see the face of Gail from the Buttons 'n Bows shop.

A small box tumbled off the heap, bounced, took two turns, and landed at Cheryl's feet.

Gail came to a halt. "Goodness. I was afraid that might happen."

Cheryl bent to pick up the gray cardboard box. A second box surrendered to gravity, knocking Cheryl in the head before angling to one side.

"Oh dear," Gail said, "this just gets worse."

"No harm done." Cheryl gathered both boxes and straightened up.

"Just put them right here," Gail said, "in the crook of my right arm."

"Are you sure?" The position seemed precarious to Cheryl.

"I don't have far to go."

"Looks like you've been on a shopping spree of your own." Cheryl tried tucking one box back within Gail's grasp but immediately could tell it would not stay there.

"I found a young woman over in Berlin who makes the most beautiful things. She has four daughters and knows just what the girls like. I bought almost everything she had on hand, but I couldn't find a parking place close to my own store."

Cheryl could hear the clock in her head gong as if it were Big Ben, knocking her buffer zone to the curb like one of Gail's boxes.

"Let me help you," Cheryl said. "I can carry a few things for you."

Altogether, Cheryl lost eight minutes walking with Gail to Buttons 'n Bows, greeting Gail's daughter Kim, who was minding their shop, and politely excusing herself. By the time she reached Yoder's Corner, she was five minutes late instead of ten minutes early.

Greta greeted her. "Having a late lunch on your own?"

Cheryl scanned the restaurant. Three quarters of the tables were empty. The lunch rush was over. Seth might have resisted waiting if he didn't see her, but surely Levi would have given her a few minutes to arrive.

"Have Seth and Levi Miller been by?" Cheryl said.

"I saw Naomi this morning," Greta said, "but not the men."

Cheryl's shoulders eased. "Then I'll need a table for three, sort of out of the way."

"We can do that." Greta led Cheryl to the same back wall where Chief Twitchell had talked with Seth and Cheryl listened from around the wide post.

Coming full circle.

"What can I get you?" Greta said.

Cheryl's stomach was a jumble of nerves, but hunger was about to overtake her brain, and she couldn't afford that. "Whatever sandwich you're pushing today."

"That would be chicken salad with a side of coleslaw."

"Sounds perfect."

"Iced tea?"

"Yes, please."

Greta's skirt swished away, and Cheryl settled herself against the back wall of the restaurant where she could see who entered. She checked the time. Maybe Levi was late because he was unable to persuade his father to come.

Greta returned with the tea. No Levi.

The sandwich came. No Levi.

Cheryl cut the sandwich into quarters to eat with less mess. She managed two quarters. No Levi.

Maybe the open cart had broken down.

Cheryl picked at the coleslaw with a fork, pushing around more than she ate.

The door opened and closed. Customers arrived. Others paid their checks and left. Greta refilled Cheryl's glass of tea. Seth and Levi were half an hour late now.

Finally father and son came through the door. Cheryl pushed her plate away and watched as Levi spoke to Greta, and Greta pointed. Halfway through the restaurant, Seth and Levi paused at another table.

They were greeting Rueben Vogel. When had he come in? It seemed impossible that Cheryl would not have seen him come in and sit down, but there he was, not all that far from her. Greta broke into her huddle with a plate-sized cinnamon roll, and Rueben's blue eyes lit up. Seth laughed, offering a trace of the twinkle Cheryl hadn't seen in his eyes lately. She caught Levi's eye and then watched as Seth shook Rueben's hand before moving on.

Seth and Levi took the chairs opposite Cheryl.

"Thank you for coming," Cheryl said.

Seth's face had sobered as soon as he left Rueben's table. "I came because my son asked me to, and I honor what kind of man he has become."

Cheryl nodded. "I wanted to talk about what's been happening over the last ten days."

"I figured so," Seth said, "though I do not believe we have much to speak about."

Cheryl's eyes began to drift toward Levi's but she pulled them back. There would be plenty of time for Levi's reaction later.

"You know that I saw you pick up that oar last Monday night."

"I do."

"And I know that this time of year is difficult for you."

Seth crossed his arms.

"I think those two things are related," Cheryl said. "I think the reason February is hard has something to do with the oar."

"I have told you several times that you did not have to worry about the oar," Seth said. "It is personal business, and I have dealt with it."

"By reuniting the matching oars," Cheryl said. "I saw them in the hardware store a few hours ago."

Seth put his forearms on the table and leaned toward her, silent.

Greta appeared. "Ready to order?"

"Just kaffee, please." Seth raised his face for a quick smile at Greta, who removed Cheryl's plate and disappeared again.

"Your whole family is dear to me," Cheryl said. "Naomi is a true friend. Esther is such a help in the Swiss Miss. All of you have welcomed me into your lives and helped me love living in Sugarcreek."

Seth nodded. "We value hospitality."

"That's why it's been so hard for me to know something was not right—something that is never right at this time of year. Your children have made no secret of the way you seem to withdraw, and I've seen it for myself."

Greta was back with a pot and three mugs.

"None for me," Cheryl said.

"You sure you do not want something to eat?"

"Thank you, no," Levi said.

Greta poured two cups of coffee and set them in front of the men. "Let me know if you need something else."

Seth glanced at his firstborn and leaned in toward Cheryl again. "My children should not speak out of turn."

"Please don't blame them," Cheryl said. "They love you and Naomi."

"Surely you wanted to talk about more than my moods," Seth said.

Cheryl laid the manila folder on the table. "Maybe you remember that my uncle took a lot of photos."

"He kept his distance, so we never minded."

"Everybody loved Uncle Ralph." Cheryl slid one photo out of the envelope and centered it between father and son.

Levi hunched toward the photo. Seth stiffened.

"Are these our church members?" Levi asked.

"Maybe you recognize some of them," Cheryl said. The photo she'd selected first featured clumps of people lined up along the shore of the river. Some engaged in conversation. Women held tightly to their little ones' hands. Others, of all ages, leaned forward and looked in one direction as if fixing their eyes on the same point.

In the second photo, which Cheryl laid out now, Uncle Ralph had trained the lens on a huddle of teenage girls. Young women. By Amish standards, some of them were old enough to marry without the panic that would beset Englisch parents at the thought of daughters throwing away a chance at an education to have babies, perhaps before they were twenty. Somehow he had positioned himself above them—in a tree, maybe—and looked down on a circle of bobbing heads.

The third photo had revealed the ragged line of eight rowboats. Uncle Ralph must have been at the bend in the river that would allow him to look straight down the water at them, but he hadn't used a long lens. The picture caught the panorama of the day, rather than close-up faces, but it was enough to put Seth in the scene. Even Naomi had recognized him.

In the fourth photo, Uncle Ralph had caught one fair-haired, blue-eyed girl looking over her shoulder. This was the image that had launched Cheryl's suspicions in the middle of the night. The resemblance was too strong not to matter, the girl's features echoed in eyes and cheekbones she saw on a regular basis. The slant of the nose. The shape of the hairline.

Levi's eyes. Levi's nose. The same color hair as if the same salon had done the highlights.

His brother Caleb's face carried the wide measurement of the girl's cheeks. Their sister Sarah, whom Cheryl saw less frequently, mirrored the feminine version of the family features. Cheryl hadn't shown this photo to Naomi. If she could spot a younger Seth, surely she would have discerned the face of the woman who birthed three of the children she raised.

Seth's Adam's apple slid down his neck.

"Daed," Levi said softly.

"Yes," Seth said. "Your mother."

They both lingered over the image.

"I have never seen a photograph of her," Levi said.

"Neither have I," Seth said.

"I had almost forgotten what she looked like." Levi's voice choked.

Cheryl gave them an elongated moment, trying to imagine living without photographs of loved ones only to see a stunning image from so long ago. Ruth Miller's eyes had shifted to one side, as if she wanted to watch without being seen. A corner of her mouth turned up in a motion that perhaps became a full-fledged smile a few seconds later.

"She was lovely," Cheryl murmured.

She slid the final photo out of the envelope, another close-up. A young triumphant Seth had pulled to the front of the race. Around the edges of the photo were scattered bows of other boats, disappointment flushing through the faces of the rowers. Seth had released his oars, which were bracketed to the boat, and raised his hands in the victory.

Cheryl watched Seth's face. His eyes glistened, and the muscles in his face went lax.

Levi pulled the picture closer. "It is you."

Seth nodded.

Levi put the photos of his parents side by side. "Before I was born."

"Before we were married," Seth said.

"You loved racing." The truth rippled through Levi's face. "You loved being on the water."

"It was a long time ago." Seth's voice was hoarse.

"But the oar," Cheryl said gently, "it's there in that picture too."

Levi looked more closely and put his finger on the only other rower who might have had a chance at catching Seth that day. The painted stripes were still fresh on that shimmering day.

"I do not understand," Levi said, still mesmerized by the images of his parents. "What does this have to do with...how you feel about the day Maam died?"

"There's one more thing I want to say," Cheryl said. "I was out walking last night. I'd lost a glove, and even though it was dark, I wanted to try to find it. I heard something on the water—a boat. I could see you weren't alone."

"Daed," Levi said, "you were on the water?"

"You would have found your glove if you had been there a few minutes earlier." Seth reached into his coat pocket and laid Cheryl's missing glove on the table. "I went looking for more than a glove."

"I go there because it's peaceful," Cheryl said. "But it hasn't been lately, not since I saw you pick up the oar. I want the peace back, and I think you do too."

Seth nodded.

"I'm sorry I treated you with such suspicion the last few days," Cheryl said. "You weren't the only one looking for peace on the river last night. Who were you with?"

Levi put his finger on the face of the man with the oars. "This man?"

CHAPTER TWENTY-NINE

Abel." Seth supplied the man's name. "I ruined the river for both of us."

Cheryl looked at the triumphal photo. "It was just a race. I don't understand."

"I told myself it was the race we were always meant for, that inevitably it would come down to winning that race in order to win everything."

"Daed, what do you mean?" Levi scraped his chair back a few inches and turned toward Seth.

"We were all young together," Seth said. He was facing the back wall of the restaurant, but his eyes seemed to look beyond it to another time. "It was just like you and your friends, Levi. Every time the church came together, for worship or a frolic, you disappeared with the boys your age. Then, when you were teenagers, you found things to do to include the girls."

"So it was that way with you and Maam?"

Longing quivered in Levi's eyes, a boy remembering a mother's touch.

"The Englisch would say she was an artist," Seth said. He rotated his coffee mug two turns counterclockwise. "She saw the colors everywhere—the shades of wheat in the fields, the way she arranged flowers in the garden, the turning leaves in the fall. By the time she was twelve, she was making her own dyes. Many women were buying dress cloth by the bolt in the general store, but she liked to dye her own. Ruth didn't stray too far from the colors the other women wore, but her dresses were always a closer match to the summer sky or the earth at planting or the field at harvest. She made her first quilt from scraps left from cotton she had colored, but the patterns she arranged were like no one else's."

"It sounds like she had a gift," Cheryl said.

"That was my Ruth." Seth blew out his breath. "My Ruth. As if I owned her."

Cheryl waited, her hands still in her lap.

"Then we started rumspringa. We were not a wild bunch. There were no cell phones in those days, and none of us had money for a car. If we were going to dabble in Englisch ways, it would be more subtle. Ruth was helping to look after the children of an Englisch family. She saw what their house was like—electricity, television, air conditioning. But what interested her most was the wife's studio full of canvases and paints and brushes. Whatever money she saved, she spent on art supplies of her own."

"I never knew this," Levi said. "I remember her quilts, but all the rest of this is brand new."

"It was rumspringa. She put it all aside when she was baptized."

"I want to hear more," Levi said.

Levi craved these unknown memories of his mother, so close to being lost forever. Cheryl knew the story would eventually lead to the oars—and the victory photo.

"The races on the river were popular in those days," Seth said. "In the summer heat, everyone enjoyed the water, even just being splashed or sprayed. We all had our favorite oars, the ones that felt the best in our grips. Someone had the idea for Ruth to paint patterns on the handles and paddles. The Englisch did it all the time. Still do, I think. She did it for several of us—different colors, different kinds of stripes. Anyone could tell our oars apart at a glance."

"Were you friends with Abel?" Cheryl asked.

Seth shrugged. "We were part of the same group of friends. Did that make us friends? I am not so sure."

"Then what, Daed?" Levi said. "Something happened between you and Abel?"

Seth rotated his mug back in the other direction. As far as Cheryl could see, he hadn't taken a single sip of the cooling dark liquid it held.

"Your mother had a way about her. Everyone liked her. I am not sure she ever realized how beautiful she was, or how much people relished the way she paid attention to them. She was at peace with the world and everyone in it. She took seriously the apostle Paul's admonition to live at peace as much as it depends on you. Eventually we knew our rumspringa would come to an end, and we would all have to decide to take our baptismal vows and join the church. Of course, that meant we could also marry."

"And you started to think of Ruth more seriously?" Cheryl prompted.

"I drove her home from the singings as often as I could," Seth said. "Sometimes a group of us took a picnic down to the river, and I would try to talk with her alone or invite her to walk along a path."

"And Abel?" Cheryl said.

"He tried to do the same. In fact, it seemed to me that if he knew I was planning to ask Ruth for a walk, he would intentionally beat me to it. Then when she was not looking, he would give me a cocky grin."

"That sounds mean," Cheryl said.

"I thought so too. For the longest time, I was not sure whether Abel really cared for Ruth or if he just took pleasure in besting me."

Levi again examined the two photos of his parents as teenagers. "Why do I have the feeling that if the race had turned out differently, I would not exist?"

"Because you are right."

Cheryl pointed to the photos. "The oars have something to do with this particular race?"

"Abel and I were the strongest, fastest rowers. One Sunday afternoon I would win, and the next time he would. That seemed to be the way our whole lives had been—competing back and forth in every kind of context, from spelling bees at school to the best hits in a church baseball game."

"Or in love," Cheryl said.

"I was in a cocky mood myself that day," Seth said. "Everyone knew either Abel or I would win any race we were in. We weren't always in the same group of racers, but that day we were. Abel had been taunting me for weeks, gloating that he was spending more time with Ruth. On that day in July, I wanted to put an end to it once and for all. I took Abel aside and proposed that the winner of our race would get to court Ruth. The loser would step aside."

"A wager?" Levi sounded shocked.

Seth nodded. "I am not proud of it."

"Surely it is against the teaching of the church."

"I was not baptized," Seth said. "I was not yet bound to the *Ordnung* in that way."

Cheryl ran a tongue across dry lips.

"This is why Maam chose you?" Levi said. "Because you won a race?"

"I loved your mother, Levi." Seth's voice cracked. "I loved her wholly and completely. But I will never know whether she would have chosen me. We gambled with our lives and futures—and Ruth's—and I won the race that day. Abel kept his word."

Levi traced a finger over his father's face in the photo. "You look so joyful to win the chance to court Maam."

Seth exhaled slowly. "If only I could say that in truth. I am ashamed of that moment, ashamed that I took such pleasure in defeating Abel and taking from him something—someone—he might have truly cared for."

"You don't know that Ruth would have married Abel," Cheryl said. "If he saw courting her as another competition, he might not have genuinely loved her. You can't know that you wouldn't have ended up with Ruth anyway."

"You are right," Seth said. "I stole that certainty from myself. I like to think we were happily married, but I know she was confused when Abel backed away with no explanation."

"He never said anything to anyone?" Levi asked.

Seth shook his head. "He got out of his boat that day and heaved his oars into the woods. Someone tried to retrieve them, but Abel got angry and stopped him. He never wanted to see those oars again, he said. He did not race again, and neither did I."

"And the racing petered out after that," Cheryl said.

"I suppose people somehow knew that something happened when neither Abel nor I wanted to race. It was not the same after that. We hurt the whole community with our foolishness."

"You could have confessed," Levi said softly. "People would have understood. You were young and on rumspringa."

"I was a coward. I could not risk losing Ruth over it."

"What happened to Abel?" Cheryl asked.

"Ruth and I got married that fall. Abel was there—the whole congregation was, of course. By the end of the day, he disappeared and his parents did not know where he had gone. He never came back."

"Until now." Cheryl's eyes went to the second-place boat in the photo.

Seth nodded.

"He was Abel Vogel, wasn't he? Rueben's son."

Seth nodded again. The note Naomi found in his pocket made sense. Abel believed Seth had stolen his life away in that momentary gamble.

"And you went out in the boat with him last night, didn't you?"

"It was time to put things right. Abel borrowed his brother-in-law's boat. It seemed best to go back to the spot where everything went wrong."

A heart at peace gives life to the body.

"And did you?" Cheryl said. "Put things right?"

"The grace of Gott takes many forms."

A choked sob startled Cheryl. A form stepped out from behind the pillar that shielded the table.

CHAPTER THIRTY

"Naomi!"

As he rose, Seth knocked his chair off balance and grabbed for it.

Levi rose more slowly. "How much did you hear?"

Naomi's face blanched, her lips moving but no sound coming from her mouth.

Cheryl pushed her chair back now and closed the distance between her and Naomi. She took Naomi's elbow. "Sit with us."

The wide pillar, the captivating photos, the heightened emotions—all of this had conspired to keep any of them from noticing Naomi had entered Yoder's Corner. The scenario Cheryl had hoped to avoid by not driving out to the farm to see Seth now crashed in on them. Naomi had heard plenty. Cheryl was sure of that.

Naomi lowered herself into a chair opposite Seth. After a moment, her eyes moved from his face to the photos of Seth and Ruth still in front of Levi.

"Cheryl, you did not show me all these photos," Naomi said.

"We got interrupted," Cheryl said.

"But that is not the only reason."

"No."

Eyes brimming, Naomi turned back to her husband. "This is what you have been guarding all these years."

"I did not want to hurt you by dwelling on Ruth."

"You loved her. You wanted her more than anything. Enough to do this...thing."

"Yes."

Seth's voice was barely audible. Cheryl held her breath to listen.

"And to think I was there that day," Naomi said. "I did not remember who was racing."

Seth's eyes widened. Cheryl gently reached across the table and pulled out the photo of onlookers on the bank of the river. Both Levi's and Seth's eyes scanned the image. Cheryl put her finger along one outside edge, and their vision settled.

Seth smiled as he breathed in and out several times. "A beautiful child. Just like our own Esther. And so innocent. Who knew that Gott would someday knit us together."

"You wanted to be knit together with Ruth. And you were." Naomi gestured toward Levi. "She gave you your first son, plus two more children."

Cheryl reached into her bag and produced a tissue for Naomi.

"Naomi," Seth said, his voice wobbling, "you are not second best. You are first best in Gottes perfect timing."

Naomi wiped her nose. "Cheryl tried to tell me you had a reason for picking up that oar. I never imagined anything like this."

"I did not go looking for the oar," Seth said. "Never. When I stopped rowing, I got rid of my oars. And suddenly, when I stumbled on that oar, it was as if I held a lost piece of Ruth. I was touching something she had touched, something she created."

"But we still have some of her things," Levi said. "Sarah has her wedding quilt. I have her Bible."

"This was different," Seth said. "This was something from before I tainted her memory with my own selfishness. Something pure. Something joyful. Something given freely from her heart."

"But it was Abel's oar," Levi said. "Surely..."

"Yes," Seth said. "Along with reminding me of Ruth, it reminded me of my own actions—and my doubts whether she would have chosen me if I had never proposed a sinful wager. Ruth was not a prize to win. She was a woman who deserved unsullied love. And I could never give that to her, not after the way I won her heart."

"But you did win her heart," Cheryl said. "Even if she was confused about Abel, she didn't have to marry you if she did not freely choose to."

"Can her choice have been free if it was bound up in my sin?"

For more than a week whenever Cheryl saw Seth, his face was stoic, unyielding. His words were cryptic, untelling. Now the torture of his own conscience wracked his familiar features.

"And I have made Naomi pay the price as well," Seth said. His gaze fixed on Naomi's dark eyes. "If I have made you, even for a moment, feel that I have not loved you as I loved Ruth, I beg your forgiveness."

Cheryl swallowed hard at the intimacy of the moment. Naomi deserved to hear these words from her husband, but Cheryl had not expected to witness them.

"And the note?" Naomi croaked. "The one demanding a meeting on the anniversary?"

Seth's features softened, as if in full relief. "You saw it."

"Cheryl was with me when I was going through your pockets to do laundry."

Levi straightened his shoulders and looked at Cheryl. "Is this the note you would not tell me about?"

"*Couldn't*," Cheryl corrected, though in the end she had.

"It came the day before I found the oar. Just turned up on top of my toolbox in the barn. It is of no account now, but it explains Cheryl's persistence these last few days."

"So it was from Abel," Cheryl said.

Seth nodded.

"And you took the oar to the hardware store?"

"Last night, after we brought the boat in. It was wrong for me to take it, wrong to keep it, wrong to hide it. It belongs with its mate, and they both belong in the past."

"You will still see them every time you go in the hardware store," Levi said.

"But now they are complete, together, rather than torn asunder. I can look at them and know all is reconciled. All is forgiven. All is grace to the undeserving. None of us will live in the shadow of my secrets any longer."

Cheryl believed Seth. Naomi's fingers were inching across the table toward Seth's. Levi stacked the photos and handed them back to Cheryl before laying his hand on the place where Seth's and Naomi's touched.

"I have one more minor question," Cheryl said.

Six eyes looked at her.

"Who has been leaving the candy hearts?"

"Candy hearts?" Levi scrunched up his features.

Cheryl dug into her bag and pulled out the heart-shaped tin. "I found the last two this morning."

One by one, she laid them out in the order, by pairs or trios, in which she had found them.

Be True. Start Now. Do Good. I'm Sure. My Pal. It's Love. Choose Me. Love Bug. Be a Sport. Puppy Love. Forever.

"They are just candy," Seth said. "There must be hundreds of those little hearts still around town."

Cheryl shook her head. "That's what I thought at first. But the way they showed up seemed more than coincidental. And now they make sense. The story they tell was about pals—friends. Young love. A choice. A sport. Somebody knew what they were doing. And they wanted me to stick with it."

"Rueben," Seth said. "He is Abel's father. Never once has he said anything that blamed me for Abel leaving. I did not think Abel told anyone, but maybe I am wrong."

"Rueben has a sweet tooth," Levi said. "Everybody knows that."

"He was right over there when I came in," Naomi said.

They all looked. Rueben's table was empty. Greta was about to clear the dishes.

"Wait!" Cheryl jumped up.

Startled, Greta's hands froze midair.

Cheryl raced to the table and scooped up two more hearts.

My Girl. Take a Walk.

CHAPTER THIRTY-ONE

Cheryl closed up the Swiss Miss at five on the dot. She locked the afternoon's cash in the safe and left miscellaneous paperwork and straightening up for the morning.

My Girl. Take a Walk.

That was an invitation Cheryl couldn't refuse, and the sooner she got out to the river the less chance she'd have of missing the opportunity. Ten minutes later, Cheryl put her house key in the lock and turned it. Beau greeted her by walking circles around her ankles.

"Glad to see you looking like your old self." Cheryl scooped him up and scratched behind his ears. A quick look at his food dish assured her he was eating. In the bedroom, he wriggled out of her arms and landed on the bed. Cheryl squatted in front of the open closet door to rummage for her hiking boots, still mud-caked from the night before. She exchanged a pullover sweater for a comfortable sweatshirt, grabbed her jacket and car keys, and headed for the front door. Beau followed.

"I'm going to leave you just for a few more minutes," Cheryl said. "I promise when I get back, we'll settle in with a fire and a book. A nice quiet evening at home. You'll like that, won't you?" She certainly would. For the first time in ten days she could relax without being preoccupied with Seth's odd behavior, missing oars, or threatening notes.

Beau meowed.

The car was in the driveway. Cheryl nudged the cat away from the door and turned the knob. With barely enough space for Cheryl to put one foot out the door, Beau darted through the opening.

"Beau!" Cheryl raced after him. He didn't run far, stopping beside the blue Ford. "You want to come?"

He stared at her, unmoving.

"Okay, but you have to let me carry you. I can't have you running off at the river."

He squinted.

Cheryl opened the car door. "Okay, in you go."

At the river a few minutes later, Cheryl parked in her usual spot. Holding Beau, she stood in front of her car and looked in both directions down the walking path. Rueben might still be coming from his farm, or he could be farther along in the other direction. It was too bad candy hearts didn't have times or locations stamped on them. Cheryl opted to take her usual route but walk more slowly and pause to look around from time to time.

"You're being good," Cheryl said to the cat, who nestled in her arms without protest. "Thanks for the company."

When she reached the farthest point of her customary route and still hadn't spotted Rueben, Cheryl considered whether to proceed or turn around and walk toward his home. In her moment of hesitation, Beau turned his head and meowed. Cheryl tightened her grip on the animal as she looked around for what might have caught his attention. Rueben was off the path, standing on the soggy riverbank.

Each fist was wrapped around an upright oar—with blue and purple bands.

"Rueben!"

He turned at the sound of his name. Cheryl waved and then looked down to find her footing and descend to meet him. This was the same spot where Seth picked up an oar ten days earlier. Rueben returned his gaze to the water. Cheryl braced her feet in the spongy ground and took watch beside him. At their feet, the river lapped and sloshed in soothing constancy. Cheryl's shoulders settled and her breathing slowed. This was what it should feel like to come to the river.

"You got my messages," Rueben finally said.

"You are one clever man," Cheryl said.

"I do not like to draw attention to myself."

Rueben's ubiquitous presence on Main Street, especially at the Swiss Miss, had hidden his plot well. Nothing he'd done or said had been noteworthy.

"I guess you heard us at Yoder's Corner."

"I saw you go in during the middle of your day and found that unusual."

"You have a keen mind," Cheryl said. "Are your ears just as good?"

"I am an old man. It serves me well to choose what I want to hear."

"Clever *and* sneaky!"

"I always suspected something about that day changed my son, but I never knew what. I never confessed that I did see the mess on the beach that night we first ran into each other."

"Then you saw the oar."

"Ja."

"Why didn't you pick it up?"

"It did not belong to me." Rueben bent his wiry frame to pick up a pebble and tossed it into the river. "When Abel first lost his spark, we thought he was sick. Then when he refused to race again, we thought he was prideful. Every day for a week, I led family devotions on what the Bible has to say about pride. It was not until the day Seth and Ruth married and I saw my son's face during the ceremony that I realized he was heartsick. And then he was gone."

"Until last week," Cheryl said.

"His sister heard from him every now and then. They stayed in touch somehow. He knew she had married, had children, when we lost his mother."

"What about now? Will Abel stay in town?"

"He was gone before breakfast this morning."

"Oh, Rueben. I'm so sorry. Thirty years is a long time to miss your son. Do you think he'll come again?"

"I cannot say. Hope so."

They stood listening to the water, soaking up long-awaited peace.

Rueben moved his hands together, bringing the oars side by side in front of him.

"How did you get the oars?" Cheryl asked.

"I went into the hardware store and made Doug an offer. Gave him cash on the counter and promised him another set of old oars. He will not know the difference."

"But you will."

"Ja."

"It must have been hard seeing Abel's oar up on the wall all these years."

Rueben shrugged. "When it was just one, I did not want it. It was something broken. Incomplete. A mangled question mark. But now I know the truth, so I wanted what belonged to my son. I suspect he had malicious intent toward Seth, but when he saw Naomi around town and visited the petting zoo, he changed his mind. He did not want to steal away someone else's life in revenge. In the end all he wanted was to be on the river one last time and remember Ruth."

"I'm sorry he's lived with so much pain all these years."

"Me too."

"Maybe now he will be at peace."

"Hope so." Rueben turned around. "I should get on back to the house before that daughter of mine knows I am gone."

Cheryl laughed. "Do you really think she doesn't know?"

"Maybe. Maybe not. I am not taking any chances."

"We could walk to my car and I could drive you the rest of the way."

"No thanks. It is better if I finish my constitutional."

Rueben marched off without waiting to see if Cheryl would walk with him. He climbed the bank to the path, and she lost him to the shadows.

Beau, who had been content in her arms to this point, squirmed, and Cheryl was too slow in tightening her grasp. He leaped out of the confines of her grasp.

"Beau!"

He darted away, not up the bank but toward a collection of small boulders.

"Come back here!" Cheryl grunted and took her phone from her pocket to turn on the flashlight app.

Beau sat on one of the rocks, looking comfortably pleased with himself. As Cheryl approached, he stood and circled the edge of the stone. In the illumination of Cheryl's phone were two tiny pale yellow hearts. The cat meowed again, and Cheryl scooped up the candy.

Thank You. Cloud Nine.

Author Letter

Dear Reader,

Several years ago at a conference at the YMCA of the Rockies—a spectacular setting for sensing God's grandeur—I took the opportunity to walk a prayer labyrinth. This is a slow, winding walk toward the center of a circular labyrinth with space there to listen to God. All of us experience seasons when we face difficulties but don't see the purpose. This was one of those seasons for me.

As I arrived at the center of the labyrinth, I felt the word *peace* impressed upon my heart. While I left the center and wound my way back out to "real life," I pondered the ways I might learn to live from a center of peace rather than a center of questions about what everything meant.

This was not an easy process, but gradually I let go of some of the things I was struggling against and began to look at my circumstances through a lens of how making decisions from a place of peace, rather than struggle, might change my attitudes and reactions.

Writing *Peace Like a River* has made me remember that experience with gratitude, and I hope reading about the journey toward peace of the characters in this story has inspired you to take your own journey.

In God's peace,
Olivia Newport

ABOUT THE AUTHOR

Olivia Newport's novels twist through time to find where faith and passions meet. She began writing Amish stories when she discovered a family line that traced back to some of the earliest Amish to arrive in the original Lancaster County, Pennsylvania. Married with two grown children, Olivia is an Illinois native happily transplanted in Colorado, where daylilies grow as tall as she is. Sun, chocolate, and hammocks are at the top of her list. To learn more, visit olivianewport.com.

Fun Fact about
the Amish or Sugarcreek, Ohio

The *Budget* newspaper that is popular in Amish communities across the United States was first published as the *Sugarcreek Budget* in 1890. The first publisher of the paper intended it to be a biweekly paper aimed at local residents of the Sugarcreek, Ohio, community. Almost from the start, though, the paper featured items from as far away as Arkansas. The next year it became a weekly paper, and by 1899, the *Budget* routinely had letters from thirty correspondents in different church districts across many states.

In the beginning, the paper served both the Old Order Amish and the more progressive Amish Mennonites. Then the publication went through a time of being owned by Amish Mennonites and serving primarily a Mennonite audience. When the Amish Mennonites formally joined the wider Mennonite church, the paper was sold to a Lutheran! Rather than turning the *Budget* into a Lutheran publication, though, the new owner cultivated more Old Order readers and contributors.

For well over a hundred years now, the *Budget* has been a forum for Amish communities to share news and announcements. While the general culture around the Amish moved on to more modern forms of communication—telephones, radios, television, Internet—the *Budget* has stood the test of time as a way to connect Amish districts.

SOMETHING DELICIOUS FROM OUR SUGARCREEK FRIENDS

Egg-in-the-Nest

4 tablespoons butter, softened
4 slices of bread (thicker is better)
4 eggs
Salt
Pepper

Spread softened butter on both sides of each slice of bread. Use the rim of a drinking glass to cut a round hole in each slice. Heat a skillet over medium heat and place the prepared bread in the skillet. Crack an egg into each hole. Brown the bread for three to four minutes and then use the spatula to flip both bread and egg together. Brown the other side. Add salt and pepper to taste and enjoy!

Read on for a sneak peek of another exciting book
in the series Sugarcreek Amish Mysteries!

Simply Vanished
by Nancy Mehl

"Sugar and grits." Cheryl Cooper slowly hung up the phone, a frown wrinkling her forehead.

"Is something wrong, my friend?"

Cheryl looked up to see Naomi Miller standing on the other side of the counter. She held a basketful of new goodies for the Swiss Miss.

"No. I mean..." Cheryl paused and smiled at the Amish woman's look of compassion. "It's nothing. That was my mother. She and my dad are coming here. For my birthday."

Naomi's eyebrows shot up. "*Ach*, your birthday? I did not realize..."

Cheryl laughed lightly. "There's no reason you should. I don't really celebrate it anymore. After I moved away from home, it just didn't seem important."

"Birthdays *are* important, Cheryl," Naomi scolded. "They allow us to celebrate *you*."

Cheryl shook her head. "You don't need to celebrate me. You make me feel special every day." She gazed into Naomi's eyes, amazed by the strong friendship they'd developed ever since she'd moved to Sugarcreek, Ohio, and taken over her aunt's gift shop.

Naomi returned Cheryl's smile. "'Friendship is a plant which must often be watered.'"

Another Amish proverb. She was learning that the Amish had a proverb for almost everything. She'd also learned that Naomi didn't need proverbs about friendship. She was a walking proverb.

"You water me often, Naomi. Thank you."

"And you do the same for me, Cheryl." She cocked her head toward the phone sitting on the counter. "Do you wish to tell me why you do not seem pleased that your parents are coming to visit? I remember you telling me how much you missed them."

Cheryl sighed. "You're right. And I meant it. But now that they're actually coming...I don't know. It's complicated." She realized Naomi was still holding the loaded basket. "I'll try to explain it later. First let's see what you brought me."

Naomi put the basket down on the counter. "More cheese, of course. Your customers certainly seem to like it. Especially butter cheese, *ain't so?*"

"My customers love everything you make." Cheryl reached in and began to remove items inside the large woven basket. Besides the cheese, there were jams and jellies and several boxes of Naomi's fudge. "This won't last long," she said, lining the items up on the counter.

"Ach, you speak the truth," Naomi replied. "Levi is bringing some caramel pies and friendship bread later this afternoon. I hope that will hold you for a while."

"Thank you. The new refrigerated cooler should be installed soon. I'm definitely running out of room in my small coolers."

Just then a customer stepped up to the counter, and Naomi moved over to give the woman room. She held two jars of apple butter in her hands and a large jar of honey against her chest. As she set everything down next to the cash register, her eyes locked on Naomi's delivery.

"Oh my," she said softly. "How much is the strawberry jam?"

Cheryl quoted a price, and the woman nodded. "Can I have two jars?"

Cheryl picked up the jam and added it to the woman's order.

"And a box of fudge too, please."

Cheryl glanced at Naomi and winked. Much of Naomi's delivery wouldn't even make it to the shelves. She rang up the woman's purchase and carefully wrapped the jars so they wouldn't break. Then she placed everything into a bag with the shop's name printed on the front. As the woman walked away, Cheryl sighed.

"Maybe I should just keep your food on the counter. That way I could sell it before I have to put price tags on it."

Naomi chuckled. "You certainly keep me busy. I am so happy that *Gott* is blessing you. When He blesses your friend, He blesses you as well."

"Another proverb?"

"Just me this time." The smile slowly slid from her face, and she patted Cheryl's hand. "About your parents?"

Cheryl glanced around the shop. There were only a couple of customers. One was inspecting the shelves, and the other was talking to Esther, Naomi's daughter. Esther usually worked from noon to three every day, but she'd come in early today since Cheryl's other assistant, Lydia, hadn't shown up for work again. Even though Lydia didn't have a set schedule, Cheryl still counted on her for various tasks. It had been at least three weeks since she'd stopped by to see if Cheryl had any work for her. Frankly, Cheryl was getting worried. Esther and Lydia were both participating in *rumspringa*, an Amish custom that gave young people a period of time to decide if they wanted to be baptized into the church. While Esther seemed happy with her Amish life, Lydia had taken full advantage of her newfound freedom. She'd rejected her Plain clothing, started wearing makeup, and acquired a cell phone. She was also spending more time with some of the young people in town who weren't Amish and less time with Esther who had once been her best friend. Cheryl knew Esther was hurt by Lydia's rejection, but she did her best to maintain a positive attitude, something she'd learned from her mother.

Cheryl waved at Esther to get her attention. Then she motioned toward the office, letting the girl know she'd be away from the counter for a few minutes. Esther smiled and nodded and then turned her attention back to her customer. Cheryl felt blessed to have her helping at the Swiss Miss. She was bright and diligent. She was also completely capable of handling the shop alone if Cheryl wasn't there.

"Let's go into my office," she said to Naomi.

The Amish woman came around the counter and followed Cheryl to the small room at the back of the store. Cheryl closed the door while Naomi sat down in one of the chairs in front of Cheryl's desk.

Wondering just how she could explain her recently strained relationship with her mother to a woman who valued family above everything except God, Cheryl plopped down in her desk chair and took a deep breath. "My parents are great, and we've always been close. But after Lance and I broke up, I could tell they were disappointed. They didn't say it, but it was obvious. I'm turning thirty-one, I'm still not married, and I don't have any prospects. I know they're worried about me, and I understand that. Even so, things seemed fine. They weren't thrilled when I left the bank, but they seemed to understand my decision. They didn't try to talk me out of it. My mother and I have a long-standing habit of talking to each other every Sunday afternoon, but the past few weeks things have been…strained."

"What do you mean by *strained*?" Naomi asked.

Cheryl paused as she tried to find a way to explain something to her friend that she didn't understand herself. "My mother started changing the subject when I brought up the shop…and Sugarcreek. It's as if she doesn't want to hear about my life now. And that's hard because I have so much I want to share. She's rather short with me, which isn't like her. And suddenly she got too busy to talk to me on Sundays." She frowned at Naomi. "Frankly, she's started treating me like Matt, my brother."

"I do not know what you mean by that." Naomi looked as confused as Cheryl felt.

"Matt got into a lot of trouble as a teenager. Since Dad was pastoring a church, I think he and Mom were embarrassed by him. When he was nineteen, he left home." Cheryl shook her head slowly, remembering the day her mother called to tell her Matt had moved out. She was devastated. Cheryl could still hear the pain in her mother's voice. "They don't hear from him that often, but when they do, my mom is pretty cold toward him. She doesn't like talking to him on the phone."

"But I cannot believe any parent would be disappointed in *you*," Naomi said, a look of confusion on her face.

Cheryl felt a rush of affection for her friend. She was an honest woman who didn't say things just to make others feel better. Cheryl was certain her comment was from the heart.

"Thank you," she said. "My dad seems fine, but my mother is definitely upset about something. Lately she's made several negative comments about Sugarcreek. She never understood why my aunt loved this town so much. Now it looks as if I'm following in Aunt Mitzi's footsteps. I don't think this is the life my mother planned for me."

"But your father lived here as a boy, ain't so?"

"Yes, but once my dad left for college in North Carolina, he never really came back. Just for an occasional visit. As few as possible."

"Yet Mitzi never left."

Cheryl nodded. "This was always home to her. I'm sure my father has some good memories, but my mother never really understood its charm." She smiled at Naomi. "I wish they could see this town through our eyes."

Naomi made a clucking sound. "All parents believe they know what is best for their children. It is hard to watch them make their own choices—especially when you believe them to be wrong."

"I guess," Cheryl said. "Maybe I'm blowing things out of proportion. I hope when my mother sees how happy I am, she'll be happy too."

"I will certainly pray that she will. When do they arrive?"

"They'll get to town on Friday. My birthday is Saturday. They're staying at the Village Inn B-and-B. I told them they could bunk with me, but they don't really get along well with Beau."

Naomi frowned. "I do not understand. Your parents do not like animals?"

"They like them in their place. Which is in another room. The idea that I let Beau get on the furniture horrifies my mom. Her house is always picture perfect. Just like her."

"I see. And when do they leave?" There was no judgment in Naomi's voice, but Cheryl knew her friend's heart for animals. Cheryl was certain it was hard for her to understand how her parents could be ambivalent toward them.

"My mother didn't say. Probably after she gets me straightened out. Since it's already Wednesday, I guess I only have two days to prepare myself."

"Oh, Cheryl, perhaps their visit will be a blessing. As you said, perhaps you have misunderstood your mother."

"Maybe you're right. I guess I need an attitude adjustment."

Naomi stood up. "It is not for me to say, but I will pray for all of you. Family is so important." She reached up and adjusted her prayer covering. "How do you intend to celebrate your birthday?"

"I haven't really thought much about it. We'll probably go out to dinner."

"Nonsense," Naomi said huffily. "You will come to our house on Saturday. I will make you a wonderful birthday luncheon. If you still wish to go out to dinner later in the day, you will have plenty of time."

"Oh, Naomi, I don't want you to put yourself out like that. It's too much work and not much notice."

Naomi chuckled. "I believe after all this time we have spent together, you know me better than that, ain't so? I love to cook. It is not drudgery to me." She studied Cheryl for a moment. "If you do not think your parents would be comfortable in our home…"

Cheryl got to her feet. "Oh no, that's not it at all. I'm sure they'll love you."

Naomi nodded, her expression resolute. "Then it is settled. You will bring your parents to our house on Saturday where we will have lunch and cake as we thank Gott for bringing you into the world—and our lives."

Cheryl was touched by Naomi's offer, but even though she hadn't admitted it, she was a little worried about her mother. She had no problems with the Amish—at a distance. Her father had grown up around the Plain People. He would be gracious and accepting. If there were any problems, they wouldn't come through him. Usually her mom was very careful to follow her husband's lead in public. She saw supporting him as her calling. As Cheryl considered this, she felt a little better. Besides, who wouldn't love the Millers?

"Naomi, I can't thank you enough. I would be so honored to bring them to your home. This will be a wonderful birthday—because of you." She walked around the desk and gave Naomi a quick hug.

"Ach, I must get on my way," Naomi said when Cheryl released her. "You were only my first delivery today. I have two more stops." She started toward the door but then turned back to look at Cheryl. "I believe you said work would begin this week on your new cooler?"

Cheryl nodded. "Chuck Watson is putting it in. Several people recommended him. Actually, he's coming tonight to tear out the wall. I don't want my customers exposed to all the dust, and the work he's doing tonight will be pretty messy. By tomorrow, Chuck said he'd have a plastic sheet hanging up to keep any dust from getting into the shop. Hopefully, it won't be too bad. I'd rather not close if I don't have to."

"What about the food that is back there now? Do you need help moving it?"

"Thanks, but I'll take care of it. Only the food closest to the construction needs to be relocated. I'll do that sometime today. Most of the other food can stay where it is. The sheet should keep it safe."

Naomi nodded. "And how long will the work take?"

"Chuck said it would take less than a week, but I don't know. Knocking out a wall seems like a big deal to me."

"There does not seem to be much space in that corner."

"Chuck says there's a dead space."

Naomi's eyebrows shot up. "A *dead* space?"

"Yeah. An area where drywall extends out a few feet, but he doesn't think there's anything behind it."

"That seems very unusual." Naomi pursed her lips. "I am not experienced in building and renovations like Seth and Levi, but I have not heard of anything called 'dead space' before."

"Me either. But if he's right, with that area opened up and using part of the bathroom"—she pointed to the bathroom connected to her office—"Chuck says we'll have enough room for the new cooler."

Naomi smiled. "I will pray that everything works out the way Chuck says." She squared her shoulders. "Well, I must be on my way. Seth will pick up Esther when her shift is over."

"Thanks again, Naomi. I'm closing at noon on Saturday. We'll head over to your house after that. We should be there a little before twelve thirty. Will that work for you?"

"That will be fine, Cheryl. Do not rush. The food will still be there when you arrive." She grinned. "As long as I can keep Levi away from it."

Cheryl laughed and walked her friend to the front door. Then she got back to work adding the goods Naomi had delivered to the shop's inventory list. After tagging them, she put them on her shelves.

The rest of the day went by quickly. At five, she closed the shop. Beau immediately ran to the back room and stood next to his crate. Cheryl stroked the large Siamese's fur. He had certainly settled in nicely to her routine and her customers. Everyone seemed to love him. "Not yet," she said gently. "We have something else to do first."

A knock on the front door got her attention, and she hurried out into the shop to let Chuck in. He looked relieved when she opened the door. Temperatures were hovering in the twenties, but the wind made it feel much colder.

"It's a little chilly out there," he said as he stepped inside the shop. Chuck was a large man, tall and stout with muscular arms. He wore his graying hair short. With his deep, booming voice and distinctive look, he was certainly unique. He reminded Cheryl of a Marine drill sergeant.

"Yes, it is," Cheryl said with a smile. "But it's nice and warm in here."

Chuck had a large tool box in one hand and a rolled-up piece of heavy plastic in the other. He headed to the back of the store and set everything down on the floor.

"I haven't moved the food out yet," Cheryl said. "I can do that now."

Chuck nodded. "Might be best. I'm gonna make a pretty big mess at first, but it will be cleaned up before you open tomorrow. I just wanna remove this drywall and get to the studs. I'll hafta do the same to the bathroom. As I told you before, you won't be able to use it for a couple of days."

"I understand." She'd already talked to Kathy Snyder, the owner of the Honey Bee Café across the street. Kathy had told her she and her staff could use their facilities until the bathroom was put back together.

Cheryl quickly began unloading cheese, cream cakes, and butter from the cooler closest to the area where Chuck would be working. Once she moved everything, she asked him about the other coolers.

"Nah, they'll be fine. I'll put some extra plastic sheeting over them just in case. After tonight there won't be much dust—until the final drywall goes up. Then I'll have to do some sanding, but I'll come back at night and get it done so it won't disturb business." He nodded at her. "A little inconvenient, but in the end, it'll be worth it."

"I believe it will." Cheryl smiled at him, but he didn't smile back. She didn't take offense. Chuck's dour expression never seemed to change. To be honest, he had the kind of face that didn't seem to fit a smile. Kind of like a basset hound having a bad day.

"I'm gonna start tearing out this wall in just a bit," he said. "I'd rather you hang around until I can see what's behind it. I've located all the water pipes and the ductwork for your central air, so I don't expect any surprises, but with these old buildings you just never know what you might find. One time I took down a wall and discovered a stash of drugs and a roll of one-hundred dollar bills."

"In Sugarcreek?" Cheryl knew drugs were everywhere, but Sugarcreek, Ohio, was the last place she expected to see that kind of activity.

Chuck shook his head. "Nah, it was a job in Cincinnati. I've found some odd things here too though. Lotsa old shoes."

Cheryl frowned. "Old shoes? I don't understand."

"Folks used to believe putting shoes inside the wall of a house being built would bring the owners good luck."

"Really? How funny."

"Lots of razor blades too. There used to be a slot in bathrooms where men would dispose of their razor blades when they became dull."

"Sounds kind of dangerous."

"They're usually so dull it's not a big deal." He sighed. "Of course, I've found lots of dead animals, rats and such." He paused for a moment. "Once I found a book and some toys. Obviously belonged to a child. Put there many years before the current owners moved in. Never did find out why they were there. That one still bothers me a bit." He shrugged. "Well, I'd better get to work."

"Thanks, Chuck." His stories about things behind walls left her feeling a little unsettled. As she turned to walk away she realized Beau was sitting a couple of feet away, staring at them. She pointed at him. "You're going in your crate. Trust me. You won't enjoy the noise and the dust."

As if agreeing with her, Beau meowed.

Cheryl picked him up from the floor and took him back to the office. As she worked on the day's receipts, she heard her stomach growl. Lunch had been a long time ago, and she was looking forward to the veggie hummus wrap she'd picked up from the Honey Bee Café earlier in the day. A tiny compact refrigerator in her office allowed her to keep food fresh for lunch and supper.

Suddenly Cheryl heard loud pounding from inside the store, and the building shook. Even though she'd been expecting the noise, it startled her. Inside his crate, Beau jumped and yowled with surprise.

"It's okay," she said soothingly, not sure if she was trying to console him or herself. Evenings at the Swiss Miss were usually very quiet. After some further pounding, there was a pause in the racket.

"Miss Cooper?" Chuck called out. "Can you come here a moment?"

Hoping he was going to tell her everything was okay and she could leave, Cheryl got up from her desk and headed to the back of the store. A large plastic tarp hung from the ceiling, hiding the corner where Chuck was working. Cheryl pushed it back and found him standing on the other side, an odd look on his face. Cheryl's heart skipped a beat. Uh-oh. Was this going to cost her more than she'd hoped? She coughed at the dust floating in the air.

"I found something odd," Chuck said as she came near. "Took me a minute to figure out what it was."

Cheryl prayed he hadn't uncovered something that would have to be moved. It could add significantly to the cost of the project.

He pointed toward the place where drywall had been torn out. Cheryl's eyes followed his finger. Inside the wall was a wooden boxlike structure with a small door. Chuck reached in and pulled the door open. Something was inside the box.

"I don't understand," Cheryl said slowly. "What..."

"It's an old laundry chute," Chuck interjected. "Not unusual for older houses. But it should have been removed before the drywall was put up. And that's not the weirdest thing." He reached inside and pulled out two dusty items that he placed on a nearby sawhorse. "Who puts a woman's purse and a valise in a laundry chute and then covers it up?"

A Note from the Editors

We hope you enjoy Sugarcreek Amish Mysteries, created by the Books and Inspirational Media Division of Guideposts, a nonprofit organization that touches millions of lives every day through products and services that inspire, encourage, help you grow in your faith, and celebrate God's love in every aspect of your daily life.

Thank you for making a difference with your purchase of this book, which helps fund our many outreach programs to military personnel, prisons, hospitals, nursing homes, and educational institutions. To learn more, visit GuidepostsFoundation.org.

We also maintain many useful and uplifting online resources. Visit Guideposts.org to read true stories of hope and inspiration, access OurPrayer network, sign up for free newsletters, download free e-books, join our Facebook community, and follow our stimulating blogs.

To learn about other Guideposts publications, including the best-selling devotional *Daily Guideposts*, go to ShopGuideposts .org, call (800) 932-2145, or write to Guideposts, PO Box 5815, Harlan, Iowa 51593.